Your Wife Is The OTHER Woman

CREATED BY

TALANA T. BROOKS

F
BROOKS
T

Thanks to ...

First, I would like to acknowledge Our Lord. Without Him, nothing is possible. He has blessed me with a talent that I am allowed to use today.

I would like to thank all my cousins, aunts, uncles, nieces, nephews and my grandma who inspired me to be me and continue with my dream. My parents Willie and Doris, sisters and brothers Tracy, Michelle, Latrell, Martell, Jerry, and my late brother Coley, who all supported me 100% and believed in my talents even when at times, I didn't believe myself.

Special thanks and blessings to my beautiful daughter Amaya, who gave Mommy the strength every day to continue on, and was ever so patient and understanding when I was too distracted with work. I love you Puddin' with all my heart. This is for us!

To my friends Tracey, Akilah, Tomeka, Raven, Dynette, Tonie, Vicki, Kita, Cothie, Adam, Brandon and the entire 750 Entertainment family; especially Skippa, Skeeta and Rico. Thanks for the motivation and the laughs to keep me going strong! If it weren't for some of you I probably wouldn't have had the idea for the book (just kidding).

I didn't forget about you Carl. You pushed me towards my vision and kept me going. For that I thank you.

BIG THANKS to my editor & graphic designer, Lisa Taylor, who worked long hours helping make my dream come true. I will never forget your dedication!

For all my readers who bought the book or spread the word, I say thank you. Hopefully you have been entertained and maybe even positively influenced somehow in your life. Thanks for your support.

Lastly, I thank all who believed in me and those who I had to make into believers. Dreams do come true.

CHAPTER 1

"Open the door you whore!" the woman pounded and yelled at my front door.

Now I'd really done it this time. How could I be so stupid? I don't know what I was thinking. Out of the many times I'd scolded Gabrielle I should have listened to my own advice. Instead I was in the same boat.

But Eric was so suave, so clean cut, so sexy...so rich. He was just everything a girl could ask for. He had it all. The good looks, great personality, successful profession, and don't let me get started on his big.....feet. He was so charismatic! He knew exactly how to wine and dine me. Whether we lay in bed together and wasted the day away or if we were out on the town it was always a good time with him. He knew how to make a woman love him. He was every woman's perfect catch but no one loved him more than his woman. Excuse me, his wife.

"Be a woman!" she yelled through the door. "You can fuck my husband but you can't come outside and face me like a woman!"

She was screaming to the top of her lungs in my little remote, quiet suburban community of town homes. I wondered what the neighbors were saying. Did they all think that I was a whore now because of this raving lunatic at my door?

Thank goodness that nosy Miss. Witherspoon was in Florida this week. She would have probably invited the girl in for tea just so she could find out all the dirt on me and Eric.

My phone rang. "Hello."

"What's going on?" Eric's voice echoed on the other end of the line.

"Your wife, that's what's going on. She's yelling and screaming and trying to kick my door in!" I made her seem like the big bad wolf when indeed she had every reason to be angry.

"Where is she now?"

"Are you listening? She's at my front door." I was impatient with the situation.

How could he be so stupid? How could he allow his wife to come to my home and invade me like this? Didn't he know how to keep better tabs on the situation? Men never knew how to do anything right.

"I'll be right over." he said.

I was partly relieved but I still didn't know what to expect when he got here. She would probably go off even more if he tried making her leave. I mean really, what was he going to do? He already allowed it to escalate this far. What could he do now?

I contemplated calling the police but figured I should at least give him a chance to work his magic.

My thoughts rushed as I waited for him to arrive. How could I put myself in such a situation? I'd always vowed to never entertain a married man.

I remembered the time when Gabrielle told me about her affair with Todd.

"You have to meet him." She said with bright eyes. I frowned my face and tore her apart with my words. I know she felt less than dirt after I was done with her. No matter how she tried justifying being with a married man, I ate her up.

2

"Two wrongs don't make a right." I said as she tried explaining that Jack, her husband had been caught and now it was his time to pay. "That was your choice to stay with him after you caught him. You're doing the same thing to that woman that the other woman did to you. That doesn't make you any better. If anything it makes you just as bad. If you wanted revenge you should have messed with her man, not someone else's."

Guilt settled in. She'd felt the worse of my wrath so I lightened my tone. "I just want you to realize that you're playing with fire, girl. So many lives are involved. You have to worry about more than just you and Jack. What about Jackson?"

I drifted into my thoughts, juggling the consequences and the affect they would have on their four year old son. Little Jackson was adorable and a complete reflection of his father which is why they called him Jackson because he was Jack's son. I thought it was cute. Gabrielle always thought it was more of a last name than anything but since she refused to have a junior as a son she settled with Jackson.

"What if he was pulled into some unnecessary bull?"

The reality shook her. My words served their purpose. They hit home. Shortly after, she ended her affair. Now here I was beginning mine. How did this happen? How did I allow myself to be put in such a horrible predicament?

"Come outside!" Eric's wife yelled and pounded at my door repeatedly. "You home wrecking hoe!"

Chapter 2

One Year Ago...

It was hot as hell! Sweat blanketed my forehead. My silk gown was glued to my skin. An aroma filled the house. Everyone could smell and hear what I was doing and yet I still couldn't believe it. It had been so long and I was totally out of practice.

"Ouch!" I exclaimed as the scorching grease caught the inside of my forearm. "Ouch! Shit!"

I had three flames going, one for bacon, another for eggs and the last for pancakes. A meal fit for a king. "Slow down take your time girl." I warned myself. I wanted everything to be perfect. Presentation is everything. I knew he would sleep for at least another hour if I let him. I had plenty of time to chill his orange juice, warm the syrup, arrange a small bowl of fruit, and grab the daily newspaper to make it the perfect presentation. I was in Martha Stewart mode, determined to please my man. With everything almost done and a little time to spare, I quickly gathered in the bathroom for a little "me" time. I checked my makeup, wiped myself down, changed into a see through lace gown with the robe to match, and fixed my hair. I was perfect and ready to be served on the platter with the rest of meal. Hey, I couldn't give him hot breakfast in bed without all the sides. Like I said, presentation is everything.

The door creaked as I opened it slowly. There he lay still, unaware of my inexistence. Quietly I crept near him. I lay the tray table neatly on the bed next to him and gently rubbed over his face with a fresh cut rose from our garden.

"Ahhh!" he screamed flapping his arms and legs in a panic. Breakfast flew everywhere. It covered the floor, the sheets, and the both of us.

I stared at my masterpiece frozen with fright and consumed with disgust. He wiped himself while returning from his delirium.

"Cory! What in the hell is wrong with you?" I finally asked.

He immediately began to laugh. I didn't see what was so damn funny. He'd ruined everything. I looked at the orange stain on the bed and the stream of brown syrup that led from the comforter to my legs, arms, and lace lingerie.

"I'm sorry baby," he finally said. He laughed hysterically. "I was having a bad dream about...."

I didn't want to know what it was about. I tuned out his excuses and started pulling the sheets from the bed. "You got stuff everywhere." I complained. "I'm all sticky."

He ignored my remarks and stepped into our master bath to clean himself while still laughing. I could have killed him.

I heard the thump of his clothes being thrown to the floor. The next minute I could feel his breath on my neck.

"It looks like it would have been good," he joked.

But I wasn't in a laughing mood. "That's not funny. I spent so much time trying to serve you a perfect breakfast in bed."

"You know I can still eat it. You want me to eat it?"

"Off the floor too?"

"Baby if it makes you happy...," he grabbed a slice of bacon from the bed and ate it slowly. "I will lick every drop."

"I see you didn't eat any from off the floor though did you?" I teased feeling a little better. If he wasn't upset then why should I be?

"Some got right here too?" he asked holding my arm. With his tongue he licked the syrup from my fingers and hands.

My fingers swished around in his mouth.

His lips were so soft against my sweet skin. It gave me chills down my back. My nipples were at full attention. How could he have such a powerful affect after two years?

"Where else? Did it get anywhere else?"

I pointed to my thigh. He instantly got to his knees and began licking my thigh.

"Right here?" he asked.

"Yes," I moaned.

He moved further up. "How about there? Some get right here too?" He grasped my backside tightly. My body grew limp in his palms. "Lay down," he demanded.

I obliged by his orders. He stared devilishly at me. His eyes were on the prowl scanning every part of me through my lace negligee. He was plotting to steal my womanhood. How dare he plot when I would give it to him willingly.

His eyes, now devious, squinted as the sun's rays glimmered through the drapes. Slowly he removed my thong from underneath my thigh high gown. He proceeded to lift my favorite see through lace lingerie above my breasts. He then grabbed the last remaining strawberry in the bowl. I at first thought he would feed it to me but I knew he was more creative than that. Then I thought he would play a game of hide and seek but I wasn't sure if I was kinky enough to attempt that. The whole idea of going to the gynecologist because of strawberry residue inside me wasn't appealing at all.

Instead of either of the above, he squeezed the juice on my breasts and drew a trail down, down, down to my vagina. It leaked from his fingertips. He showed me the juice before making me lick it from his hand while he rubbed my clitoris seductively. I bit his fingers softly as he went through the motions of playing with my pussy.

My mind ran rampant. What was next? When would I get it? How would he give it to me? I moaned in aching antici-pation as he cleaned the juice from my breasts with his tongue. He worked his way down to the pit of my stomach. Just when I thought I couldn't take it any longer he made me wait.

His face was lost between my thighs. He was sucking my life away and I enjoyed every second. It was pure agony but the best fucking agony I'd ever experienced. He teased me with sensual licks. Then he sucked maybe as hard as he could before he blew on my clit. It was driving me crazy!

"Fuck me Cory. Pleeeeaaasse, baby. Fuck me right now!" I begged.

It must have been more juice in that strawberry than I realized.

He rose to his feet. His penis stood straight out at me like a witch on a broom stick. He grabbed one leg at a time spreading them as far as they would go and held onto my calves while he slowly placed his manhood at the tip of my now juicy pussy. After a few quick adjustments, he slowly pushed his never ending hard wide dick inside me. At last I was full of him. After what felt like hours of teasing, pleasing foreplay and multiple orgasms, and making passionate love on the carpet, the bed, and the dresser, we lay exhausted.

"Come on," he slapped my bare thigh. "Let's go to IHOP."

*   *   *   *

Hours later Cory and I walked into the filled restaurant and waited for a table. We thought we had ingeniously beaten the morning rush but I guessed the Sunday patrons decided to attend early morning service today. Besides, the quickie in the shower before we left couldn't have helped our timing.

"Let's just go," Cory said. His patience was wearing short. I didn't blame him. It felt like we'd been sitting there forever. The both of us were starving.

"We've waited all this time, we might as well stay. As soon as we leave they'll be calling our name," I told him.

Like a child, he was restless in his seat. He quickly excused himself and ran to the bathroom. More people entered into the restaurant.

"Wow!" one girl said. "I told you it would be a ton of people. I wonder how long the wait is."

"I'll go check," the tall big stature girl excused her way through the crowd to the host at the counter.

"Have you been waiting long?" the other girl asked.

"About twenty minutes," I said. "It was a thirty to forty five minute wait when we got here."

She pouted and slid her hands on her hips. "Thank you," she said politely.

Her friend returned. "They said it's an hour wait," she informed. "That's not bad."

"Your fat butt is just hungry." They laughed and exited the restaurant. "Let's go. I'm not waiting an hour for anybody."

I waited patiently for Cory to return. As soon as he did he started up again.

"Let's just grab something quick to eat and go to the park or something." He tried convincing.

It sounded like a nice plan and we did have four more people ahead of us. But I had a taste for French toast. I looked at Cory who was now standing near the door, almost outside the restaurant.

"Alright let's go," I said freeing him from his misery.

It was like someone lit fire underneath his feet. He rushed out the door while I slowly strolled admiring how beautiful a day it was. I listened as the birds chirped and the cars drove by with their music playing. Then all of a sudden the music stopped. The red Toyota Camry approached slowly. I'm surprised they didn't get whiplash when the driver slammed on the brakes. Cory kept moving as if he didn't notice the surprising glares from the two girls.

The thinner girl got out first followed by her big friend. Neither seemed as friendly or happy as the minute I saw them inside the restaurant.

"Hello," she said in a snotty tone.

"Hi," he said trying to avoid the girl.

"That's it?" she asked. "You're not going to introduce me to your friend?"

Friend? What friend? She couldn't have been referring to me. There must have been another friend out here.

"Yeah, I'll introduce you," he said reluctantly.

The girl folded her arms and switched her hips from one side to the other.

"Lisa this is Mikayla. Mikayla..... Lisa," he vaguely introduced.

What in the hell type of introduction was that? Now I was only Mikayla? And the way he said it was like she and I were on the same level. Like he and I never spent two years together. Like we didn't live with each other for the last six months. Like we didn't just spend the morning making love for hours. I was livid but I was never the type to lose my cool, especially in public and especially in the presence of another woman.

9

"And who the fuck is Lisa?" I asked in a calm yet demanding tone.

"Yeah Cory, who the fuck am I?" she asked.

Her friend stood by her side, never interrupting once. She exchanged evil stares between Cory and me. I could care less about her. I wanted to know what the hell was going on.

"A friend of mine," he said.

"Oh so now I'm a friend?" she asked.

"Why are you acting crazy?" he asked her.

"I'm crazy?" she repeated. "Oh I'm crazy? I'm acting crazy because you're here with another woman and you're acting like you don't see me? Why do you think I'm acting crazy?"

Another woman? I waited for him to defend me and our relationship. He tried ignoring her.

"That's your girl now?" she kept asking. "That's your girlfriend?"

"Come on lets go," he told me and that was it. Both Lisa and I stood with our mouths open.

"You're not going to answer her?" I wanted to know. I needed to know. He wouldn't answer. He couldn't because he was caught and I was pissed.

"You better open your mouth and say something," I told him.

"Kayla, it's not that serious."

"Not that serious?" I snapped.

"I mean she's going off like we're together or something," he explained. "We're just friends."

She was appalled. He'd denied her.

"Then tell her who the hell I am. Tell her we've been together for two years and we live together." I demanded.

"Really?" Lisa asked. "That's funny because we've been dating for the last four months. I didn't know anything about you sweetie."

I cut my eyes at her then at him.

"I thought you moved in with your cousin Cory. What happened to that lie?"

"Man, whatever," is all he said. "We haven't been dating for four months," he told her.

"You're a liar, Cory," she said.

"A big liar," her friend cosigned.

"It's going on five months Cory!"

He continued to deny her accusations.

"Have you been seeing her Cory? Tell the truth," I asked.

"Kayla, no."

Lisa threw her arms in the air. Her friend laughed.

"Just tell me the truth," I pleaded.

He contemplated his next words before he said, "That is the truth."

"You are a lying bastard!" she said. "Honey I've been in his car and everything. The day he bought it he picked me up and we drove around and 'christened the car'." She held her fingers up like she was quoting him.

I knew she was telling the truth. He'd used those same words to me when I returned from my weekend conference the day after he bought his car. My eyes got low as I gritted my teeth.

"You're crazy," he told her and began to walk off. "I swear something's wrong with you."

She grew more and more agitated as did I. "Is that why? Is that why you wanted me to have an abortion last month?"

"What?" I couldn't breath. The once fresh summer air now choked me.

"That's right. Your boyfriend of two years got me pregnant last month and told me to have an abortion," she spilled all the beans.

That was it. I couldn't take it anymore. I felt suffocated. I felt helpless. I felt so naïve so stupid. I felt like....like...fighting. "You got her pregnant?"

He twisted his lips and turned his head. He tried lying about it but his mouth wouldn't let him. I'd given him a chance to defend himself. He failed. Rage filled my chest. I could feel the adrenaline rising from my throat and the smoke erupting through my ears. I curled my fingers into a ball and with all my might I punched the SHIT out of him!

The surprise blow to the head almost forced him to ground but he managed to maintain control after a few stumbles.

The parking lot was filled with spectators. My mind wasn't on them.

"You hear me talking to you!" I yelled while trying to hit him again but he blocked it along with every other punch I threw. And when it seemed I couldn't get to him, I pounced on top like a lioness on her prey.

He was stunned. He'd never seen me behave in such a way. Not quiet, well reserved Mikayla. I couldn't believe it myself but after dedicating two years to a relationship he should have known not to mess with me. I bore my heart and soul into this relationship. How dare he disrespect that?

I was out for blood, all over him scratching, punching, and kicking. He tried pulling me off but couldn't. Finally, he escaped to the other side of the car. I followed behind but couldn't catch up. Every time I came close he ran again. Lisa stood in his way still nagging him with questions and yelling in his ear. The two exchanged words and when I came near he ran again. The next time around she grabbed his arm while I jumped him again. He flung Lisa to the ground and ran.

"Kayla stop!" he demanded. "Would you just be cool and let's talk about this?"

I wasn't trying to hear it. Lisa's friend helped her up. Embarrassed, she too chased him. We both cornered him and we all tussled around. In the midst of all the commotion I got thrown to the ground. I could hear him arguing with Lisa some more. "Would you get out of my face?" he yelled but another voice screamed as well. The voice in my head yelled 'Enough of this BS!' and before I knew it I reacted on it.

"Ahhh!" he yelled and screamed, "I can't see! I can't see!" he shouted.

Lisa and her friend coughed profusely. They'd also been caught in the whirlwind of pepper spray. Police sirens play in the background and that little voice spoke again. This time it said 'girl get your ass out of here.'

I grabbed the keys from the ground where Cory dropped them, jumped into his BMW, and sped off.

I couldn't believe it. How naïve of me. How had he managed to pull the wool over my eyes for four months? I always thought we had the perfect relationship. It had its ups and downs but what relationship didn't?

Now that I thought about it the last three months were different. It was great when we first moved in together. Neither of us could get enough of each other. After it became routine, things seemed to die down. Cory would go out more and I wanted him to stay out. We both longed for that "me" time, that time by ourselves or with our friends. So his outings didn't bother me. Never was I jealous or suspicious. I'd always convinced myself that a man should have the opportunity to roam and if he strayed in the wrong direction then it wasn't meant to be. And well, I guess it wasn't meant to be.

But my heart was broken. I couldn't believe it. How could I be so dumb? More importantly, how could he do me like this? I thought I did everything right. I cooked as often as I could. I kept the house clean. I even put on for some of the bills. And to top it off, anytime he wanted a 'lil' taste' as he called it, I was there ready and willing with my legs spread wide open.

So what was the problem? What did he want? Wasn't I pretty enough? Honestly, Lisa wasn't by far better looking than me. Seriously, she wasn't. Her short, thin frame, light complexion, and long hair was no comparison to my tall medium built voluptuous body, long wavy hair, and hazel sometimes green eyes. Truly she was no competition. At least I would have thought.

Really what did he want? Did I not do it good enough to him? I did everything the man could possibly ask for without him having to ask for it. I treated him like a king in the bedroom. Most of the time I had him screaming.

'Tell me it's mine. Promise this is the best pussy you ever had.' I would command and he would do it. Well I see now he was a liar. It was all bedroom theatrics and he was just another actor. Another man pretending to be in love, to be interested, and to be faithful. But with all men, the truth shines through one day whether he confesses on his own or if it walks right up to him in the parking lot of IHOP.

"Gabrielle you will never believe what just happened."

"What?" she asked concerned. She could hear the distress in my voice.

I tried to let it out but my anger turned into sorrow. I was so heartbroken and .....

"Are you okay?" she asked through my sobs. "Where are you? What's the matter?"

"Cory.....Cory was sleeping ....." I tried catching my breath.

"Cory was sleeping and what happened? Is he okay?" she tried piecing the puzzle together.

"No!" I yelled.

"No, he's not alright? What happened honey?"

Finally I calmed myself, "He was sleeping with another girl. He got her pregnant."

14

"Wait, what?" she said in disbelief. "Cory has a baby on the way by another girl?"

"He would have but she had an abortion."

"Oh my God," she said, "Where are you?"

"I'm leaving IHOP. I'm going to grab some clothes. Can I stay with you and Jack for a few days until I get things together?"

"Yeah come on. You want me to meet you?"

"Okay."

"I'll be there in ten minutes."

I began planning my disappearance. I needed to make sure I got home and got my things packed before Cory found a ride and caught me there. I wasn't sure if he'd come home explaining or trying to choke the shit out of me. He had never hit me but I'd never maced him before either.

One blink after another the tears fell loosely from my eyes. I tried holding back but it only blurred my vision. Through the haze I managed to see the red and blue lights flashing in my rear view mirror. It was 5-0 and they were pulling me over. Great! What do I do now?

The officer, a tall cocky man approached my car. His partner, a short stout female walked around the opposite side and stood near the trunk. I wiped my tears and rolled down the window.

"Yes officer?" I put on an innocent face.

"Would you step out of the car please ma'am?"

I obliged by his request. The last thing I needed was to be arrested by Officer Friendly here.

"Is this your car?" he asked.

Why did they ask stupid questions like that? He knew damn well this wasn't my car. The female officer searched the car.

"No sir, this is my boyfriend's car."

He looked into my eyes. I tried being tough by not showing any signs of weakness but he saw right through me.

"Was that your boyfriend at IHOP?"

"Yes."

"You want to tell me what happened?"

I took a breath and turned my head in embarrassment as I fought back tears and shook my head "no."

"Another no good bastard?" he smiled.

"Yeah." I smiled and sniffed. Few tears escaped.

"It's okay. Don't cry. Some people aren't worth a good woman's tears," he lectured.

His smile was warm and his words were filled with compassion. His partner wasn't as gracious. She walked over and put the pepper spray on the hood and gave me a look like, 'bitch stop crying, you're not as innocent as you look.'

"6511," the dispatcher called and the female officer answered.

"He probably deserved it," the male officer told me.

I laughed a little. He lightened the mood somewhat. I felt he, unlike his partner, understood my actions. I explained my side of things while his partner continued her conversation with the dispatcher.

"And I'm sure she's never heard or seen this other girl before," she sarcastically interrupted my story.

"I haven't."

"Yeah okay."

What was her problem? Why was she being mean for no reason? I mean my goodness, was she sleeping with Cory too?

"We're going to take you back to the restaurant. Unfortunately there are two sides to a story," she told me.

I gave a great sigh. This heifer was getting on my nerves. She was lucky she had my pepper spray.

"It's just procedure," Officer Butler coached me. He hesitated for a moment before taking the keys out of the ignition.

"Do you have any other weapons we should know about?" Officer Kerry asked as she frisked and handcuffed me.

"Nooo," I whined and cried. I was never so embarrassed in all the days of my life. People drove by staring. I wanted to bury my face. "Why do I have to be handcuffed?"

"It's just procedure for our protection," she said coldly. "You'll be fine."

I cried the whole way to IHOP. By this time the lot was lined with people gaping at the display. Bystanders smiled and pointed fingers as I returned in the back of the police car.

When Cory laid eyes on me he went ballistic. "No! No! No! Let her out of the car. It was an accident," he carried on. "She didn't mean to do it. It was an accident." He lied in my defense but I'd already told the truth.

He banged the window. I turned my head. I was too angry, disgusted, and embarrassed to even look his way. The officers made him move and calmed him. He nodded his red, swollen face as the police spoke and he pleaded. There was no way out. The two girls had made an even bigger mess of things by saying I sprayed them as well. Lying little bitches. I wish I had. With that said, I was going to jail, straight to jail. Do not pass go or collect two hundred dollars.

Again I cried a river the whole way there. Officer Butler tried consoling me but there was no use. "I'll hurry up and get you processed so you can get out soon."

He fingerprinted me, had mug shots taken and all. They even took the laces from my shoes. But the icing on the cake happened right before I went to have my fingerprints and mug shots done. I stood in the middle of the room lined up with four other girls. We all were told to undress. 'Are you serious?' I thought.

The lady in lockup looked at me. The broad shoulder, short haired, man-looking lady wasn't going to ask again. Shyly, I pulled my shirt off, followed by my rhinestone cut BeBe Capri jeans. And I stood there nude with four other girls.

"I need each of you to bend over and cough like this," the officer demonstrated. Then she directed us one by one as to what she wanted us to do beginning with a six foot dark skinned girl who looked like she had been through hell. Scratches and scars from head to toe.

"Huh?" the girl asked with a deep voice.

"Turn around," the officer told her. Frankenstein's cousin turned around and spread her cheeks like it was no problem. Then she gave a loud smoker's cough when directed. We all tried not looking. It was most disgusting, but I couldn't help but take a peek every now and then. I was curious knowing that whatever they did to her they would do to me as well.

They inspected her lightly. I don't even think they wanted to come close to that.

Then it was my turn. I listened closely yet numbly to the guard's directions. I turned this way and that way and spread and coughed until my turn was up. I didn't pay attention to anyone else who went after me. I'd had enough. I never wanted to ever go to jail ever again! But I might be making another visit after I get out and kick Cory's ass.

"Come on. You're outta here," the officer said six hours later.

I picked myself out of the corner grabbed the little bit of dignity I had left and walked outside to Gabrielle.

"Are you alright?"

"Girl, what a day. What a day!" I explained the whole ordeal on the drive home.

"But how good did it feel to mace his ass?"

I thought for a second. We both laughed. "I'm not

going to lie to you. Seeing him on the ground screaming and crying, 'I can't see! I'm blind! I can't see!' It felt so good."

"I wish I had spray when I found out about Jack and his little heifer. I would have sprayed his ass, her ass and whoever else was around."

"But Lisa didn't know anything about me."

"I don't care. And she had to know something. Why couldn't she come to his house, you know? And even if she didn't know, then I'm sorry bitch, you were in the wrong damn place at the wrong damn time."

We laughed so hard until we both were in tears. After arriving at her place we showered, drank champagne, and men bashed all night until we passed out.

Chapter 3

Tonight was the night. I'd avoided all Cory's calls and surprise visits. He couldn't catch me at work because I'd called off for the last two days. He refused to release any of my things to Gabrielle and every time I drove by to get my car I noticed his car outside. He too hadn't returned to work. And since I refused to talk to him I couldn't get my keys.

But tonight was the night. While he slept we plotted to steal my car. Gabrielle kept a spare key to our condo and all I had to do was use that to get me in. I knew my keys were on the rack in the kitchen which was only a few steps away from the front door so the plan was simple.

"Okay, you wait outside while I go in and get the keys," I instructed Gabrielle.

"This is crazy! What if he wakes up while you're in there?"

"Cory sleeps rock hard. He won't wake up. Trust me."

She didn't seem so sure but I crept inside anyway. I gently put the key in the hole and turned it softly. The lock disengaged and my heart beat boldly against my chest. I prayed he didn't catch me and hesitated to turn the knob but it was now or never.

I opened the door slightly. The shadows of the playing television reflected on the living room walls. There he slept heavily on the couch. I contemplated leaving but his snores egged me on. Like a ninja, I stayed low and inconspicuous. I was dead silent as I crawled behind the couch to the kitchen. Slowly I rose to my feet. With all eyes on him, I grazed my hand on the empty key rack. My keys were gone. Cory cleverly moved them. I checked everywhere in the kitchen but they were nowhere to be found.

I refused to panic. He still lay unaffected by my presence. His mouth was wide open and one leg hung off the end of the sofa. I inspected the living room. The keys weren't on the tables near him. I slipped into the bedroom and searched. Finally, there they lay on the nightstand next to his cell phone. I contemplated my next move. Should I, or shouldn't I? Did I really want to know or care anymore? You damn right I should and hell yeah I cared! No woman could resist going through a man's cell phone. It was like gold in my hand.

I scrolled to his list of calls. One after another there was a call dialed to me. But as I continued down the list I came to notice more uncommon numbers. I didn't know Lisa's number so I wasn't sure if he'd talked to her or not. Being the smart guy that he was he didn't put her in his phone book so her name remained anonymous to her number.

Cory still snored in the distance. I was safe for now. And with a little extra time to spare, I escaped the call log and went directly into the text message screen. Bingo! Messages to and from his phone for Lisa. I could tell by how the conversation read that it could only be her.

"I can't believe you played me like that," she said. "Don't try to call me now that your girlfriend left you," she wrote. "You must love her seeing how you treated me," "I can't believe I considered having your child."

He only responded, "I wasn't trying to hurt you," and, "Please answer your phone."

I wanted to see more. I wanted to know what he had

to say to her. I knew they talked because the number she texted from was the same number in his call log. They talked for twenty-eight minutes the first time and thirty-two the second. I wanted to know what about. He must have been laying it on pretty thick because the second time she actually called him.

My mind ran rampant. Was he still sleeping with her since we broke up? Was he doing it to her without a condom? He had to. He'd done it before and got her pregnant. Of course he was now. Did he love her? Was he putting his mouth on her nasty.....Uuggghhhh!

That was it. I was upset all over again. That little voice started speaking to me again but instead of wrecking some shit, I grabbed my keys. Both sets. Now he wouldn't even have a spare.

I even grabbed clothes from the closet before walking into the living room. Now I was bold. If I was nuts I could have done all types of things to him while he slept. "You ever heard of Lorraina Bobbitt?" I thought. I could be more creative than that. How about 'the hot grits poured all over him idea?' That's creative.

So many thoughts ran through my mind as I stood gaping at him. I was so angry I wanted to end his life. I stood watching as he slept so peacefully when all of a sudden his eyes opened. My body froze with fear. What was I thinking? I should have got my keys and clothes and got the heck out of dodge. Now I was caught. I stood still until his dozy eyes closed again. He rolled over and broke out into a coughing frenzy. I dropped to the floor. He sat up as I made a dash on my hands and knees, for the kitchen pantry. I stood inside and held my breath. He walked inside and fixed a glass of water. I observed as he leaned on the counter and drank his water. Only two feet away, I watched as he gazed away in deep thought holding onto his empty glass. I wondered about his thoughts. Was he sorrowful over me or her? Whomever, I hoped he was suffering.

He looked a mess. His hair hadn't been cut in days and he needed a shave badly. I knew he hadn't been out of the house since I left. He was too much of a pretty boy and wouldn't be caught dead looking the way he did.

He slammed the glass on the counter and retired to the bedroom. I waited until I heard what I thought were rumbles in the bathroom. I snuck out the front door, jumped into my 2005 Maxima, and darted out of the driveway.

Cory ran out in his boxers yelling and screaming my name. Gabrielle followed behind as we both sped to her house. Paranoid, we ran inside and peeped through her blinds.

"What—" We both jumped as Jack snuck up from behind, "are you two doing now?" he continued.

I looked at Gabrielle. She looked at me. The two of us began to laugh hysterically. We'd done some crazy things before but this was one that would take the cake.

My phone rang. It was Cory. I didn't know whether to answer or not. I looked at Gabrielle for advice. She gave me one of those 'don't look at me,' type of looks.

"Hello."

"Why couldn't you talk to me? Why'd you have to sneak into the house and steal your keys?"

"Are you serious? Do you know how you sound? How can I steal something that's mine?"

"Mikayla, I only want to talk to you."

"About what? Huh? About what?"

"About getting things clear and explaining the entire situation. I love you Mikayla and I'm not trying to argue or lose you."

"Is that why you were having sex with another woman for five months? Because you love me so much? That's why you're getting another woman pregnant because you love me so much, right?"

He couldn't speak.

"That's what I thought."

"Baby..."

"Baby? No you have me confused. You aborted your baby remember?" I said harshly.

"Mikayla, I'm not going to sit here and say I didn't do anything wrong. I've had three days to sit here and think about everything I did—"

"And it took you three days to realize you were wrong?"

"No. I knew it a long time ago. That's why I left her alone. Why do you think she was so upset? She's mad because I'm not seeing her anymore. Couldn't you tell that?"

"I'm sorry I was too busy wondering why my man was fucking another woman in the first place."

I wasn't giving him a chance to recover. Everything he said I came back with cold, well deserving ridicules.

"Can we talk? I just want to talk in person not over the phone. Please, I miss you baby. I can't sleep."

"Seems like you were sleeping just fine to me."

"On the couch? When do I ever sleep on the couch? I'm up half the night trying to go to sleep so I won't think about our situation?"

"I'm sorry victim," I said sarcastically.

He smacked his lips. "I'm not the victim. I know you're the victim."

"No, I'm not the victim sweetie. You did us a favor."

"Well whatever. I'm only saying I want to work past this. How can we do that?"

"Cory...it's over between us. I want my things from your house—"

"Our house," he corrected.

"Like I said your house. It's time we move on. There's no need in prolonging the situation. Let's just get it over with so you can move on and I can too."

"I don't want to move on."

"No you want to do whatever while we're together."

"Mikayla please."

"I'm sorry. Did I hurt your feelings?"

He gave a sigh. "So there's nothing I can do? That's just it between us?"

"That's it. I could never trust you again in life. Would you want to be with someone who doesn't trust you?"

"If it means you and I will be together, then yeah I would," he gave the perfect answer. "I can live with that."

"Well I'm sorry I can't," I said coldly. "Why are you calling me? Shouldn't you be calling Lisa?"

"I'm not worried about anyone but you."

I gave a sarcastic giggle. I started to tell him that I'd been through his phone and that I saw that he practically begged her to answer his calls but I didn't. It wasn't worth my breath. I was beginning to see that Cory cared just as much for Lisa as he did for me. He could talk all the game he wanted but 'you can't hold shit above water,' my Granny used to always say.

He paused, in search for the right words. "I love you. I never meant to hurt you—"

"What?" I interrupted. I couldn't believe he was using the same words as he'd texted to Lisa. It burned my soul. "You never meant to hurt me?"

"No, Mikayla I didn't. I would do anything to get you back. What can I do?"

"You know what? Die slow bitch." I slammed the flip of my cell phone.

It would be the last time I would speak to him. I had it

all figured out. Numbers would be changed and in a week or two I would have a new place to live. All access would be destroyed. It was time for something new.

CHAPTER 4

I'd kept busy for the last two weeks. So busy that I didn't have time to change my phone number but after telling Cory to 'die slow' for some reason I didn't receive as many calls. I guess words do cut as deep as a knife.

Better news came when Jack informed me of his client's last minute decision to back out of a deal for a townhouse in a nearby suburb. I could sign the papers to close in two weeks. I couldn't be happier. I wanted Gabrielle to have her house back. Although I knew she enjoyed my company and I enjoyed hers like old times at Penn State, every good thing comes to an end. She and Jack did benefit from having a babysitter on hand all the time. So neither ever complained. I didn't mind either. Jackson was so fun, so different, and so sweet. If ever I had kids I wanted one just like him.

"Auntie!" he screamed as I returned from work.

"Hey little man! What's going on?"

He schooled me about his day and drilled me about taking him to the park like I promised.

"Alright little man," I said, "let me fix a sandwich first then we can go."

"Yeaaaa!" he went screaming through the house.

"Hey." I spoke to Gabrielle who sat on the phone still wearing her corporate America suit.

She gave me a wave. "Tomorrow at five? Let me check," she covered the phone. "can you watch Jackson tomorrow?"

I gave a nod.

"Yeah, tomorrow at five. That's fine. Alright. Thank you."

"What's going on at five tomorrow?"

"Hello nosey!" she said. I laughed at my prying. "Tomorrow I have a meeting with some people from the design team for this new project I'm working on."

"Yeah, yeah, yeah. Whatever. I don't want to hear about your advertising projects and stuff like that," I teased.

"Well then don't ask. You're just mad because you're a boring teacher," she came back.

"You're right and don't ask me to watch your kid while you get to go on fun advertising dinners and dates."

"Trust me, it's not all that glamorous."

I ate my sandwich as she looked over her notes.

"I'll be out of here in a couple weeks," I said.

"Yeah then what will I do about a sitter?"

"I'll still get my son."

"Your son? If you're going to take the credit for the child after I went through nine months of pregnancy and fourteen hours of labor, the least you can do is take him with you."

"I don't like him that much."

"Bitch," she called me.

"Hello," I smiled and answered my phone.

"Mikayla?" my sister asked.

"Hi Paris," I said not enthused.

"Have you spoken to mom?" She was so rude sometimes. Not even a 'hello how have you been Mikayla?' Or anything.

"No I haven't. Why?"

"Well you know her birthday is coming soon and I've decided to have a surprise birthday for her. It'll be on the tenth and I'll send you an invitation. My reason for calling is to inform you that I told her that you and I would be taking her to dinner. I wanted to make sure she hadn't called and you ruined the surprise."

Her tone was the same as always. A better than my sister type of attitude reflected in her voice every time we spoke. I couldn't stand it. We never got along. She was always perfect in my mother's eyes and I was the misfit child.

With her industry and A-list friends, I fell way low on the totem pole of success in my family. I learned long ago to stop competing. And since then it seemed that every bit of misery in my life made her feel more significant.

"Auntie, is it time to go to the park yet?" Jackson tugged at my leg.

I fanned him off. "No I haven't talked to mom so your surprise isn't ruined."

Gabrielle gave me a look. She experienced the boiling blood between our sibling rivalry.

"Great. I'll send you and Cory an invitation. Also let Gabrielle know I've sent her one as well."

"I'll do that."

"And I'll give you a call so you'll know where to meet on the day of and all the other details."

"That's fine."

"Okay. So I'll talk to you soon."

So formal. No one would ever suspect we're sisters. I mean who needed an invitation to their own mother's surprise birthday party in the first place? It was ridiculous but it was just another way for her to say she did it all by herself. And she could have the credit. My mom's love wasn't worth its cost.

"Another big shin dig for Mrs. Vivian Parker," I told Gabrielle. She pretended to be surprised. "And guess what? You're invited too."

"Well how wonderful is that? I'll just have to go and get that dress I bought to wear to the Grammy's and wear it there instead," she joked.

"Tisk, tisk. No white attire after Labor Day."

We both laughed at the thought. Neither of us enjoyed the functions. The people were always so stuffy and snobby. They only mingled amongst each other. And every time someone asked my profession there was Paris explaining why I chose to be a teacher. Then she'd give a nod as if she'd done me a favor. But I could care less if I were accepted by her friends.

Actors, lawyers, doctors, marketing executives, the entire network of people were to be made fun of. The way they dressed. How they held their glasses and drank their champagne. How they stood with their hands in their Dockers pants pockets or sat with their legs crossed like a queen on her throne. They were all to be made fun of and I was just the one to do it with the help of Gabrielle, of course. The same people I kept away from were the same people I looked forward to seeing when I got there just so we could laugh all night long.

You couldn't tell them anything. They knew they were the best thing that ever walked the earth. And my mother validated it with her constant compliments and butt kissing. She stood proud among her eldest daughter and her high and mighty friends. Appeased by the way Paris could always draw a crowd, she would tell me, "You need to learn how to blend more in a crowd. You stick out like a sore thumb." I could have called her many things but I bit my tongue as I had on so many other occasions.

What did she want me to do? Most of the men barely escaped her overly flirtatious behavior. Did she want me to carry on the legacy of being the slut of the party? It wasn't my style. She wasn't fooling me. She may have fooled Paris, but not me. I knew she slept with at least two or three. I was sure about the first two but the third was questionable.

I am so happy my dad isn't around to see his wife act a total fool. He'd died ten years ago from colon cancer. The sweetest man you could ever meet. He'd give his last dime and his shirt off his back to anyone, especially me.

"Come on Jackson. Let's go to the park."

"Yeaaaa!" he screamed.

"You coming?" I asked Gabrielle.

"No, you guys go ahead. Have fun. I'm going to take a shower and get some rest."

"Alright."

Jackson and I stayed at the park for hours. I was trying to tire the little boy out but I think he got me instead. We both were tired by the time we got home. Jack sat quietly inside.

"I thought you were Gabi. Is she with you?" he raced to meet us at the door.

"No she was here when I left."

"I called her phone and she didn't answer."

"I don't know where she went."

Seconds later Gabrielle sauntered into the house. "Hey honey," she hugged Jackson. "Did you have fun at the park?"

"Where were you?" Jack quickly asked.

"I went to the office. I had to get some things for a meeting tomorrow," she explained.

"I called the office."

"Really? How long ago?"

"Maybe an hour ago."

"That was probably you that called. Yeah," she said flabbergasted. "I didn't pick up. I didn't want to be stuck in the office talking to anybody."

"And your cell phone?"

"It's dead," she showed him her phone. "What is this?

What's with all the questioning?"

Jack gave an unsure stare. I walked Jackson upstairs and prepared him for bed. I could hear them arguing while Jackson play in the tub.

"I'm just saying a lot of things aren't adding up lately."

"Like what?"

"All the late meetings and overtime. You never worked this much before."

"I'm working on a promotion. What do you expect?"

"Yeah, but you don't answer your phone most of the time."

"Jack, I'm not about to have this discussion with you. I can't believe you're questioning me because you were unfaithful in our marriage."

"This has nothing to do with what happened with us in the past. This is about you and how you've been acting lately."

"How? You know what, I don't even want to know," she blew him off. "This has everything to do with our past. You're afraid now that since you messed up that I might go behind your back and retaliate. Well you're not going to put this off on me. If you can't trust me or yourself then let's just end it now."

He was quiet. She had him right where she needed him. In the palm of her hand with a closed tight fist. Even if she were cheating, as long as she pulled his card and she hadn't been caught, she could get away with it for Lord knows how long.

"I'm not about to go through this every damn night, explaining where I've been and why I didn't answer my phone. When you catch me doing something, then that's when you have the right to question me. Until then, shut the hell up."

And that was that. The only thing he could say was, "You better watch who you're talking to. Don't disrespect me in my house."

"Like I said, shut up."

They exchanged few words before she went upstairs to her bedroom. I put Jackson in his bed and ran to my room. Tonight was one of those uncomfortable nights. I couldn't wait to get my place. It felt weird sleeping there when the two were at odds. As long as I stayed in my room, she stayed in hers, and Jack stayed downstairs, everything would remain cool.

* * * *

"Alright class, read the remainder of the story to yourselves. I don't want to hear any talking," I instructed my second graders. "Victor come here please."

The thin framed, usually bright-eyed boy rose to his feet and approached my desk. He seemed out of touch with things lately and missed a couple assignments. It was out of character for the boy. As one of my better students, he usually stood on top of things. But I noticed a distinct difference in his behavior and attitude towards school. He refused to work with a group or work at all. I allowed him to complete several assignments in class buying into the story of, "I left my homework at home" or "I only had a pen. I didn't have a pencil to write with."

"Where's your homework? Did you bring it with you today?" I asked him.

He gave a nod and walked to his desk to retrieve the incomplete assignment. I looked into his pitiful eyes.

"Why didn't you finish it?" I asked. "Didn't you have time?"

The boy shook his head 'no.'

"Victor, is there something wrong? Is there something you want to talk about?" I was filled with compassion. I really wanted to know. I couldn't stand to see a child so bright get lost in the system.

Again he shook his head.

"You know you can tell me anything, right? You know I'll do my best to help you with whatever the problem is okay?"

He gave a nod.

"But I can't help you sweetie, if you don't tell me what's the matter."

He wouldn't look up.

"Give me a hug," I told him and held him tight. Children were so sweet and innocent sometimes. I didn't know what was happening in this kid's life, but if anybody was misusing him I would make it my business to do whatever I had to do. "Okay honey, when you're ready to talk to me and tell me what's wrong you can. Okay?"

He gave another nod.

"Alright, go back to your desk and read the rest of the story. On your lunch, you're going to come and sit with me and finish your homework."

He sat at his desk and read. My class was quiet while I graded tests. The lunch bell rang shortly after and I walked them down to the cafeteria. Victor walked back with me.

"Hi Mrs. Johnson," I said to a coworker, "How was Hawaii?"

"Just beautiful. I'm ready to go back."

"Well take me with you when you go."

She smiled then took a glimpse of Victor standing near me with his tray, "I know he's not in trouble? Not my Victor."

"Yeah, your Victor," I looked into the timid boy's face, "Your Victor didn't finish his homework."

"Really? Now Victor, I know you don't want me to

call your mother. Do you?"

He shook his head 'no.' The older lady wasn't going for that.

"Excuse me?" she said.

"No ma'am," he corrected.

"Alright now. That's what I know. Don't think that because you're not in my class anymore you can act like you forgot."

He didn't say anything. I smiled.

"I heard that, but no, he's fine. He just didn't have enough time to complete his assignment so he's going to do it now. But he's usually on top of things. He just didn't have time last night."

I came to his defense. I didn't want her calling his mother. The boy was already experiencing something. I didn't want her prying and agitating the situation. Besides if anyone was going to call the child's mother it would be his current teacher, not his former teacher.

"Come on sweetie, so you can finish your lunch. Mrs. Johnson we'll talk to you later. I have to make a phone call."

"Okay," she dismissed us.

Cory had texted me minutes before lunch saying he missed me. It was his everyday routine. My heart remained bitter but I hadn't recovered all of my things. We needed to make arrangements to do so. I was tired of shopping for clothes and wearing repeats. And if I wore another one of Gabrielle's 'hi, I'm a successfully married, corporate America working, three year old child raising' suits again, I think I would just about die!

"Need to get my things. When will you be home?" I replied back to Cory's text.

"Seven."

I left it at that. I made plans to beat him to the house.

I still didn't want to see him. It may have been petty, but if I could avoid him at all costs then I would do just that.

"Miss Parker," Victor started. His eyes were so big and round. He couldn't hold it in any longer.

"Yes, baby," I felt like an old lady. At only twenty five I used terms like my grandma used on me.

"I finished my work."

"Okay, sit it here. Are you ready to talk now?"

"Yes," he was reluctant. I pulled the chair from my side desk. It was my teacher's pet chair for my students who were only exceptional that day. They could sit and have a treat and color. It was a huge privilege to sit in that chair.

"Alright, what's been happening? Whose been messing with Miss Parker's baby?" I tried lightening the mood.

"Nobody."

"Then what's the matter? I don't like to see you wearing such a long face. Tell me what I can do to make you happy?" I asked sincerely.

"Can you tell my mommy to come back home?" he asked.

It just about broke my heart. I was at a loss for words. What do you say to a seven year old who's losing his family?

He looked at me for reassurance. I had nothing. His problem was bigger than me. The bell rang. Lunch was over. I hadn't been happier in all the days of my life to get my class back so soon.

"Sweetie," I searched for words, "you know how I sometimes tell Jonathon to do something but even when I tell him to do something he still won't do it?"

"Yes."

"Well, I can't yell at him or make him do it because I'm not his mommy. It's just the same with your mommy. I can try and tell her to come home but I can't make her or yell at her if she doesn't because I'm not her mommy. You understand?"

He gave a disappointing nod.

"But I will give you a letter to take home today to your dad okay? Now don't let me forget. You have to remember to remind me. That'll be your job, okay?"

"Okay."

"Alright, sweetie pie. Let's go and get the class."

It was all I had. I didn't know what else to say. Poor baby, I thought to myself.

* * * *

"I can't believe I'm doing this again," Gabrielle complained as we approached the house. "I've got to be just as crazy as you."

"This will only take ten minutes. He doesn't get in until seven. I'm just going to run inside while you keep lookout."

She gave a sigh and rolled her eyes. "I don't know why your crazy, stubborn ass won't just talk to the man face to face. Why do we have to keep sneaking in his house?"

"If I see him he's just going to beg and—"

"So what? Then you tell him to kiss your ass. It's just that easy."

"It's not that easy."

"Yeah it is. You know what it is? You're afraid that he'll convince you to come back and you'll go for it."

"No I'm not."

"Yes you are."

"Whatever, Gabrielle. This is not the time to discuss this. Please give me the keys."

She handed them over. "Hurry up. I have plans for me and Jack to get busy tonight so don't take all day."

I ran to the front door and fumbled the key in the hole. It didn't fit. The sneaky bastard got the locks changed.

"What happened?" Gabrielle asked as I returned to the car.

"He changed the locks," I said contemplating my next move.

"Now you don't have any other choice but to see him."

"No, there's another way into the house. The bedroom window is broke. You need to—"

"Me? I'm not going through the window. Do you see this short skirt I have on? And I'm wearing a thong. There's no way you are getting me to go through anybody's window."

"Alright fine, I'll go through the window but you've got to give me a boost."

We walked over to the bedroom window. She struggled to give me a boost.

"Ouch!" I screamed as my stomach pressed against the window pane while I squirmed and scrambled to get the rest of my body inside.

In an instant, the bedroom door flung open and there stood Cory. I tried to pull myself out the window but I guess Gabrielle thought I was falling and she pushed me back up. Cory sprinted over the bed and pulled me inside. "Get your ass in here," he said.

I screamed to the top of my lungs.

"Let me go Cory!" I yelled.

"Kayla are you okay?" Gabrielle yelled from outside.

I was too busy fighting Cory off to answer. "Would you let me go?"

He pulled me into the bathroom and slammed the door. I tried escaping but he wouldn't let me pass. He blocked the door and stared without speaking.

"What?" I finally yelled becoming frustrated, "What do you want?"

Still, he didn't speak. He just stood there looking at me emotionless.

I put my hands on my hips, "What?"

"I miss you," he said still with no emotion.

I folded my arms. I wasn't trying to hear him. I made another attempt for the door. He cut me off.

"You miss me?"

"Kayla what's going on in there?" Gabrielle yelled from outside. "Open the door."

"I can't, Cory has me locked in—"

He covered my mouth. I bit his finger.

"Owe!" he yelled.

I tried escaping again but he wrestled to keep me in.

"What?" she yelled.

I bit him again and he yelled.

"Would you stop biting me?" he said.

"Stop putting your hands on me."

"I don't want you to leave."

"Too late, I'm already gone."

"Baby, I love you. Can't you see that? I messed up. I don't want anybody but you," he tried grabbing me when I pushed him off. "Baby, please I love you. I love you. I love you," he held me tight. I wanted to push him away, but it felt so good to be held by him again. I felt warm inside as he squeezed the bottom of my back and tugged at my hair. I refused to let our lips meet but I didn't stop him from kissing anywhere else.

I heard a loud thump as Gabrielle hit the bedroom

floor. She finally made it inside.

"Kayla!" she called. Her voice was in a panic.

"I'm in here, Gabi. I'm in the bathroom."

Cory looked at me hoping that I wouldn't leave. He still held my hair in his hands. His breath lay on my neck seducing every bone in my body.

"What's going on? Are you okay?"

"Yeah, I'm fine. We're just talking."

"Oh, okay. Well...,I was just asking 'cause I didn't know if I had to bust the door down," she said. "You know I've been doing my new TaeBo," Gabrielle teased.

"I know girl. Good looking out," I laughed

"Yea, fo' sho.' Um...just let me know if you need some aid and assist. You know I always got my strap," she had her big boy voice going.

"Alright, Gabi. I will." Cory and I both laughed.

"Okay! I'll just be in the kitchen....putting some ice on my bruised knee," she squealed returning to her womanhood.

"You look nice." He said still trying to seduce me.

"Thanks."

"Have you missed me?" he asked.

I didn't answer.

"Because I have missed you so much," he hugged me as tight as he could. "Ah, baby it feels so good to feel you again. Damn! I am so sorry. I never want to lose you again."

"You don't love me," I said still trying to hold on to the past. I couldn't give in so easily no matter how good this felt.

"Don't say that. I have missed you everyday you've been gone."

"When you love someone, you don't hurt them."

"I would never try to hurt you."

"But you did. And aren't those the same words you told to your girlfriend? You weren't trying to hurt her."

"What?"

"Cory, don't lie. I saw it in your phone the first time I came over to get my car. I saw that you talked to her for over an hour. I saw that you begged her to answer your calls."

He took a breath. "You saw me trying to clear the situation. I was trying to get closure. I'm not going to lie to you, I went out with her a couple of times while you and I were together but nothing happened."

"Yeah, right."

"I'm serious. Nothing like she made it out to be. She was never pregnant. We never had sex in my car. I never had sex with the girl. We went out and we talked on the phone. For the last two weeks leading up to the IHOP incident I hadn't seen or talked to the girl. Why do you think she was so pissed?"

"Because you were with me and acting like you didn't know her."

"You're right. The only person I was thinking about was you. I wasn't worried about her. I wasn't trying to hurt her, but if it came down to it and it was you or her then, hey," he said. "I see that she's a liar and she's crazy."

He continued to explain his side and was slowly winning me over.

"Let's go in the bedroom and makeup."

"Gabrielle is here."

"Let her take your car. Spend the night at home baby. Come back home."

I wanted to so badly. He kissed my neck and then my lips. I loved this man so much. I couldn't resist. He tugged at my pants. He was going to take me right there in the bath-room while Gabrielle iced her knee a few yards away in the kitchen. And I was going to let him until his phone rang.

It was a different ring tone. A kind of love tone that I couldn't quite put my finger on at the time. But it wasn't a tone that he would use for one of his guy friends.

"Who is that?"

"I don't know," he said trying to ignore it.

I stopped his kisses. "Pick it up and find out."

He hesitated, deliberately trying to let his voicemail catch it. "I'm busy," he said.

"You can't answer your phone now that I'm around?" I asked suspiciously.

"I can," he stalled. "You want me to answer?" The phone stopped ringing. "It stopped."

"I know it stopped because you waited so long." I became frustrated. "Forget it. I'm about to leave."

"What? It stopped ringing. What do you want me to do? You want me to call it back?" he bluffed.

"Yeah. I do."

"Alright, fine." He went into his phone and tried to be slick. Instead of redialing the last number into his phone he went to the call right before that. "It's John. I got his voicemail. See." He put the phone to my ear so I could hear John's voicemail.

"Let me see."

"What?"

"Can I see your phone please?"

He reluctantly handed it over.

"You must think I'm a stupid bitch. That wasn't John that just called you," I pointed out. "It was Lisa and you couldn't even answer your phone while I'm around."

"Mikayla, I can. I just don't want any more trouble."

"Shut up with your lies."

"I'm trying to get things right with us."

"How? By lying to me?"

"No, by avoiding her calls. If it makes you feel better the next time she calls I'll answer."

He couldn't have spoke it at a better time. The phone rang again. It was the same ring tone, Marvin Gaye's, 'Let's Get It On.'

"I suppose you're going to tell me that's John again with the ringer set at 'Let's Get It On,'" I asked him.

He didn't say anything.

"Should I call you a liar now or later?"

He reluctantly opened the cover on his phone and barely whispered, "Hello."

"Hi!" she bellowed, "What's up?"

"Nothing," he cleared his throat as he looked up at me timidly, "What's up with you?"

"I was going to head on over to——"

"Can I call you back?" he quickly interrupted.

"Why? You busy or something?"

"A little."

I grabbed the door. I wasn't going to clown or act a fool. I was done with the situation. I couldn't believe I almost allowed myself to be tricked into being a fool again. He stood in front of the door and held up one finger telling me to wait.

"No, fuck that. You're going to sit in my face and talk on the phone to that broad?"

He closed his flip phone. "You told me to answer!"

"Yeah, but you act like I wasn't even here."

"What did you want me to do...announce your name?"

"It's not about announcing me."

"What is it about then?"

"Cory, if you don't know by now then you will never know." There was no stopping me this time. I grabbed as many things as I could. Gabrielle, swollen knee and all, helped me pack my suitcases and laundry bags. Cory didn't stop us. He was full of confusion and frustration. He was fighting a losing battle.

"Is that everything?" Gabrielle asked.

I took one last look around. The closet was bare. The dresser was free of my jewelry and pictures. Nothing of mine remained. Not even a memory.

"Yeah, that's everything."

We prepared to make our exit.

"Lisa wait," he called to me.

I whipped my head around. Gabrielle couldn't believe her ears. Cory couldn't believe his mouth. I couldn't believe my reaction. Like a kid swearing before his mother he covered his mouth quickly. I could have slapped his face or burst into a rage, throwing things and tearing the house apart. I could have done a lot of things, but this time I walked out. I didn't even slam the door behind me.

CHAPTER 5

Today was the big day. So many things had to be done and I had so little time to do it. I had to pick up my dress from the cleaners, get my car washed, have my mother's gift wrapped and, to top it all off, I was due to meet with a parent today. Victor's dad, Mr. Lareau, called for a surprise meeting at the very last minute to discuss his son's behavior. After two weeks of sending letters back and forth to each other he finally found time to schedule a meeting with me. Of course it was on his time and at his convenience. No wonder Victor was having so many different issues. It seemed you needed an appointment to talk to the man.

It couldn't have fallen on a worse day, the day of my mother's surprise party. I had so many things to do and it all had to be done by six. Because it was report card week, I hadn't devoted my time to anything else. But I couldn't, I just couldn't break today's meeting. If I didn't speak to Mr. Lareau today then there was no telling when he would be available again.

The boy's mother was an even bigger task. It had already been clear that there was no use trying to reach her. My best option was to continue with notes and messages.

I wiped the chalk board while waiting on my three o'clock appointment. Unexpectedly, he arrived early at a quarter to.

"Ms. Parker?" he said standing at the door.

I turned to see him. I'd never met Mr. Lareau before. I'd never needed a reason until now. When I dismissed the children from school it was the boy's babysitter, Patricia, who always picked him up. I'd even spoken to her a few times telling her to forewarn Mr. Lareau that we needed a conference. She sent messages back saying, 'he said he'll call you with a date.'

And now the busy business man stood before me, suited and booted for the occasion. He looked as though he just left a press conference. His arm lay on the brim of the doorway just above his head. His seemingly Armani suit jacket hung perfectly above his wrist exposing his diamond embezzled Rolex watch. His freshly polished shoes shined underneath his tapered pants. He stood inquisitively and waited patiently before being invited in.

"Yes," I finally spoke, "Mr. Lareau?"

He smiled a very attractive smile as the scent of his Issey Miyaki cologne preceded him.

"Come in and have a seat, please," I finally invited.

The tall, fair complexioned man walked inside with a certain swagger about himself. It wasn't an 'I think I'm the shit' type of swagger, or a 'This is petty, I have more important things to tend to' type of swagger. It was more of a nervous, but 'let's get this done and over with,' type of swagger.

"You're not what I expected," he said.

"Really?" And I could say the same. He appeared to be a concerned parent which shocked me seeing that he took two weeks to meet with me.

"No not at all. I pictured an older lady at least early forties with gray hair. I guess I imagined my old second grade teacher."

"I get that a lot from most parents."

He sat in my teacher's pet chair. I wouldn't mind him being my pet for a day. I tried staying focused and professional. His lips, his nose, his goatee, his everything was sexy as hell. I tried to be on point and avoid the thought of straddling him right there in that chair right now.

"I'm sure you already know why I called for this conference," I started, "Victor has been really withdrawn lately. He isolates himself from the class. He barely hands in his homework which is very unusual for him. He discussed with me that his mother isn't in the home anymore. He wanted me to tell her to come back home."

He rolled his eyes in the back of his head and put his head down. "Is that so?" he seemed surprised.

"Yes. I'm not trying to pry or—"

"No, I understand you're doing what any good teacher would," he complimented. "I'm just surprised that's all."

"Haven't you noticed any differences in his behavior?"

"Actually I haven't. Victor's mom and I are going through a separation. But before we began having problems she was rarely at home anyway. We both work and travel a lot. Patricia usually handles everything for Victor regarding school. When I see Vic he acts like everything is cool."

I thought to myself, 'How messed up is that?' I don't care how successful parents are in their careers, children should come first.

"I'm sorry to hear about that," I told him but was I truly sorry? Of course, I was!

"Things happen," he said, "People make mistakes. We married too young and had Victor even younger. I'm still learning how to be a parent and maintain a successful career. I came from a middle class family, but dad was just fortunate to keep our heads above water. I tried not having that for my son. I pay for karate lessons, summer camps, basketball camps, you name it."

"I understand, but don't you miss the fun things in life that money can't pay for? What about sleepovers at your cousin's house and playing Mr. Freeze all night? Or, what about pillow fights, family nights, and catch a girl kiss a girl?"

His eyes lit up as I spoke about the good old days. He rubbed his freshly clean cut goatee.

"Victor is missing out on a lot of things that money can't afford. He might be in this and that sport but socially he's underdeveloped."

"I used to coach his little league and basketball team until things got really crazy, but you're right, I have to put my son first. Like I said I'm still trying to figure this whole good father thing out. Do you have children?"

"Yup."

"Seriously? How many?"

I directed his attention to the twenty eight desks aligned in the room. "Twenty nine if you include my God son."

He smiled. "You don't look like a woman with twenty nine children." he teased.

"Well thanks," I teased back.

"So baby momma," he started.

He was silly. Not at all like I pictured him either. His down to earth and humble attitude made me feel at ease when speaking to him. He was a cool parent, unlike some of the snotty, rich parents I'd spoken to when their sweet innocent Timmy misbehaved.

Mr. Lareau showed a deep concern, "What do you suggest I do in this situation? I should only ask an expert."

"I'm no expert but I think you should first start by making yourself more available. I don't know what you do professionally, but—"

"I'm part owner in a private airline company."

"Oh," I said. It was a demanding job. I could see how

he would keep so busy. 'Damn! He must be loaded,' I thought to myself. 'What in the hell is his wife thinking?'

"Well," I continued still impressed, "when you're doing whatever you're doing maybe you can set a certain schedule to follow for clients as well as Victor. Maybe begin by having every other Saturday a Victor day or something."

"Sounds like something I could do."

"And when you're out of town you should check in at least once a day, not to see what he's done but to see how he's doing, so he won't feel totally abandoned during the separation." I suggested. "What about his mother? Is she willing to see him?"

"Yeah, but she's in Australia. She won't return for another two weeks."

"Can he call her?"

"Yeah. We were trying to give each other time apart."

"My last suggestion is for you to try to work things out. I'm sorry but this isn't just your problem. You have a child involved," I told him. "Excuse me for being so direct."

"No please," he said. "We need all the help we can get."

"I'm glad you're at least doing this much."

He nodded his head attentively. "Thank you."

"No problem."

He stood to leave.

"We have a fieldtrip coming up. I'm taking the kids to see Disney on Ice if you would like to chaperone."

"Sounds like a plan."

"Is that a promise?"

"Yup. You got it, baby momma."

I laughed.

"Maybe I could do weekly checks with you to see how he's progressing in class. Is that okay?"

"I think that's a great idea. Just call the office."

"I'm going to leave my cell number so you can call me anytime...to talk about any problems... with Victor, I mean," he cleared the air.

"Alright."

He wrote his number on a Post-It and handed it to me but snatched it back as I reached for it. "Did you really play catch a girl, kiss a girl?" he smiled and teased.

I smiled back. 'Bad girl,' I thought for wishing it was him I played with instead of buck tooth Frank.

"Bad girl," he said almost reading my mind.

He and I talked until the school was just about to close. The administrative staff usually left by five and it was a quarter to. I would definitely be late for my mom's party and with that in mind my feet still stood planted in the concrete of our captivating conversation. I wanted to hear more about his life and how he became an owner of a multi-million dollar private airline company.

"You're still here," Mrs. Lewis the principal's secretary said walking by.

"Yeah, I'm having a meeting with a parent. We're just finishing up."

"Okay. I'll see you Monday. Have a good weekend."

"I'll try. You do the same," I said.

"I'll walk you to your car," he invited.

"Thanks." I grabbed my things, locked my room, and swiped myself out. "I am going to be so late."

"You got an important date tonight, huh?"

"No, unfortunately I'm not that lucky. I have to go to my mom's surprise birthday party."

"That doesn't sound so bad," he said. "Here let me help you with that."

Mr. Lareau took my teacher's bag that weighed about ten tons and threw it over his broad shoulder as if it weighed less than a feather. I stood impressed. A man with strength and shoulders like those, I wondered of other things he could lift so easily.

I banned the thought and changed my gears to park. I wasn't in the habit of perusing the streets of infidelity especially with married men.

"What's so bad about that?" he carried on.

"My sister is a talent agent so she knows a lot of top notch people that she's invited. I just don't feel like being bothered with the whole industry crowd tonight. The phony conversations and the whole stuffiness of the party isn't my style."

"I know what you mean. My wife's a model. I'm always at her little industry parties. The glitz and glamour isn't all what it's cracked up to be," he said. "I wonder if your sister knows my wife. The two may have crossed paths before. I wouldn't know. I refuse to go to another party where they only feed you sushi and cheese crackers."

"I know. I'm not into caviar and stuff. I'm guess I'm too ordinary."

"You don't seem so ordinary to me."

"Excuse me?"

"That's a compliment." He smiled and kind of just stared into my eyes for a moment. I gave a flirtatious smirk myself. There was no denying the attraction. The man was fine with his cute dimples and sexy, bushy eyebrows.

All too soon, we reached my car. I unlocked the doors and he placed the bag on my seat.

"Well it was nice talking to you," he said.

"Same here."

"Sorry I made you late."

"That's okay. It was worth it," I couldn't believe I said that. I didn't want him to take it out of context so I added, "Victor should do better now that we've talked."

"Yeah, I think so." he smiled again. His pearly white teeth shinned from the sun's reflection. "Have fun tonight and I'll be in touch."

"Okay, Mr. Lareau," I said regaining my professionalism.

"Stop with the Mr. Lareau. You're my baby momma now. Call me Eric."

I smiled, "Alright, baby daddy and you can call me...." Wait, what's my name? Oh yeah, "Mikayla."

"You sure," he laughed.

"Be quiet," I said embarrassed. "Yeah I'm sure. You just make sure you have your tail on that fieldtrip come November eleventh."

"I will."

He acted as if he didn't want me to leave. I didn't blame him because I acted the same.

"Here let me give you my email address just in case you have any problems or need anymore advice."

He was pleased. I figured it was just email. That was completely harmless. It would be different if it were my cell number or something.

We both stalled before we made our separate moves. I pretended not to watch as he walked to his car but I gave one last wave goodbye as I drove by.

"Gabrielle, do me a huge favor," I called desperately. "Are you dressed?"

I knew there was no making up for the time I'd lost while talking to Eric. Gabrielle had to help. She listened to my orders and quickly ended our phone call.

I arrived at my sister's condo almost an hour late. No one was there. I tried calling but Paris didn't answer her phone.

Gabrielle called in on my other line. "Hello."

"Where are you? Paris and your mom just walked in," she told me.

"I've been trying to call Paris. Tell her to answer her damn phone!" I calmed myself. "I'll be there in a minute. I'm sitting in front of Paris' house."

"Alright. I put your gift on the table."

"Okay, thanks."

People at the party danced and mostly mingled the night away. Gabrielle sat tucked away in a corner with two men who fought for her attention.

"Hi! You finally made it!" she escaped the men and gave me a 'get me out of here look.'

"Yeah I made it. How's it going so far?"

"I'm sorry, excuse me guys," she gave them the slip. The men waved her goodbye as she walked to the other side of the room with me. "Well, Mrs. Vivian was very excited to say the least. Paris questioned me about your whereabouts only a second ago. I told her Cory had an emergency and you had to drop him at home."

"Good looking out dog," I cheered.

We made our way to another corner of the room where the food sat. I noticed my mom and Paris in the midst of an attractive conversation as they sashayed from one person to the next with great poise and posture.

"Can we get some real food in here?" Gabrielle complained to me as she poked around the cheese crackers with mystery toppings.

"I stopped by White Castle on the way over. Can you believe they left me?"

"Yes I can, but let's talk about that White Castle. What did you have?" Gabrielle questioned.

"Chicken rings, a double cheeseburger, onion rings, and a milkshake."

"Damn!"

"Yeah, I know. I have to eat when my nerves are bad."

I reminded her.

"You could have saved a little for me. Look at this. Really, what is this?" Gabrielle held the cracker. "I can handle cheese crackers but what is this?"

I turned up my nose at it. "So what else did I miss?"

"Well, I think that guy," she pointed, "is Paris' new fling. And that guy," she pointed to another guy, "is Vivian's want to be fling. She's been hanging on his shoulder ever since she got here. And that guy too," she pointed to the guy next to her.

I scoped out the guy's behavior. Vivian, my mom, kept giving him the eye. How ridiculous.

"Oh my," Gabrielle said, "Here he comes."

"Who?"

"That guy with the green on. He's been giving me the eye all night."

I turned to see a slender, nerdy man edging near us. He tried to look cool and collective as he approached but someone bumped him on the way over and almost made him spill his drink. It was like something from a movie. He tried wiping himself but managed to only make the stain on his shirt bigger.

We turned our backs and laughed.

"Glad to see you made it," Paris snuck up from behind.

"Yes, I had a bit of a delay but I made it."

She didn't seem pleased or interested to hear.

"Mom seems to be having a good time," I said.

"Yeah," she looked over at our mother as the fifty-five year old woman hung on her new boyfriend, "Yes she does."

"Is that your boyfriend?"

She gave a 'how did you know' stare. "Yes, that's Martin. We met in Hawaii on a photo shoot."

"That's nice," I said returning a 'good for you' smirk.

"Where's Cory? I hear there was some emergency?" she stared suspiciously.

She knew something but searched for more. I needed rescuing but Gabrielle was wrapped in a conversation with Pointedexter. It seemed she needed rescuing herself.

"Can I have everyone's attention please," my mom spoke on the mic.

For the first time I was thrilled to hear my mother's voice.

"I just want to thank everyone for joining me tonight in celebration of my twenty-fifth birthday."

Everyone laughed.

"But seriously, I am so happy tonight to see so many semi-pretty faces..." the crowd laughed more. "What?" she played into it, "Anyway, I can't remember a better time than what I've had tonight and it's all because of a special person...my daughter Paris. Where is she?"

They all pointed to Paris who stood beside me waving her hand and smiling modestly.

"Come up here!" Mom demanded.

Paris ran up and stood beside her mom.

"Everyone, this is my heart, my best friend. A mother couldn't ask for a better child," she handed her a glass of champagne and everyone toasted to the mother and her perfect child.

I felt a tap on my elbow. It was Gabrielle. "Let's get out of here." She tilted her head towards Pointedexter hinting that she was ready to get away from him. I knew Gabrielle all too well and the truth was she was trying to escape for me.

I agreed and we both made our getaway. Gabrielle followed behind me to my new suburban town home that Jack helped me get. I got out while she sat in her car fumbling around.

"What are you doing?" I asked looking in. She

unlocked her door. I noticed the clear plastic bag on her lap. She looked up at me.

"I thought this would be the perfect night," she said. "So what's up?"

I sat in her car. She lit fire to the joint and took a pull before she passed it. For a second I held it in my hand. It had been so long since I got high but tonight I would break that streak. What would my kids think if they knew their second grade teacher smoked pot? After so many do not use drug lectures I sat here in my best friend's car with a joint squeezed between my two fingers.

I inhaled deeply, held it, and let it go. "You are a bad influence," I laughed taking another pull.

She held her hand out. "I needed this."

"You needed this? Huh, I think I needed this a little bit more than you."

"Yeah that could be true. You have been through some things."

"Tell me about it. I don't know whether I'm coming or going. Tell me Gabi, why is it that I find every no good man out here?"

"Oh, trust me there are worse. At least you didn't have to worry about a man bashing your head in."

"No, they just bashed my heart in." I took a pull and spoke with a weed smoker's voice. "I did everything for that boy. What else could he have wanted?"

"Well," she stopped.

"Well what? What? Tell me," I insisted.

"You did too much for Cory. You cooked, cleaned, washed, ironed, you catered to his every need."

"What's wrong with that? I always hear men complaining that they cheated because their girl didn't do this or that. I didn't want to be a product of that."

"Now you're a product of something else."

"What was I supposed to do?"

"Not tell him your every move. You would call him if you went to the grocery store. I don't care what anybody says, if you know you can steal and get away with it, then one day you're going to try."

"Yeah well he got caught. I'm done with relationships for a long time. Where's Mariah?"

I fumbled through her CD selection and found Mariah Carey's latest CD. The first song played and we danced our high butts off. It was my new theme song.

"No tears, no time to cry, just making the most of life!" I sang along. It was our moment to exhale.

It was late and we both began to doze until a knock bellowed at the car window. I turned to an older lady with extremely big glasses, wearing a moo-moo and a frown. I gave Gabrielle a few taps. She stared strangely at the woman.

"Who in the hell...." she whispered as I rolled down the window.

"Hello," I said politely.

"Hi. You girls okay?" Her tone didn't sound concerned as she looked past me at Gabrielle and throughout the rest of the car.

I knew she could smell the smoke as it seeped through the small crack of the open window. I wished I could go with it. How embarrassing! Being caught smoking weed by an old lady. It was on the same level as the time in high school when my boyfriend's grandfather walked in on us getting it on. Yeah, it totally blew my high then too.

"We're fine. We were just getting ready to go in."

"I was just checking. I know you girls been out here a long time."

"Yeah we were just...out here talking," Gabrielle

covered our mess, "But thanks for checking."

Even after the noticeably clear attempt to blow her off, the nosy old lady still wouldn't leave.

"I'm Miss Witherspoon. I live right here in twenty-two-o-four," she said. "You moved in here not long ago right?" she chatted to us at four in the morning in her slippers and moo-moo.

"Yes ma'am."

"Um hm," she said, "This is a quiet little village. I think you'll like it here if you the quiet type. We don't throw wild parties or hang out all night. It's very quiet around here," she informed but mostly warned.

"That's great," I laughed with Gabrielle at the nosy neighbor as she chattered on and on. Finally she left but we took notice of her constant peeps through her lace curtains.

"I am never coming over here again," Gabrielle teased.

"Can you believe that shit?"

"This is too much for me. Would you look at this...." We stared at the lady who stared back at us. "This is way out! You know what your ass is bad luck. Every time I'm with you crazy stuff happens. Climbing in windows, sneaking in houses, and now you got Grandma Moses looking at us. I promise you this is the last time you will see me at 2206 Hawthorne Drive."

I laughed so hard until tears fell from my eyes. Gabrielle kicked me out of her car and Miss. Witherspoon watched me go in. It was a very strange night. A very strange night.

Chapter 6

Buses loaded in front of the classroom window. The children cheered. They awaited their adventure of popcorn, cotton candy, glow lights, and Disney characters parading around on ice. I must admit I couldn't wait to see Cinderella myself. She was my favorite character of all time. Whenever I felt bombarded by my mother and Paris I would always imagine my dad as the prince to save me. There wasn't a time that he didn't save me until he died. So most of the ten years after that I had to rescue myself. Then I met Cory who made me feel like I was his everything. My empty life was filled with compliments, romantic evenings, great sex, and just down right good times. We fell in love so fast. He was everything I could ask for.

But that was old news. He is a closed chapter of my life.

I prepped the parents on their duties as chaperones. Mr. Lareau promised to attend but it was ten minutes before our departure and neither he nor Victor were present. I'd be lying if I said I wasn't disappointed but it was probably better that he didn't come.

I gathered the children and loaded them on the bus. Just before the driver stepped on the gas a green Jaguar blocked us. The tall man dressed in a button up shirt and faded jeans to match got out of the car with his son at his side. The two were dressed almost exactly the same in cute brown casual boots and three quarter length leathers. They were too clean.

My heart dropped. I was so happy he made it. I got off the bus to meet them.

"Hi, you made it," I said.

"I told you I would," he smiled nervously.

I checked my watch. "Come on. We're on this bus."

He and his son followed. I intentionally sat the two of them across from me. I briefed him on which students he'd be responsible for and he proudly accepted his responsibilities.

"They're not going to run all over me are they?" he asked uncertainly.

I laughed. How cute was that? He was afraid of second graders.

"They might."

"I may need the chaperone," he joked.

We arrived at the event in good time and took our seats. Eric sat next to me. I felt like we were on a date. Butterflies crowded my stomach.

"I emailed you," he continued to talk through the show.

"Really? I didn't have a chance to check. I had a busy weekend. What did you say?"

"Only thanking you for your time and that it was nice to meet you. Nothing fancy."

"Oh, you're welcome," I said modestly.

"You'd be proud of me this week," he bragged, "I took some time off work."

"That's nice to hear," I gave him his props.

"I'm trying to make an impression," he smiled.

I didn't know whether he meant for me or for his son. I left it alone.

He grabbed my hand and I instantly broke out into a sweat. He gave it a quick squeeze before he let go. I would have probably melted the ice had he held it any longer. I prayed there wasn't a puddle on my seat when I got up, and I'm not talking about from the sweat, either.

The show ended rather quickly. The children ate their lunches and we arrived back on school grounds just in time for my class to go to gym. Eric walked inside with me as most of the chaperones did.

I gave thanks for their help while he patiently waited his turn until the last parent left.

"You survived!" I teased.

"Yes, I guess I did. I made it."

"Thanks for helping out. Fieldtrips can get a little chaotic. I'm assuming this will be the last time I have you as a chaperone."

"No, I might try it out again. It wasn't so bad."

"Good. I bet Victor enjoyed you being there."

He gave a mannish giggle.

"What?" I asked.

"Nothing. I'll keep that one to myself."

Again I let it go.

"How was the party?"

"It was everything I expected."

"That bad huh?"

I shrugged my shoulders.

"We could have spent that time over dinner talking about our plans."

"Our plans?"

"Our plans for Victor," he covered.

"Oh," I understood. "That's what email is for."

"What good is email if you don't check it?"

"You're right. I apologize. I'll have to make it my business to check my emails everyday for messages from Mr. Lareau."

"Mr. Lareau? I told you Eric. For a teacher you don't learn very well."

I laughed at his comment. The last bell rang. We'd been talking the entire time. It felt like ten minutes every time we spoke instead of the actual time it was. He waited in the classroom while I got the children. I gave them free time. Soon the dismissal bell would ring and he'd be taking Victor home. For the first time I wasn't looking forward to dismissing my classroom. But that time came quickly.

"Take care," I said to him.

"Check your mail," he reminded.

"I will from now on."

I cleaned the room as everyone left. Before I could leave it was killing me inside to know what he said in his message. I opened my mailbox and a thank you greeting card popped up. The color filled email contained a boy saying 'Thank You' to his teacher by giving her a half eaten apple. It was cute.

I read his message. He wrote.

Hi Mickayla,

I enjoyed meeting you today. Thanks for the words of wisdom and advice. But for the record if I had a teacher that looked like you, I would have problems concentrating too. If you need anything (like a knight to save you from tonight's party) don't hesitate to call your Prince Charming.

Signed,
Your Baby Daddy

It sent chills up my spine. He offered to be my knight in shining armor. How poetic was that? And the cute little thank you card, he must have really been thinking about me. Wow! I was so impressed. I read it over and over again excusing the fact that he misspelled my name.

I lay back in my chair. The man is married not to mention his son is my student. I had to stop thinking about him. But I couldn't.

*　*　*　*

I chopped the vegetables slowly laughing to myself. "What?" Gabrielle asked.

"Nothing, nothing I was thinking about something," I concealed my secret inside.

If Gabrielle knew I laughed about the email Eric sent today she would have a stroke. I couldn't tell her I was talking to a married man no matter how innocent our relationship was. I couldn't tell her especially after I scolded her about her affair.

Eric and I carried on everyday emailing each other back and forth. The conversations grew a bit more flirtatious but not too outlandish. We were just friends and it would remain that way as long as his child was my student and he was married.

His wife was home and he said they were talking and possibly trying to work things out for Victor's sake. He said she continued with her selfish ways and seemed disinterested in their relationship. He described her as too involved in her career and wrapped up into her model friends. He even confided that he believed she was having an affair. Through all this he still wanted to stay. He was a good husband.

I laughed out loud again.

"Okay bitch," she said, "That's the third time you've laughed now tell me what's so damn funny."

"I was just thinking about something one of my parents said today."

"Today? You saw a parent today?"

I forgot all about today was Thanksgiving. We didn't have school today.

"I meant yesterday," I lied.

"Whatever. You know you've been acting real strange lately."

"Like how?"

"Like you got yourself a new piece and aren't sharing."

"I wish. I'm so sexually frustrated I don't know what to do. I'm almost desperate enough to call Cory."

"Hey, sometimes you gotta do what you gotta do."

"Naw, I don't want to go that route. I do, but I don't."

"I know what you mean."

"But I do miss it. He called me twice this week. I couldn't even pick up. Every time I see his number I see a big dick on the other end."

"You are too crazy!" she laughed.

"Girl, I'm serious. Cory was the biggest and best I ever had. That's why it's best I stay away. As long as its been, I'll probably end up pregnant."

"Shut up," she told me.

"Yeah I have to stay away from him," I convinced myself.

"Don't you have a vibrator?"

"Noooo," I squealed. "I wouldn't even know how to work it."

"You need to purchase one. Believe me you'll figure it out."

"Ugh, Gabi."

"Oh grow up. That should have been on your things to do list when you and Cory first broke up. Get your things, get a place, and buy a vibrator," she ran off the list.

"I don't know where to get one," I laughed.

"There's a place right off of eighty seventh. It's a girl's dream. We can go this weekend. I need to pick up some things."

"I always knew you were a hoe."

"How do you think I got my husband," she gave me a wink.

I continued to prepare Thanksgiving dinner.

"By the way, I forgot to tell you a friend of Jack's is joining us for dinner."

I put the knife down. "What kind of friend?"

"Just a friend he works with."

"Is this just a friend, friend or a let's fix Mikayla on a surprise blind date type of friend?"

"It's a let's fix Kayla on a surprise blind date type of friend."

"I knew it! Okay tell me the damage. What does he look like? How many kids does he have? How many teeth is he missing?"

"Matthew is very cute. I've seen him a couple of times and he's very nice looking. In fact I requested him for you. He's about the same height as Jack. He dresses nice. He's not married but has two kids and he has all his teeth."

"Sounds pretty decent. I'll have to check him out when he gets here."

"Yeah give him a chance."

"I wish you would have told me. I would have brought better clothes for the occasion."

"You'll be fine."

We finished our meal. The men watched their football

game before we served them. I had to be honest, Gabrielle did a great job choosing Matthew. He wasn't bad looking at all.

The nervous man introduced himself politely as I accepted his hand. It wasn't a strong grip like I was used to more like a flimsy female handshake. I believed he didn't want to seem too intimidating.

The night was short, yet long. We ate, talked, drank, and joked until it was time to go. Matthew walked me to my car. I could see the blinds moving as Gabrielle and Jack watched like concerned parents.

We exchanged numbers and decided to meet again for dinner the following night. He kissed my hand and said 'good night.' I could tell he was the romantic type. I took charge in our conversation and knew I would probably have to take charge in the bedroom. My body was so hot and horny that sex was all I could think about. I didn't care how strong I came across I needed sexual healing. Tomorrow Matthew would get it. He didn't have to say the right things or bring roses to my door. All he had to do was show up and be breathing.

Morning came and night fell. I responded to most of Eric's emails throughout the day. He pretended to be jealous when I told him I had a date. At least I think he was pretending.

Matthew showed up at my doorstep as planned and we left for the restaurant.

"You look very nice tonight," he said

"Thank you."

We ordered our meals and carried on basic conversation. I wanted to rush the night along and skip past the desert and foreplay. I initiated a steamy conversation by asking him if he thought sex was important in a relationship. Of course it was a spin off from a previous conversation so I had a legitimate excuse for bringing it up. I couldn't seem too desperate or too big of a whore.

"I think...well ...." he nervously stumbled through the question.

"Honestly, Matthew. I'm not looking for a right or wrong answer. I'm only looking for your opinion."

"Yes, I think two people have to be compatible sexually in order for things to work."

"I agree."

He gave a look. I returned with the same look. The next thing I knew he was asking for the check and we were in my bedroom undressing each other. At last I would finally get some action! I couldn't wait. He pulled his pants down and slipped on the rubber while my eyes scanned for more. There had to be more. 'Don't tell me that this is all!' I thought. I felt around for him. At first I thought this better not feel like it looks. But then I threw the thought out of my mind. I'd have to settle for what I could for now. I knew from past experience that size didn't matter all the time. Then again, his size was ridiculous.

He put himself inside of me and began to stroke back and forth. I was wrong for thinking it would feel like it looked. It felt worse. I could have used my finger and got off better than this! It was a total disappointment. Not only that but it ended seven minutes after it started. What a waste of my time.

Matthew lay in my bed worn out. I directed him to the bathroom so he could clean up. I wanted him out of my house. And now! He returned from the bathroom and lay back beside me. He tried kissing me but I turned the cheek. He turned my face and forced me to kiss him in the mouth. I thought I would vomit in his face.

I lay pretending to be sleepy, hoping he would put his things on and leave. He didn't. He stayed the entire night. I couldn't believe my luck. Gabrielle had better start digging her grave.

Chapter 7

I covered my face in humiliation. Gabrielle had no shame. She strolled in and headed straight for the back. She needed no direction or assistance. She was a pro.

"Back again, huh?" the girl asked from behind the counter. She couldn't have been any older than twenty one, twenty two. How did she land a job here?

"Yeah and I got fresh meat." Gabrielle joked.

I was mortified. How could she joke at a time like this? And so openly with others around, watching and listening.

"This is a good one. The Butterfly."

"The Butterfly?" I read the package as Gabrielle moved on.

"Okay, here it is," she picked up the package, "The Rabbit." Her eyes lit up as though she held diamonds.

"What does it do?"

"It's guaranteed to give you an orgasm."

"But how does it work?"

"You just attach the straps around your legs like this," she pointed to the picture of the lady on the box, "and there's a switch that you adjust to whatever speed you want."

"Wow, that's crazy," I examined. "Oh my goodness, look at this one."

I pointed to the extremely large black penis on the shelf.

"Yeah it's huge isn't it?" she picked it up like it was nothing, "But it's just a dildo."

"What does that mean? What's the difference?"

"Vibrators work on their own. Dildo's are just like men, you have to do all the work."

"Put his ass back on the shelf then."

"That's what I'm saying," she put it back and searched around. "They don't have the one I was looking for."

"Which one is that?"

"It's called Wild Willy. It's a vibrator with the clit stimulator and rotating beads. Oh my goodness..."

"Okay Gabi, you're getting a little too excited." I looked at more toys on the wall. "They have everything here. Come here! Look at this!"

She ran over. "Butt plugs?" she frowned, "Ugh Kayla, you're nasty."

'Not for me!' I started to say but the girl in the store walked over.

"That's a nice selection," she said, "Would you like me to take it to the counter for you?"

She asked as I held the plugs. "No, I'm just looking," I said uncomfortably.

"No problem. You ladies need help finding anything?"

She was loose and unconcerned. It was like working in a candy store for her.

"No thanks," I said politely.

"I do. Hey where's your Wild Willy? Are you guys all out?" Gabrielle asked.

"Um, I think we are but," she walked away, "we have a new one in." She pulled a purple wrapped package in a shipping box. "Ready Ralphie. We just got it in today. I haven't even put it on the shelf yet."

Gabrielle inspected it. She would have the final say.

"It has five different speeds, here let me show you."

The clerk took the package from its box and inserted batteries. The object began to rotate and utter vibrations throughout the store. I was full of shame. The sales lady continued describing all the features. Then she tried to get me to touch it. "It's made of soft latex so that it feels real."

"No thanks," I declined.

"Girl, touch the damn thing," Gabrielle demanded. "Stop being so paranoid. Everyone in here is looking for the same things that you are."

She fronted me so bad.

I touched it. It felt icky. It felt rubbery and jiggly on the tip of my finger.

"Doesn't that feel real?"

"Ewe, it does."

"She'll take it," Gabrielle told her.

"Wait I'm not getting this one am I?" I asked. I didn't want the same vibrator that we all had been touching.

"No this is our demo," she explained before she wrapped it up, gave me batteries, and got my virgin butt out of there.

"I can't believe I bought a vibrator," I said getting into the car.

"I can't believe you were such a wimp about it."

"What do you expect? It was my first time in a shop like that. Why didn't you ever take me there before?"

"I don't know. You can be such a baby sometimes. I didn't think you could handle it."

I didn't know how to handle her comment. Gabrielle was so open minded, so wise, and so knowledgeable. Her head was always screwed on right. I was almost the opposite. I wondered how we became best friends. Was it because we'd grown up together? So young and only two years older than me, Gabrielle took me in. We'd grown up almost in the same house. I ate, slept, and breathed her home life and tight family core. It was my place of solitude away from home and away from my mom and Paris.

"Gabi, do you think I'm not understanding?"

"What?"

"Do you think that whatever you tell me I'll understand?"

"I think that no matter what I tell you you'll be honest about it."

It wasn't a real answer.

"Do you think I'm opinionated and closed minded?"

She thought for a minute. What was so hard?

"I mean, when you told me about your fling with Todd, did you expect me to chew you out like that?"

"Mikayla, I needed to tell someone because it was eating me up inside. I knew before I opened my mouth that you wouldn't approve. I wanted an honest opinion and that's what I got."

"So would you tell me if you continued to see him or would you hide it from me?"

"I don't know."

"Honestly Gabrielle?"

"Kayla! I don't know. The point is I'm not seeing Todd anymore so I can't hide it."

"I know but," I stopped to think. "What would you have said if I would have told you that I was seeing a married man? Would you have been as harsh as I was? I just want to know what you would have said."

"Kayla, I think I would have told you to be careful and that you're playing with fire. I would have said not to fall in love and try to make your marriage work," she stopped. "Yup, that's what I would have said."

It wasn't at all what I said to her. I told her to end her affair immediately. I told her she was risking losing her family over that man. I barely allowed her to speak about him. I basically called her a whore for sleeping with a married man.

"So what happened with him? Does he still call?"

"No. After I told him that I was going to work things out with my husband and he should work things out with his wife, we pretty much haven't spoken to each other."

"How did that happen? I mean, what makes people cheat on their husband or wife? I understand why you cheated but—"

"You do?"

"Yeah I do. I just didn't understand why you cheated with someone married."

"It was the safest route and it's not like I planned it."

"I guess." I thought some more. "Are you and Jack alright now? How's the counseling?"

"The counseling is over. That ended months ago. We're managing, but it'll never be the same and I'll tell you what, I'll never trust him again."

"I'll never trust any man again."

She hunched her shoulders wanting to tell me to keep an open mind but she didn't know if she'd ever trust another man herself. Then she thought some more.

"I don't know how it began," she said, "All I know is I was distraught and broken up about catching Jack. I had a gut feeling but I never had anything concrete and when I found the lipstick in my car and the letter torn up hidden under the seat, it was like I still didn't want to believe it. But it was real and no matter how much he wanted to deny it or I didn't want to accept it, it was real."

"You taped it back together? How many pieces were there?"

"There were like twenty pieces. You damn right I taped it together! I took it into the room while he sat on his laptop and I started reading it. 'I love making love to you. I wish you could stay all night instead of running home to her.' Can you believe she called me a 'her'?" Gabrielle asked me.

"I don't know what I would have done." I'd heard this story before a million times but I think her telling it over and over again was therapeutic. I didn't mind listening. Each time she added something new and gave a different reaction.

"He turned every color in the book," she carried on. "I've never seen a black man turn so many colors," she laughed. "He started stuttering... 'I uh...I....she...where'd you get that'?" She laughed some more. "I took my fist, letter and all and punched him in mouth. I thought he was going to cry when he saw his blood. Then I told him to call that bitch and tell her that you don't have to come home to 'her' anymore. 'She can have you!' That's when the begging began and the crying. 'Baby please don't leave me'," she imitated some more. "Then I bust him in his mouth again and left him and Jackson there."

"I remember I called that night and he sounded so sick. 'Kayla don't play with me. Have you seen Gabrielle for real?'" We laughed at my impersonation of Jack. "I was like 'what in the heck are you talking about?' He didn't want to tell me."

"Now you know Jack wasn't going to tell that. That's the only person in this world that can keep a secret. I don't tell anybody's business, but damn, I have to tell at least one person or it'll eat me up inside."

"Tell me about it."

She drifted back into her thoughts, "He begged and pleaded and told the 'I'll do anything' lies and I bought into it. We were in counseling for all of three weeks when his schedule got too hectic."

"But I thought you continued to go?"

"I did," she hesitated for a moment. I saw her reluctance to speak her next words.

"What?"

"Nothing."

I decided to leave it alone. It was her business and though we were best friends it was her decision to tell it or not. I was ready to move on to the next subject when she raced the words out of her mouth.

"That's how I met Todd," she refused to look at me.

"Huh?" I asked dumbfounded, "How?"

"Kayla....He's the counselor," she confessed.

I was thrown for a loop. She couldn't be telling the truth. She had to be lying. The only person I knew who counseled them was....

"The deacon of your church?" I asked.

She nodded her head in shame. I stood frozen. I was shocked. It wasn't that I was disgusted or anything or being judgmental. I just couldn't understand how in the hell, I mean, heck that happened.

So I asked her, "How in the hell did that happen?"

"To tell you the truth I have no idea. It was just that I could confide in Todd about anything. We first began talking about my problems with Jack and our sex life and just everything. It didn't feel like I was talking to a counselor or a deacon at all. He'd become my friend. Then we'd talk for hours on any day. He was so understanding and knowledgeable. One day the church had a celebration for the choir, you remember the one I invited you to?"

"Yes, the one that I couldn't go to because I had a principal's class that weekend?" I reflected on that day almost a year ago. She'd asked me to go but I was stuck in class. When I asked her how the celebration went she just said 'it went well' and left it at that. Now I wanted to see how well it really went.

"Yeah that one," she continued, "After the celebration everyone rallied in their cars and I asked if we could have a conference in his office. One minute we were talking about Jack and I, the next minute I was butt naked on his desk."

"In the church Gabi?" I screamed. I couldn't believe my ears.

"I know I'm going straight to hell."

"Girl, you're going under hell."

"I know but at the moment I couldn't help it. He was saying things to me that I wanted to hear from Jack. He would tell me how beautiful I am. Seriously Kayla, when I found out about Jack and that girl that really fucked me up." She trembled thinking about it. "I felt like I wasn't attractive. My body changed so much after Jackson. I figured that was why he cheated in the first place."

I looked at my best friend in disbelief. I was stunned that she felt that way. I never knew such things about her.

"Gabi, you have one of the baddest figures out here." I told her. "Mother or not."

"I couldn't see that. Todd said how beautiful I was, told me that some men don't know what they have. Just laid it on real thick, but he was so sincere." She kind of gave a soft smile just thinking about it. "He made me stand to my feet and look in the mirror. He wanted me to see the beauty in myself. He stood behind me whispering in my ear 'you are beautiful' while I recited it. I turned to give him an innocent hug and...and."

"And what?" I hung onto her every word.

"And his dick was hard," she said. I almost fell out. A deacon with a hard ding dong?

"I think he wanted to move but I kind of gripped his arm. I wanted it just as much as he did. Then he kissed me. I don't even think my husband has ever kissed me like that. I think I leaked a puddle on the church floor. Up 'til then Jack and I hadn't had sex in shoot, forever. To this day I can count on my hands how many times we've had sex since the affair."

"Really?"

"Yea."

I listened attentively as all the skeletons came out of her closet. I couldn't wait for us to have this same conversation at a later date. I wondered what else she would come clean about.

"I've had sex with Todd more times this year than I have with my own husband," she added.

I wanted to jump out of the car window. This was too much! But I concealed it all inside and maintained best friend mode.

"That's crazy."

"I just don't trust him. I can't sleep with him and be comfortable. He made me feel so self consciousness. Every time we try to have sex, I'm thinking in the back of my mind, 'did he fuck this girl like he's fucking me? Is he still seeing that bitch?' A wife shouldn't have to worry about things like that."

I thought about what she was saying. Of course Eric came to mind. I would immediately stop talking to him. If we continued, our innocent friendship would turn into a scandalous affair just as Gabrielle and Todd's. I couldn't do that to another woman. I just couldn't.

"You know you've been sheltered a little too long," she interrupted my thoughts. "Do you think Ralphie will stand up to the test?"

I laughed. She didn't need to worry I was going to put Ralphie to work tonight. My phone rang.

"Hello."

"Hi baby."

"What do you want Cory?" I signaled Gabrielle to let her know it was "him" calling me. She gave me the 'don't give in girl' look.

"I was about to drive by Gabrielle's and I was wondering if you were over there so I could stop by."

"Sorry I'm out right now?"

"With who?"

"None of your business!"

"Okay," he said. "How was your Thanksgiving?"

"It was nice. I enjoyed myself. And yours?"

"I was lonely and bored. I would have had a better time if I'd been with you."

I wanted to say 'good, suffer!' But I didn't.

Instead I commented, "Lisa isn't good company these days?"

"There's nothing between me and Lisa. Come on honey, don't start. I don't want to argue."

"Who's arguing?"

"Alright, Mikayla?" he let it go.

"Is that all?"

He smacked his lips. "Christmas is coming up. It's our special day. I wanted to invite you over for dinner."

"Who's cooking?"

"What do you mean who's cooking? I'm cooking."

"If you're cooking, I'm not eating."

"Don't be like that. You know I can throw down."

"We must be having breakfast?"

"I cook more than breakfast. You said we. Does that mean yes?"

I thought about it for a second. It would be nice to spend Christmas with Cory. It was our best holiday. He always knew what to buy me and we would spend the evening listening to old Christmas songs. I'd make Rice Krispy Treats and he'd make cocoa. I didn't even like cocoa but Cory made the best cocoa I ever tasted. Then we'd stay up late sharing childhood Christmas tales and watching the Christmas Story at least two or three times. It was always a great time.

"I don't think that would be a good idea," I refused.

"Please," he begged.

I wanted to say sure but I couldn't. "Let's wait until it gets closer to that time."

"So you'll think about it?"

"Yeah, I'll think about it," I gave in. "Alright but I have to go."

"Okay, I love you."

"Okay, bye."

He would never hear those words from my mouth again. I don't care how true he or I knew it was, he would never hear me say it.

Once Gabrielle dropped me at home, I rushed to my computer. Thirty six new messages. I scrolled through the junk and made it to the three that were from Eric.

EricsDaMan.com: Hey, This conference is so boring. Please save me. I could use some of your great conversation right now. Email me!!! PLEASEEEEE!!!

He wrote in his first message. Then he sent a second saying:

EricsDaMan.com: Hey, Baby Momma! What are you doing? Is it anything I should know about? Are you cheating on me? I haven't heard from you today. If you can give me a call. I'm still mad about your date the other night too. Don't think I forgot.

Signed,
Your baby daddy

EricsDaMan.com: Hey, I could really use some advice. Call when you get in.

I emailed him immediately. There must have been some emergency with Victor.

OKMikay.com: "What is it?"

What could it be that had him so troubled?

EricsDaMan.com: Finally you email me back. Never mind now.

OKMikay.com: You've got to be kidding? What's the matter?

EricsDaMan.com: Nothing. I was desperate to talk to you today. Where were you when I needed you?

OKMikay.com: I'm sorry I wasn't by a computer I was too busy buying a vibrator.

There was a short pause before his next instant message. It was bold of me but I figured what the heck, he was my 'baby daddy.' We talked about everything else under the sun. Why not tell him I bought a toy?

EricsDaMan.com: Call me.

OKMikay.com: No thanks. I've suffered enough embarrassment for a day. How was your day? How is Victor enjoying Tampa?

EricsDaMan.com: He loves it. We went to the zoo after my conference. He had a ball but our day wasn't as vibrating as yours.

OKMikay.com: Very funny. Question, do you find me easy to talk to?

EricsDaMan.com: Extremely. Why?

OKMikay.com: Just asking.

EricsDaMan.com: You're like a breath of fresh air. I feel like I can talk to you about anything. I'm hoping we can be eternal friends.

It was the perfect answer. I sat back in the chair. Man was Ralphie going to get a workout tonight. We instant messaged each other for hours. He continued to beg for my phone number but I continued to decline. Our conversations were personal but I wasn't ready to take it up a level. Nor was I ready to let him go yet either.

Every time we emailed I learned more and more about him. I imagined how his lips curled a certain way when he spoke or how he raised his eyebrow.

He asked me to go Christmas shopping with him. His wife would be out of town again doing a photo shoot in Brazil or somewhere. She'd be back home for Christmas but would leave thereafter. I accepted. I needed to do a bit of shopping of my own.

Next Saturday, he planned a whole day of shopping and lunch. It would be our first day alone together but in a public place. I couldn't be alone, alone. Bad things would happen. Bad things like what was about to happen to lil' Ralphie.

I cut open the package. The smell of latex scattered the room. I sucked it up. It reminded me of a freshly opened baby doll on Christmas day. At first, I stared at it. Could I really do this? Could I really put this thing on my private? Humph, why not?

I turned it on and watched it rotate. Then I turned off every light in the room, blasted the sound on the television and lay flat on the bed. I tried getting my mind right for the occasion, thinking of every possible sexy scenario I could.

I thought about Cory but that wasn't getting it. I'd get halfway there then back to square one when thoughts of Lisa popped into my head. Then I fantasized about threesomes. I was turned on by the idea of getting so much attention by more than one guy. I played with the thought some more. Cory was one and the other was Eric. It was beginning to put me over the top.

I began to penetrate Ralphie just a little bit deeper inside me as the stimulus on my clitoris intensified greatly. Ten minutes into the show I was about to explode. Pretty soon my visual excluded Cory and only Eric remained. I imagined his soft kisses below my belly line and his strong hands grasping my breasts.

He was a man with power and connections. It turned me on thinking about how he paid for the high ranking lawyer to get my case thrown out. When I asked how much I owed him, he just winked and said 'this one is on the house.' Now the pepper spray incident was behind me. I didn't have a record or anything. It was like it never existed.

I pictured him in the courtroom even though he couldn't make it because he was away on business. I imagined the judge's comments and me being free to go. He and I would celebrate right there in the courtroom after everyone had left. On the judge's stand is where he undressed me. Only a man of power belonged there and he would exercise his rights by taking advantage of me in every possible position.

My breathing became more exaggerated. There was no stopping it now. With little warning and great determination, I was at my peak. I moaned loudly and squirmed around the bed before settling comfortably into relaxation and falling asleep on a sexual high.

Chapter 8

"Good morning," I spoke gaily to my coworkers.

"Hello."

"Mrs. Maddox, have we decided on who will lead the committee meeting Friday?"

"Not yet. I'll ask Karen when she gets in."

"Thanks."

"You're in a good mood today."

"Am I? I don't know what's different."

"Me either, but you need to spread a little of that joy around here," she smiled. "By the way, you have a package in your mailbox."

"What is it?" I checked the box. "What is this?"

"I don't know. It came Fed Ex first thing this morning," she informed.

I pulled the beautifully wrapped box from my mail slot.

"Is it your birthday or do you just have an admirer?"

"It's not my birthday," I told the older white haired lady, "I'm not sure what it is." The early bell rang. "Oh shoot!"

"Come in for lunch and let me know what it is."

"I promise!" I yelled running to my class. I settled into the room writing the morning story on the chalk board. I couldn't wait to open my package but I had to complete my morning duties before my class lined up. Once everything was done I quickly settled my children, we did our pledge, and I gave them their first assignments.

I grabbed the package from my desk and opened it. Inside was a cell phone and two way pager. On the two way read:

Now we can talk whenever we want to.

I couldn't believe my eyes. Was this man crazy or what? I quickly replied back:

What are you up to Eric?

Good morning. See isn't this better?

I can't accept this.

Don't be like that. It's an innocent gift so that we can keep communication open in case we need to ask about Vic.

Yeah right.

What? You think you're that cute and this is all about you?

No.

I was modest believing that I was getting beside myself.

Well it is and you are.

I began to blush. He was so sweet. How many men would buy a girl a phone and two-way just so they could talk to her? I couldn't think of one. He was going to make it hard for me to cut him out of my life.

Keep it. I can't email you Saturday if shopping plans change.

I was convinced he was right and I would keep the pager and cell phone but after we went shopping I would give it back immediately.

Alright.

* * * *

83

I stood waiting patiently with my back against the brick storefront wall. My arms, legs, and face though bundled and protected against the winter's frigid air, now felt cold and numb. I took another sip of my hot apple cider and let it warm my throat, chest, and pit of my stomach. The steam struck my face and the warm sensation tingled against the pores on my skin.

I loved apple cider. This small and intimate coffee shop seemingly had the best I'd ever tasted.

"Twelve fifteen." I read my watch. I wondered if I should head in. He only said to meet at the coffee shop. He never said inside. There I stood watching the crowd of holiday shoppers and busy traffic. Across the way I noticed a sign, "The Poetry Corner." It invited guests to see the show from Wednesdays thru Sundays from seven to one in the morning.

Gabrielle and I would have to try the place out one day. I wondered what they'd talk about and how poetic it would be. Ideally I imagined another rendition of "Love Jones" except a better version of a sequel personally staring Mikayla. But yeah right, in my dreams! I'd keep on fantasizing. And keep hope alive.

It was probably like any other spoken word café. I pictured a tall man with dreads dressed in a black turtle neck with a green mock sweater over it. He'd wear creaseless jeans and have both ears pierced and dark Stacy Adams with a thick sole. His verses would include a speech about how he lost his woman or how the white man stood in his way of whatever.

Nevertheless, I'd still give it a try.

"Hi!" Eric snuck up from behind. I almost choked on my cider. "I'm sorry I didn't mean to scare you."

I looked into those big brown eyes of his that lay under those beautiful brows surrounded by those gorgeous lashes and it gave me butterflies. I felt like I was in high school all over again.

"That's alright," I smiled.

"You're early. Have you been waiting long?" he seemed concerned.

"No, not that long. Ten minutes max."

"Good." He gave a great big smile and my heart melted.

"What?" I asked, feeling a little shy.

"Nothing. I'm just happy you agreed to come that's all." He gave another smile.

"What?!"

We laughed it off as he and I walked to our first store. He put his arm around me. I was a little uncomfortable as I thought about his wife. What if someone saw us? What if she saw us? He didn't seem worried or at all concerned but I still found a way to maneuver myself out of his arms and out of harm's way.

I helped to pick various toys that I thought Victor would need. Eric really didn't need my help. It was more so my company that he really wanted. I didn't mind though. We enjoyed taking a trip down memory lane over all the toys we used to have and how technology has changed since we were younger.

"Oh wow!" I exclaimed, "Rainbow Brite! I loved Rainbow Brite." I examined every part of her and her pal. "I remember being younger and wanting her and all her friends but I only got the doll. Look at her. Isn't she cute?"

He agreed but barely paid any attention to the less interesting, girly toys I was involved with. I sat her back on the shelf and continued to look around while he played with every toy he bought for Victor. I didn't know whether he was buying toys for himself or for the boy. Either way, the two would have a great time playing together.

I picked a few items for Jackson. I always went overboard for Christmas. I couldn't help it. It was my favorite holiday.

Eric and I shopped around for other gifts for other friends and family. Then he grabbed his gut to suggest he was starving. We took a cab to a nearby Italian restaurant.

"So," I began and took a sip of water, "How's married life?"

He fidgeted around the table. "It is what it is, you know? It's still the same. Always will be, I guess."

"Can I ask you something personal?" I was full of questions. He invited them with open ears. "Do you love your wife?"

He thought for a second. "I do but I don't think love is good enough. I'm not sure if she loves me anymore."

"Why would you think something like that?"

He took a breath before explaining, "My wife isn't interested in making things work. She's not compassionate towards my feelings. When I'm home she doesn't want to be. When we are home together she sleeps in one room and I sleep in another. It's hell right now."

I listened as he poured his heart out about his marriage.

"I've tried everything. She accuses me of having an affair. This is the first time I've ever entertained a woman outside of her. I've never cheated on my wife. I honestly think she's cheating."

"So what are your options now? Where are you mentally in this relationship?"

"I'm out for happiness. I'm tired of stressing over a woman who doesn't want me. I'm at the point now where I don't even want her anymore. It's sad to say, but it's the truth," he told me, "I just want to be happy and move on and....I can't lie, I'm attracted to you."

It was an unexpected surprise. Nice but unexpected.

"I understand your feelings on the whole situation and I respect that but I can't say that there's no pressure, because frankly, I'm going to make it hard for you," he bluntly told me.

His assertiveness was turning me on. It was a great thing that I kept my level head. There was too much to lose. My job and my morals were at risk. No man was worth either. But if Victor wasn't my student there was a slight possibility that I would be attacking him right now on this dinner table.

I smiled at his comment. "How are you going to make it hard for me?"

"You'll see," he said confidently. He leaned back and lay his arm on top of his chair. He gave a huge grin showing off his dimples.

"Now why would you want to make it hard for me? You have a wife and family. I mean, why?"

He leaned forward again and looked deep into my eyes. His eyes were serious, his whispers were stern, "Mikayla, I want you."

"You want to sleep with me," I told him.

"Naw, sweetheart, you don't get it. We've already made love."

"Come again?"

"Just because we haven't had physical sex doesn't mean we haven't made love. That's where people go wrong. Everything starts here," he tapped his head, "Anger, sadness, happiness, love, it all starts here."

I listened closely waiting for his point.

"I'm already up there in your head," he said without a doubt.

I gave him the 'oh really?' look.

"If I wasn't, you wouldn't be here with me now."

I shrugged my shoulders, "Okay Mr. Know-It-All."

"So you're going to tell me that you don't daydream or fantasize about making love to me?" he blatantly asked.

I opted to not answer.

"That's beside the point. The fact that we connect on so many levels shows we belong together. We can talk about anything. Who else can you do that with?"

I thought for a minute. Honestly, I couldn't talk like that to anyone. Eric and I had developed such a relationship that even speaking about sexual positions with someone else was just as easy going as speaking about the weather. Let me try to talk to Cory about past partners or even present. He would blow a gasket.

"Regardless if I'm not in your head, you're in mine. I fantasize about you at night when I lay in between the cold sheets. I'm wishing you were my wife and I should be coming home to you. Some nights when my wife's cold, heartless body lays next to me I lay there getting rock hard thinking about how I would do you."

'How would you do me daddy?' I thought to myself. I wanted so badly to ask.

"I think how I'd hold you down until you just can't take it anymore...."

'That's what I'm talking about daddy!' I screamed inside. I loved an aggressive man.

"And dream about hitting it from the back and all types of other freaky stuff, all while my wife lay next to me. Now what type of shit is that?!" he said. "I shouldn't feel like that. I should be happy with the woman I'm with and right now..." he grabbed my hand. "I'm happy with the woman I'm with."

He smiled as he held my hand. I wanted to snatch away but didn't want to reject him. Luckily our waitress returned with our food.

"Here we go!" she said placing our meals on the table.

The two of us ate, finished our heated conversation, grabbed our bags and headed for the car. I drove him to his car since he hadn't found a close parking space.

"I had a nice time," he stalled to get out.

"So did I."

"We'll do it again one day?"

"Yea, I don't know about the shopping part."

"Why? Did you overspend?"

"Just a little," I lied knowing damn well I'd overspent a lot.

"You'll get that back," he said, "It's only money. You can't take it with you."

'Yeah, thanks for the piece of knowledge.' At least my stomach was full even though my wallet and checking account was empty.

He got up. "Can I get a hug or something? I bought dinner I can't even get a hug?" he teased.

"Just like a man to think you owe him something because he sprung for dinner," I teased back. "Do you want your money back?"

"No you keep it," he walked around to my side of the car.

I opened my door. "Good because I wasn't going to give it anyway."

"I know because you can't afford to." We both laughed. Then unexpectedly, he pulled me up from the car by my hand. "Come here. Give me a hug," he held me around my waist and squeezed me tightly. My entire body tingled. "I don't know when I'll see you again. I hope I didn't scare you off."

"You don't scare me Eric."

"Good," he whispered in my ear, "Let me kiss you."

Oh no! I wasn't about to go that route. He pulled my face to his. His lips were the softest I ever tasted. Oh yes! I had gone that route. I didn't stop. I'd gone that far, I might as well enjoy every second of it. It couldn't go any further in the parking lot so why not enjoy the moment?

For the longest time, the two of us were glued together. Our tongues did a dance of their own. And after that kiss...that sweet wonderful, sensual soft kiss was over, I felt light headed. It was every bit of what I fantasized, plus more. My heart dropped to the pit of my stomach. The feeling was awesome.

"Come with me tonight," he said.

"No, I can't."

"Please," he begged.

"No Eric." I was beginning to get the 'this isn't right' feeling again.

He stopped hounding and accepted my rejection.

"See you soon," he said after a few more kisses.

We both got into our cars. I waited as he started his then he jumped out and back into mine.

"I have to let it warm up," he said before kissing me again. We stay in my car kissing and touching for almost an hour until I finally kicked him out. That man really knows his way around a woman! He managed to get underneath every layer of my clothing. Nothing much happened. He felt the print of my vagina but I wouldn't let him finger me and he felt my breasts but I wouldn't let him lick me.

He vowed to get me soon and all I could say was, "Let the games begin!"

Chapter 9

I wish I could say it stopped there but I'd be lying if I did.

It was Christmas break when Eric realized he'd accidentally grabbed one of my bags. Seeing that he was in my neighborhood, I accepted the invitation of him briefly dropping it by. It was late and I refused to let him in.

"Sit outside with me for a minute then," he said.

I did but only on the condition that he parked elsewhere in avoidance of Miss Witherspoon. He agreed and we pulled into a dark parking lot of another complex. Our long talks turned into heavy petting and long deep kisses. His hands were down my panties again. This time I let his fingers penetrate me while he kissed my breasts. I swear this man had the softest lips ever! They were as soft as silk.

I tried stopping him many times but he could see in my eyes that I wanted it just as badly as he. He continued his assertiveness until my pants were at my ankles and I was in the back seat of his Range Rover. He flicked on the light.

"What are you doing?" I covered myself.

"I just want to see it. Let me see what it looks like." He moved my hands.

I was so embarrassed. This was crazy. I lay uncomfortably while he stared down on me.

"Turn the light off," I demanded.

He obliged while I tried pulling my clothes up.

"Wait. What are you doing?"

"Eric, I can't do this."

He fought against my rejections until we both settled on a compromise.

"Let me just see what it tastes like," he said, "I promise I won't do anything else."

I didn't want to at first but he held my hands and ignored my screams of 'no.' And when he put his face between my thighs and I felt that soft damp tongue, I shut up and let it be.

Afterwards, he dropped me off. Not once did he ask to come in. He cleaned himself outside with hand sanitizer and washed his mouth with a small bottle of Scope that he claimed he keeps in the car when he has to go from the airport to a meeting.

I floated inside my house and ran upstairs and gave Ralphie a workout.

Chapter 10

It was trouble in the making. Gabrielle agreed. So I began to avoid Eric at all costs. I wouldn't let him come over and refused to see him. He invited me to spend the New Year with him. I politely turned that down too. I knew the next time we saw each other there would be no stopping either of us. So until I was strong enough I would have to stay away.

It was Christmas Eve and I had a date with Cory. He didn't let me live it down.

I arrived at the house just at dusk. The Christmas lights glistened underneath the pale moon light. Although it was a great attempt of decorating by a true bachelor, it was far from the exceptional look I used to give it.

My feet soaked into the welcome mat as my trembling fingers pressed against the bell. The door slid open and Cory stood before me wearing no shirt, just a cut up chest from peck to peck, and an eight pack to match. His sweat pants slouched heavily off him exposing just a tiny little bit of his waist line.

He looked hot!

He extended his arms and we hugged. I tried distancing my feelings from his warm comfortable arms but the butterflies in my stomach turned into sweet sensations. I pushed him away.

"Wait," he said and pointed to the ceiling. A mistletoe that he'd planted purposely hung above the door.

"You'd like to see that happen," I replied.

"Come on. It's tradition. Just one little kiss."

I played his game and leaned over and teased him with a slight peck. His lips begged for more but he accepted what I gave and I slid past him inside.

A familiar aroma lingered about the house. "It smells good in here. What's cooking?"

My eyes did a quick scan of the room, looking for any trace of another woman's possible presence or left belongings.

"I made us greens, candied yams, mac and cheese and the turkey is almost done."

"You threw down, huh?"

"I tried my best." He popped his imaginary collar. "Make yourself at home." He grabbed my hand and led me to the sofa. "Can I get you something to drink?"

He treated me as though I'd never been there before.

"Yeah, sure."

He walked into the kitchen and returned with a glass of chilled wine.

"Thank you but don't try to get me tipsy," I told him.

"I'm not trying to get you tipsy," he said, "I'm trying to get you drunk." I giggled at the comment while he sat next to me. "So how have you been?"

"Great."

"Really? Don't tell me that," his face frowned.

"What should I tell you then?"

"Tell me you've been miserable and missing me."

"Boy puhleeaase. Life goes on."

"Mine hasn't."

"Whatever, Cory." I wasn't going for tricks.

He snuck a quick kiss on my cheek. "You're so cute!" he

said while getting up to check on the turkey. "Ay, come in here!" I followed his command and joined him in the kitchen.

"But really, I'm happy that you're doing so well."

I looked in his pots. It had all the symptoms of his mother's cooking. "Who helped you cook?"

"What?" he asked defensively, "What do you mean?"

"Cory, you and I both know you wouldn't know what a turkey looks like let alone know how to cook one."

"You see how much I've grown since you've been gone?"

"Yea, and I wonder who you're learning it from."

"Don't do that," he said bluntly stopping me in my tracks. "Nobody is teaching me anything. I just never had to do things on my own before."

"Maybe I should have left you sooner." I continued nosing around the kitchen.

"Had I found out about the little slut sooner I would have left," is what I wanted to say but I didn't. Instead I disregarded the grimace on his face.

"Maybe you should come back home tonight and teach me for yourself," he said.

"Maybe I should set the table."

"Set the table?" he said, "Since when have we ever set the table for Christmas dinner?"

Excuse me. I thought tonight he was trying to be impressive. Cook dinner, set the scenery, pamper and beg me instead of our usual traditional Christmas dinner.

"Do you want the table set?" he asked me. "We can have dinner at the table if you want."

I thought for a moment. Sitting in front of the television watching Christmas movies, listening to the Temptations, playing Scrabble, all sounded so much better than a boring romantic dinner together.

"No, we can eat in the front," I said.

"You sure?"

"Positive."

"Okay." He fixed our plates while I carried the drinks.

"Ah, ah." he stopped me and pointed upward. Above hung another mistletoe. He was toying with me but what the hell, I couldn't break tradition and no matter how many mistletoes he'd planted around this damn place, I was not giving him anything more than a kiss.

Still holding the plates of food, he wrapped his arms around me and stuck his tongue down my throat. I would have pushed him away but I didn't want to spill our drinks. Not to mention, damn it, I didn't want to! But now I was teasing myself.

"That's enough." I pulled back. He tried cornering me against the wall but I weaseled my way around and took a seat on the couch.

"This is pretty good," I complimented.

"I told you I'm learning."

"Well good for you."

We finished dinner. "Man that was good!"

"Yes, tell your mother thanks."

"My mom didn't have anything to do with this meal," he lied.

He could deny it all he wanted. I knew his mother's cooking from anywhere. The sage in the dressing, the amount of cinnamon on her sweet potatoes, and no one else seasoned a turkey the way she did. It was her credit and I would call her and tell how great it was.

"No I'm lying. She did cook."

"I knew it. You are such a spoiled brat."

"She couldn't resist when I told her that her favorite daughter-in-law was coming over for dinner," he exaggerated. But it was partly true. I was her favorite. And she was such a sweet woman. I wouldn't have minded having her as a mother-in-law had her son not screwed up.

We watched "A Christmas Story" in each other's arms like old times. He grabbed me close and at first I fought but ultimately gave in. Every now and then he'd give me a quick peck on the forehead to test the waters. When I didn't resist he tried to take it a little further by grabbing my breast in his hand.

"Stop!" I swatted his hand and lay my hand back on his thigh.

I could feel him contracting his penis up and down underneath my arm. It was turning me on. He grabbed for my breast again.

"Cory! Stop!" I yelled.

"Okay. Okay," he said.

Less than a minute later he pulled my face to his and tongued me. I loved every second of it but of course I pretended to be agitated.

"Stop, Cory!" I said. "You know what? That's enough lover boy."

I grabbed his empty plate and carried it to the kitchen. On the countertop lay all the ingredients to make Rice Krispy treats.

"You just assumed I'd be making treats huh?" I yelled from the kitchen.

He joined me, "You know how we do."

"Whatever." I grabbed the marshmallows and butter and put them into the pot. The fire instantly made them into soft mushy clumps as I continually stirred. Cory stood behind me with his arms wrapped around my waist.

"You're going to make me burn it," I complained.

He sniffed my hair and then my neck. It was something about my scent that always got him going. I was glad that I made sure I wore his favorite perfume. He was crazy over Perry Ellis.

"Mmmm, you smell so good. I miss this smell," he said to me.

I continued to stir the pot, trying to stay occupied before I exploded. His hands were tied tight around my waist. I felt faint by his grip as he tugged and pulled at my clothes. He slowly led his hands on my butt and private area.

"Cory, stop," I begged. I was getting weak.

He smelled his hand. "Mmmm, see I miss that smell. Give me a sample of what you got cooking down there." He licked all ten of his fingers. He was so nasty.

My smile went from ear to ear. He knew exactly where the power switch was to turn me on. I hadn't had sex in so long. I was tired of all the foreplay and my vibrator. I wanted the real thing.

"No," I rejected his offer.

"Please baby," he begged pulling his sweats down and showing his rock hard penis. "Just a little taste."

"No, you're going to make me burn our treats."

"Fuck those treats." He turned the fire off and grabbed me by my waist lifting me onto the counter. "I got a treat for you."

"No, I got a treat for you," I boldly told him.

"Yea, that's what I'm talking about."

With a little help from me he pulled my pants down. "You want this treat?" I asked.

"Yes baby, and I'm real hungry too."

"Well come and get it."

"Open wide," he ordered then took one foot and stood it at one side of the counter. He took the other and sat it at the other end of the counter. I lay back with both my knees up, legs spread, and my womanhood fully exposed.

He stood back seducing me with his eyes and mapping out his agenda. He teased me by licking his lips before leaping head first in my juices. With my eyes closed I could only hear smacks of his lips and slurps of his tongue.

"How does it taste baby?" I asked.

"This pussy tastes good," he managed to say. "Mmm. Mmm Mmm," he moaned and smacked his lips. Almost instantaneously I came over and over again.

Every so often, I would ask myself, 'had he ate Lisa out like this?" but the shit was so good, I would throw it out my brain so as not to ruin the moment.

He finally lifted his head. His face soaked in pussy juice. He took a step back. He wanted to fuck but was scared if he asked, I'd run out on him.

He decided to take a chance. "Give me that pussy," he whispered softly while tickling my now extremely sensitive clit.

"You sure you ready for this?" I asked

"Is it still that good?"

"Even better."

He was just about to put it in when a flash of Lisa flew through my mind.

"Stop," I demanded

"What?"

"Stop."

"Why?"

I climbed off the counter and grabbed my clothes from the table where he'd thrown them.

"Kayla, please wait. Please don't go," he begged.

I don't know if he begged because he really didn't want me to leave or because he didn't want blue balls.

"I'm not going anywhere," I told him and lay my clothes on the counter, "Your turn."

I demanded he lay back on the table. I was going to suck the shit out of his dick. It had been so long and I was feigning for a taste myself.

Yes, I thought about Lisa, which is why I stopped him.

This was about to be the best blow job he ever had. I intended to perform the best head of my life. And when I was done sucking the skin off his dick, I was going to ride it until I put his ass to sleep.

He lay on the table. I stood between his long legs licking my lips. Slowly, I went down on the head and grabbed his balls while I deep throated his gigantic cock. I went up and down on it just the way he liked it while I jagged it off with the other hand. He moaned in ecstasy and clawed my hair. I squeezed his dick harder arousing the both of us even more before he exploded in my mouth. I looked at him and swallowed. He was in awe. In total astonishment. I'd never swallowed before. I always said it was disgusting. But tonight I was trying to leave my mark. Fuck Lisa. She didn't have shit on me.

He lay weak on the table. His dick began to go limp. It was normal. He always needed at least five minutes before round two. I knew exactly what to do. I climbed on the small long wooden table and stood over him. My pussy stood directly in the view of his face. I played with my clit at first then penetrated myself with my finger. I pretended to be excited but the only thing that thrilled me most was that Cory enjoyed it.

His eyes grew huge. He was impressed. Houston we have lift off! He pulled me down on him. I straddled him carefully. As much shit as I talk, Cory would kill my pussy with his massive penis. I didn't want to end up in the hospital on Christmas Eve.

Gently, I pushed him inside me and rode him slowly for the first couple minutes until I got adjusted. His feet dangled off the table.

He moved my hips back and forth. I lay my hands atop his and put it on him! He screamed like a little girl as I took in all that dick. I lifted off almost all the way and fell right back on it. Then I clamped my muscles tight and wiggled my hips. Next, I leaned over him so only my ass could lift off while he sucked my tits and slapped my ass.

"Oh, I like that baby," I moaned, "You like that?"

"Mmm, hmm."

"Me too. Do it again." He slapped my ass again. "Oh yeah daddy. That's turning me on."

I'd succeeded in getting all in his head. Within seconds, he let out many wails as he climaxed.

"You cumming?"

"Uugghh!" he yelled.

"Yeah," I said still moving my hips. I should have climbed off before he climaxed but I wanted him to have it all. I hope my birth control patch was on its job tonight.

I tried getting up but he pulled me down and made me lay on his chest. He was still inside me but neither of us cared.

"Come on," I said, "get up."

"I love you." He pulled my face to his and kissed me. It felt nice. I could feel him getting harder and harder inside me. He was ready for round three and so was I.

He sat up while I rode him again. Then he lifted off the table with my ass in the palm of his hands and carried me to the bedroom.

The last orgasm took forever. I was so sore by the time we were done. My body throbbed and throbbed until finally I didn't notice the pain between my snores. I fell asleep wrapped in his arms. We both slept late Christmas morning and opened our gifts at one in the afternoon.

"Thank you sweetie. It's beautiful," I said looking at my new diamond bracelet. It had to cost a fortune. It was no comparison to the Kenneth Cole watch and Sean John outfit I bought him.

"You don't remember this?" he asked. "You saw this in the store when we went to the Bahamas last year."

I stared at the bracelet. I thought it looked familiar. "This is that bracelet! Cory, how'd you get this?"

"I called the store, described the bracelet, and even drew a picture of it and faxed it to the manager. He took a picture from an old brochure, faxed it to me. I said 'yup that's the one' and then he special ordered it because they'd sold the last one. I've been working on this for months," he bragged on all his extra efforts.

I was grateful that he'd gone through all that trouble. I gave thanks and got dressed, said my goodbyes and darted out the door.

"Wait," he stopped me. "When am I going to see you again?"

"I'll call you."

Chapter 11

I arrived at my mom's house at a quarter to three. For once I was on time. Paris and my mom sat in the front room drinking wine. Their new boyfriends sat at their sides.

"Hi honey!" my mom greeted me at the front door. She was trying to make an impression in front of her new boyfriend. "I'm so happy you made it." She kissed my cheek.

"Hi mom," I said taken back. I wanted to wash her kiss away but instead of doing so I politely sat my gifts down and introduced myself.

"Nice to meet you, I'm Martin." The first guy said.

"Same here, Martin." I turned to the next guy who sat near my mom. "Hi, I'm Kayla."

"Chuck, that's my other daughter Mikayla," she corrected.

"Hi Mikayla, I'm Chuck."

I gave her the evil eye and took a seat on the chaise.

"We were just getting ready to have dinner. Mikayla, entertain our company while we set the table."

"Sure." I sat inside while Paris and my mom went into the dining area and gossiped about their men.

I talked with the boys who seemed to be not any bit as stiff as my mother and sister. Our conversation was just getting good when my mom announced that it was dinner time.

The conversation was boring but it was what I

expected. I tried pretending to be interested but it showed all in my face.

"Mikayla, where's Cory?" My mom asked.

"Why didn't he come? Was there another emergency?" Paris added sarcastically. The two laughed.

"Actually, no there wasn't another emergency."

"What is it then?"

"It's not important." I tried avoiding the topic.

"I bet they broke up," Paris announced at the table. She was out of pocket. Was it even necessary to make an assumption even if it were true?

"I wouldn't be surprised. I knew it wouldn't last," my mother added. She too was out of line. Why did we have to discuss my love life at the dinner table? "Mikayla can't stay with one man for too long."

Did she just call me a hoe? Her insinuation pissed me off. "I got it honest," I said.

"Mikayla!" Paris said appalled.

My mom tried laughing it off.

"She's only teasing you. Why do you have to be so stiff all the time. Loosen up." She looked around the table smiling at the two men who could see the rising tension. They sank in their chairs.

"Me stiff?" I asked. "Maybe I am stiff but maybe it's because I can't relax around you two."

"Oh here we go again."

"Let's discuss this at another date," my mom now insisted since things got ugly.

"It's true Paris, and you know it." I ignored her request. Since they wanted to talk about Mikayla then Mikayla would talk about Paris and Vivian as well. It didn't make me a bit of a difference. I didn't have a man at the table.

"I know Mikayla. Mom and I always team up against

you," Paris said even more sarcastically.

"You don't see it?" I asked.

"No Mikayla, I don't see it. What I do see is you acting like the fourth graders that you teach."

"I teach second grade," I corrected my sister. I gave her a look of disbelief. How could she not know that?

"Leave it alone Paris. You know Mikayla has always had a grudge against you."

I slammed my fork onto the table. "Why do I have a grudge mom?"

"You've always been jealous of Paris since day one. You've always wanted her life, her friends, her charm, her looks," she tried down playing her words by smiling around the room. She spoke as if everyone already knew these things were true. "You've always wanted to be Paris but you will always be you."

"What does that mean? What am I?"

She became agitated. "You're the unhappy jealous little sister who sits in the shadows wanting to shine but doesn't know how."

She talked like it was nothing. As though it was normal for every little sister to behave in such a way.

I couldn't believe my ears. It wasn't the worse thing she said but it was the first time she said it. Everyone tried returning to a normal dinner routine. Martin and Chuck barely took a breath but timidly managed to take a bite of their food. I sat in my seat half defeated when something rose inside me.

"That's bullshit." Never in my life had I swore in the company of my mother. Paris had normal conversations that involved cursing and all types of vulgarities. It was acceptable for her. But let me try it and I'm "unlady like."

"Mikayla!" Paris screamed again trying to silence me.

"No fuck that Paris! I'm tired! Tired of all the bullshit

that you two give me for not being her!" I screamed and pointed at Paris. "For your information I'm very happy in my life. I can deal with being ordinary and having an ordinary job and friends. I'm happy when I'm not around you two."

"Well good Mikayla. Stay away," my mom said.

"Mom," Paris called to our mother.

"You think I don't try? You think I want to be surrounded by your sweet precious Paris, a name fit only for a princess." I threw my hands in the air to mimic her prissy motions. "You think I want to be surrounded by the princess and the queen of darkness?"

"Mikayla, you're acting like a child!" Paris yelled.

"Shut up bitch!" Wow did that feel good. I'd waited so long to get that off my chest. "Another thing, if you'd stop playing crowd pleaser and act like a mother, you would see that your sweet, popular, charming Paris is just as unhappy as you are. But you're too selfish. You're not worried about me or Paris!"

The boys held their heads down as Vivian looked to them convincingly.

"I've always done right by you girls. Paris has always had everything she wanted."

"Everything except a mother."

"I'm her best friend. You're just jealous of that."

"Jealous! I am so tired of you giving yourself that much credit in my life. Mom I don't care if we're friends. We've never been friends so I'm not bothered by that because I don't know what I'm missing."

"And you never will." She stared me in my eyes with extreme aversion. I knew this look. She'd given it on occasions before. At that point she couldn't stand my guts.

"That's great. You couldn't have given me a better gift."

"Mikayla why do you always play the victim?" My sister asked.

Didn't I tell that bitch to shut up already? But I answered her question.

"Paris, I'm not the victim. Your mother's the victim and so are you. The sad thing is neither of you know it." I was done. There wasn't anything else to say. The decision was made. I would just stay away and everyone would be happy. I got up to leave when this bitch agitated the situation.

"Whatever. Get yourself a man so you can relax," my mom laughed it off and I had fire in my eyes.

"Like you did when Paris went away to college. Sorry mom, I think all of Paris' boyfriends are taken but that never stopped you so why should the apple fall far away from the tree?"

There it was. All the family secrets exposed. Our mother was a true whore. She was stunned. In fact, everyone was stunned. The boys hid their faces in shame. They basically buried their faces underneath their plates. Chuck especially. He adjusted the collar on his mock turtleneck that now seemed to be choking him.

Martin sat motionless. I only saw the top of his head because he kept it bent down and stared at his plate. He refused to lift up for a second.

I pointed to Paris and then to my mom, "Oh please, don't act like you had no idea. And you don't act innocent. You had to know what was going on. You think Ted was hanging around the house to be surrounded by your ambiance of memories? Of course not!"

"He came over because he knew she'd be calling," my mom reminded.

"Yeah right. She didn't have his home number? Paris..." I boldly looked her in the eyes. "Ted was fucking mom. And on a daily basis. She even made him drive her to get an abortion," I spilled all the beans.

"Mikayla, you're crazy. Why would you say such things?" my mom almost cried.

"Because fortunately this whore tells the truth. I was never the one who wanted to be Paris. That's you mom, always running behind her from man to man, party to party. Why do you act like that? You are fifty-five years old."

"What am I suppose to do, knit all day?" she asked me.

"Pick up a hobby besides screwing your daughter's boyfriends. You don't think that's embarrassing? Her friends are laughing at her, not with her, and you're facilitating that. That's not how a best friend or mother acts."

"Paris you don't believe her," she pleaded.

I looked into Paris' eyes. She believed me. She knew before, I even opened my mouth. She wasn't stupid.

"She's lying," mom said. "You are a lying, jealous slut."

"I may be lot of things but jealous and a liar ain't one of them. I may even be a slut but that's an inherited trait. Hell, it may be the only thing I did get from you." I looked around the room in disgust. I could no longer stomach being in the room with them another minute.

"To hell with this. I don't need you. I've had enemies treat me better. You two have a wonderful Jerry Springer-filled life."

I marched out of the room leaving the four of them to finish their Christmas dinner as one big happy family, just the way they liked it. I didn't take anything with me not a single gift, plate, or bad memory. I was out of there.

The time wasn't even six in the evening. I contemplated calling Gabrielle but I didn't want to spoil her Christmas with her family. I thought about calling Cory but he was due to go to his mom's. I didn't want to invite myself to their Christmas dinner.

I went home to wallow away in my anger and sorrow. Even Miss Witherspoon wasn't home. Her bathroom and porch light were on. Those were true signs of her not being home.

I warmed apple cider, turned on my Temptations CD and sat in the dark and watched my Christmas lights as they blink and danced around my tree. For hours I sat on my chaise alone and then my phone rang.

"Hello."

"Merry Christmas!" Eric screamed. He was so glad I answered his call.

"Merry Christmas to you. What are you doing calling me?" I really didn't care. Right now it didn't matter who saved me.

"You know I can always make time for you," he said. "How's your Christmas?"

"What can I say? It is what it is."

"What's the matter sweet pea? Everything alright?" he asked in an overprotective tone.

"I'm fine. I don't want to bring you down on your holiday."

"Don't talk like that. You know you can never bring anything down on me." We laughed. "But seriously, what's wrong? You know you can talk to me about anything."

"I know Eric but I really don't want to talk about it. I just want it all to go away."

He meditated on the thought. "I have a surprise for you," he said.

"What?"

"I think it will brighten your day," he hinted.

"Okay. When do I get it?"

"When do you want it?"

"When can I see you?"

"When do you want to?"

"Don't act like you can see me anytime. You can't get away when you want to."

"Baby, I'm a grown man," he told me. "This is all about you. You better start believing me."

I should have called his bluff but I already knew without a doubt he wouldn't pass the opportunity to spend Christmas with me.

"When are you going to come and get it?" he asked. There was a sexual undertone in his voice.

"I'll get it soon," I flirted back. "I got something for you too."

"When can I get that?"

"That depends on if you've been a good boy. Have you been a good boy?"

"I'm trying to be bad but you won't let me. But I promise when I'm bad it'll be reeaaal good."

We carried on for a bit when I heard a knock at my door. I gaped through my peephole and noticed Cory standing on my step.

"Eric, can I call you back?"

"Yeah, sure."

I open the door. "Hi. What are you doing here?"

"I stopped by your mother's on my way from mom's. I brought you a plate." He held the plate of food for me to see. "My mom says hi and to come visit her."

I invited him in. My house was pitch black. He didn't attempt to turn on the lights. I warmed my plate of food. What a wonderful surprise. I was starving. Because I was so angry, I stormed out before eating.

"Thanks. I'm so hungry."

He sat on the sofa and watched the lights. Not once did he interrupt while I ate.

"Did Vivian tell you what happened?"

He hunched his shoulders. "Somewhat."

I sat my plate on the table. "I bet she made it all seem my fault."

He waved his hand for me to come over to him. I did and he kissed my forehead. "I'm a witness to your family. That's why I'm here."

He wrapped his arms around me tight. I lay my head on his chest. "You still love me don't you?" I needed love right now.

"Always."

"Tell me why?"

"You're always there for me. You're sweet, understanding, patient, beautiful inside and out. You're my best friend."

"But that wasn't enough?" I asked. "Talk to me Cory."

"What do you want to talk about baby?"

"I want to know what it was. I thought our relationship was perfect. I thought we could tell each other anything. Why couldn't you tell me I wasn't doing my job. Why couldn't you tell me you wanted to sleep with another woman? We were best friends. I just don't get it."

My tone was solid but non threatening. It was true. Cory and I were best friends since day one. You can't mold a relationship like that. We could have talked about anything. He knew my feelings for him. What would make him wander and hurt me so bad?

"Kayla, it was something I...." he started but lost his words, "I don't know."

"Cory, you do know. Just tell me what it was."

"Baby," he rubbed through my hair, "it was just me being stupid. It was a mistake."

"How can you make the same mistakes for five months?"

"The time flew by. And in the beginning I didn't even see her as much. We maybe saw each other once a week for the first month. After that maybe twice a week. It was something to do."

"Why couldn't you do me?" I sat up and looked into his eyes. All the pain came back. Tears filled my face. "Why'd you have to go out and do someone else?"

He wiped the tears away. "Mikayla I love you more than anything in this world. Baby please don't cry. I never wanted to see you cry tears over me."

"But you hurt me," my voice quivered.

"I know baby but I promise you if you give me another chance that will never happen again. I promise you," he hugged me tight. "We can move back in together and get married tomorrow and I promise you won't ever hear about Lisa or any other woman again. I only want you."

He swore by his mistakes and I was willing to at least listen and think about giving our relationship another try. Maybe it was what we needed. Maybe he needed to cheat to get it out of his system and I needed to catch him so I wouldn't be so free with him. Maybe this whole experience is something we both needed.

I didn't know. I would have to think about it.

Chapter 12

"Do you think you're going to take him back?" Gabrielle asked me on our way to church. She'd invited me to a New Year's celebration. Jack was supposed to go with her but the two were at each other's throats.

I didn't mind. I was eager to see Todd. I'd been to her church a dozen times and I couldn't remember which one he was.

"I don't know. I'm thinking about it."

"I knew it wouldn't be long before you two got back together."

"It's been almost five months. I just hope I could trust him again."

"Don't I know what you mean."

We arrived at the church right on time. Patrons ran inside to grab a good seat. We did the same. The pews were packed with people eager to confess their resolutions to the Lord and make changes. I had a few resolutions of my own.

"That's him," Gabrielle whispered about Todd who now approached the pulpit.

He was a tall, tall slender man. He wore glasses and a fitted black suit. I watch as his wedding ring glistened in the lights as he adjusted the microphone. He cleared his throat and began to make announcements. "Let the church say Amen," he said.

"Amen!" Gabrielle shouted. I looked at her as she gazed at him. Her eyes lit up. I thought to myself 'what in the hell' I mean 'heck does she see in this man?'

If the big fat lady in the first pew with the big, purple hat were to breathe too hard his frail body would blow in the wind. And when he spoke, his voice was not strong like a regular deacon or pastor, it was weak and shaky.

Me being a teeth person, I did notice right away his perfect smile. It seemed sweet and innocent. That was about all I noticed. But Gabrielle stood in awe. She listened closely as he gave announcements like her life depended on it. I tried to figure out what she saw in him. Finally, I gave up. Hey, if she liked it I loved it.

He led the choir in a quick song. "No way I can make it without you! I can't even raise my hands! I can't even do my dance!" he sang. The crowd clapped and rejoiced. Then he said a prayer for all the sinners who praise God in the day, and follow Satan at night. I thought to myself, "and you're one to talk?" I tell you about church folks. They're always the first ones to point something or someone out.

Then Todd gave thanks for everyone's attendance before announcing the pastor and taking his seat in the back. Gabrielle followed him inconspicuously with her eyes until the Pastor began his sermon.

It was an awesome sermon. The pastor preached about making New Year's resolutions versus making a life plan. He talked about working on the plan God has in order for us. He spoke about putting positive things and positive people in our lives. I took so much from his preaching, teachings, and prayers. I couldn't wait to make changes in my life.

Of course I would begin with Eric. He wasn't lying when he said he would make it hard. He called me everyday, all day non-stop trying to see me to give me my surprise. He even invited me to spend New Year's with him. I opted to spend it with Gabrielle though. I was very curious about my gift but my spirit was convicted and I felt so guilty. No matter how bad their situation, Eric and what's her name were still married.

"Deacon Mills, this is my best friend Mikayla. The one I was telling you about."

He extended his hand. I took the fragile little thing and shook it. "It's very nice to meet you."

"Nice to finally meet you," he said. "How'd you enjoy the service?"

"Oh wow, I loved it. I thought it was great. The choir, the sermon, everything was very nice."

He was pleased with my answer. "I'm glad you enjoyed it. Maybe we'll see you next Sunday."

'If I can get my lazy ass out of bed,' I thought to myself.

He barely looked at Gabrielle. "You have to bring her more often Gabrielle."

She smiled, "I keep trying. I'll think she'll be here next week."

They spoke cordially as friends as if they'd never owned a personal relationship.

"Good bring her back tonight," he suggested. He went on his way about his business and fellowshipped with other members of the congregation.

Our stomachs growled so we made a run to Boston Market to get a meal for the entire family.

"So what do you think?" Gabrielle asked.

It was the inevitable question that haunted me ever since I laid eyes on Todd. And still I hadn't thought of any good answer.

"He seems very nice."

"He is. He's so sweet," she glowed, "I don't know what I'm going to do with myself."

"What you mean? I thought you stopped seeing him."

"I did," she said, "it's just that....sometimes I miss him. You know?"

"Girl if don't nobody know, I know." Lord knows I knew. I thought about Eric the entire ride to her house.

Jack and Jackson played in the living room while taking down the Christmas tree. He barely spoke as we walked in the door.

"Soups on!" Gabrielle yelled from the kitchen. I sat to eat. She joined her men in the front. "Are you ready to eat?"

Jack refused to answer.

"Hello? You don't hear me talking to you?" she snapped.

"Gabrielle, please just leave me alone," he told her.

"What is your problem?"

"I've asked you nicely just to leave me the hell alone!"

I sucked my food down and jumped out of my seat. It was time to go.

"If you can't tell me what I need to know then we don't need to talk," he told her.

"I'll call you later, Gabi," I said grabbing the doorknob and leaving out. I did not want to be around while they bickered and argued about whatever. It seemed most days they were so in love and others they couldn't stand each other's presence.

I drove aimlessly. Now I had nowhere to go. Gabrielle wasn't going to service tonight and those were my only plans. I sure didn't want to take Eric up on his invitation and join him in bringing in the New Year. I decided on stopping by Cory's. If he wasn't doing anything then maybe he wouldn't mind starting our relationship fresh.

At first sight I instantly noticed the red colored Camry parked nicely in my old parking space. My heart beat almost through my chest. I needed to be smart. I parked directly in back of Lisa's car blocking her in. Then I dialed his number from my cell phone. He didn't answer. I was livid! I called a second time. Again no answer.

Almost cartoon like, my feet raced at light speed. I was a mad woman running up the walkway to his condo. If anyone would have seen me they would have thought I'd lost my mind. My hair swayed back and forth as I sprinted toward the door in my church dress and high heels. The sounds of my heels chummed against the pavement.

I banged as hard as I could. I could hear rumbles behind the door.

"Who is it?" Cory asked.

"You know damn well who it is Cory. Open the door," I huffed and heaved not because I was out of breath but mainly because I was so fired up. I couldn't believe he had the audacity to have this trick in his condo when just last week he was ready for me to move in and everything. The nerve!

I banged on the door again.

"I'm coming out Kayla," he said. He took a step outside and closed the door behind him. I put my hands on my hips and waited for an explanation or an invite inside.

"Before you go off—" he started.

"No, before you lie let me just tell you this,"

"Kayla—"

"Shut up!" I yelled at him. "You are the biggest liar and hoe I've ever seen. I don't want to hear your excuses. I wanted you to know that I caught you. You're nasty! You're sleeping with me one day and her, the next. Then you bring your ass outside half dressed and leave her inside and keep me on the porch."

"Kayla I'm not sleeping with her."

"Stop lying!"

"Kayla, she's inside because I don't want you inside tearing up my place."

"So I'm ghetto now?" I asked knowing darn well that if he let me in that's exactly what would have happened.

"No but—" he stopped himself, "okay so, you're telling me that if I let you in you won't go in there and try to fight the girl?"

"Hell no, I'm not saying that."

"See."

"So you're protecting her now?"

"No, but I don't want a replay of what happened before. And I don't want my apartment tore up."

"Fine then tell her to step outside. We can go head up since she wanted to lie and say I sprayed her. I'm gonna spray her ass alright."

"Kayla, baby hold on," he said. "Calm down."

"Don't touch me. I don't know where your hands have been." I took a breath as things marinated. I couldn't believe I was outside trying to get into a place that used to be mine while this broad sat inside safe and sound. I couldn't believe he was doing this to me. He should have told her to sneak out the back or something. Then I could have at least caught her ass as she tried unblocking her car. He was disrespectful for keeping me outside. You don't treat your main girl like the other woman.

"You know what Cory? It's not worth it. You're not worth it. Lets just forget that any of this happened." I began to walk away.

"Kayla baby please just hear me out," he grabbed me.

I snatched away. "I told you don't touch me."

"Wait. Don't leave. You can come inside. I'll let you come inside." He opened the door.

Part of me wanted to turn back and go inside and

whoop that hoe's ass and flaunt in her face that he'd let me in and was kicking her out. But the other half, the better half, said 'just leave his ass the hell alone.' It shouldn't have taken this much convincing for him to let me in. I was prideful. So I listened...to my first half. Hey, he gave the bitch up so why not take advantage of the opportunity.

I damn near knocked him out of the way to get inside before he changed his mind.

"Kayla promise you won't start anything."

"I'm not promising shit," I told him, "and you can keep protecting this bitch if you want to."

He shut his mouth while I looked around. Nothing was out of place, and there was no one in sight. I looked in the bedroom. The bed was made and there were no condom wrappers laying around neither there or the bathroom. I couldn't find her. The scary bitch had slipped through the cracks but not for long.

"You got her out of here huh?" I asked him.

"I didn't tell anybody to leave. She must have left on her own."

It burned my soul. I could have killed him. I ran for the front door but he stopped me.

"Let her go," he told me. "Leave her alone."

I fought to get away. "Let me go. I'm going home. Fuck you and her!" I was serious. I did want to go home. I didn't have time for his petty games. I was tired. I felt like a damn fool. I was done with the situation. But if it just so happens that I catch her outside by my car well then, you know...what can I say? Somebody deserves an ass whoopin.' The fact that she ran out the back told me that she knew she was doing something wrong. Plus, I still carried a grudge about her lies of my spraying her.

"I'm trying to tell you she's nobody. I'm not messing

around with her."

He followed me to my car. Lisa sat inside hers trying to maneuver her way out of the jam. Her windows rolled to the top I laughed in her face and gave her the finger. If she would have said one word to me I would have demolished her.

"Just get in your car Kayla," Cory told me.

"Why, so you're little girlfriend can come back inside?"

"No! That's not my girlfriend. Why don't you come inside so we can talk?" he stood toe-to-toe with me. He wanted to grab me but I would have taken my church shoes off and cracked him across his head so many times.

"Oh, now it's my turn to talk to you? What was I, your three o'clock appointment?"

"Mikayla."

"Go to hell Cory."

Lisa still tried getting out of the parking space. She was stuck bad. I jumped into my car and drove home. I didn't wait to see if she got out or anything. To hell with him. To hell with both of them.

Chapter 13

I knew Cory would be over my house later that night trying to explain. I didn't want to hear it. In fact I wasn't going to be home to hear it. I would stay at a hotel tonight and do a count down on my own. It was going to be torture but I couldn't call Gabrielle. She had problems of her own.

"Hello?" I answered my second cell phone. No one but Eric had the number so I knew it could only be him.

"What's the matter?"

I told him about the whole Cory situation and what my plans were. We talked for hours as I packed my suitcase. He told me not worry about it. But nothing he said really mattered. I was still pissed more than anything.

Knowing I couldn't afford it, he arranged a suite downtown.

"Do it up real big," he said, "order room service, movies, get a massage tomorrow, just treat yourself. It's all on me."

He was sweet. I appreciated it. I planned on doing it real big too.

I arrived at the Pennisula Hotel as early as eight. Everyone gathered around in their evening wear heading to parties while I headed to my suite. I'd brought a good book to read just in case I couldn't get my mind off the whole Cory episode.

The door opened to a beautiful junior suite overlooking the city. It smelled of fresh flowers and potpourri. Everything was clean and intact. The maid had even turned the bed down already. I immediately threw my things down, turned on the television, and picked up the phone to order room service. I was starving. I hadn't had a chance to enjoy my food earlier at Gabrielle's. It seemed that every time I went over there to eat, an argument would ensue and I'd end up leaving on an empty stomach. I'd lost many meals that way. If I continued to go to Gabrielle's house for dinner, I'd soon, begin to lose weight.

I always loved my figure. To me it was perfect. But maybe not to anyone else.

It was New Year's Eve and the hotel was packed. Room service was running behind by about two hours. That left more than enough time to soak. I added a couple of sifts of complimentary bubble bath that lie on the sink and turned on the Jacuzzi. It roared loudly.

I pinned my hair and undressed myself. My body was bare before the huge mirror that surrounded the tub. I examined every inch, every single detail. Flawless skin. Not a stretch mark in sight. No cellulite. Small waistline. Great ass. Firm breasts. Everything seemed to be just like it was three years ago when Cory and I first met. Why had he gone astray?

I looked further. It had to be something. Maybe my breasts weren't big enough or hair wasn't long enough or my complexion wasn't light enough. There had to be something.

"You're perfect," I heard a voice from behind. I turned my face to see Eric standing in the doorway smiling with a handful of roses and a bottle of champagne. I hid myself with my hands.

"Don't hide it," he said. "It's beautiful."

I blushed, ashamed that I'd been caught staring at myself. He must have thought I was so totally vain. I grabbed the hotel robe and wrapped myself in it.

"What are you doing here? I thought you were going to a party with your wife."

"I have business here," he smirked. "You don't think I would leave my favorite woman alone on New Year's Eve do you?"

"I think you should leave. Your wife may be looking for you."

"I don't want to be with her. I want to be with you. Why should I spend my night putting up this façade of us being a happy family when we're not?"

I didn't know why.

"Go ahead. Get in the tub. I won't touch you. I won't bother you. I'll just sit and talk with you," he swore. "I'll even turn around while you get in."

I accepted it. The Jacuzzi was filled with bubbles that lay over my body.

"Here." He handed me a glass of champagne. He sat on the stool just outside of the tub in the vanity area. "Lay back."

I lay my back towards him so that he could massage me. I almost went to sleep from the heat and his hands. My hair fell and forehead sweat. He kissed my neck.

"Don't start Eric."

"That doesn't feel good?"

"Yes but—"

"Shhhh." He sucked my neck and gripped my breasts. "You are so beautiful," he whispered.

"Thank you," I said shyly. I knew it was about to go down and I didn't think there was any stopping it. Then there was a knock at the door.

"Room service."

It was bitter sweet. I was safe for now but did I really want to be?

He paid the man a heavy tip. I could tell by the grateful tone in his "Thank you!" I closed my eyes and waited for Eric to bring my food. He returned naked with a bowl of strawberries that I'd ordered and a huge gift bag.

"What are you doing?" I laughed.

"I'm going to join you. My back hurts leaning over to massage you. It'll be easier for me to get inside with you. Is that alright?" I wasn't convinced but didn't deny him. "But first..." he handed over the bag.

I opened it and found an entire Rainbow Brite collection. I was so excited. Just when I thought he was so interested in his boy toys he was actually listening to me carry on about wanting the collection as a child. It was a sweet gesture.

"Now I just have to buy Rainbow Brite," I said noticing that she was missing.

"Rainbow Brite isn't in there?" he asked confused. "How could I not have her?" He looked into the bag but there was nothing left. "I must have forgotten."

I was content with that. It didn't matter. I could always buy her to add to the collection. He ran into the other room and brought in yet another huge gift bag. I smiled as he handed it over. The gift tag read 'Maybe this will Brighten your day.' I knew exactly what it was and the words couldn't have been more precise. I pulled the doll out of the bag. Bling! Bling! No Rainbow Brite doll I ever saw wore ice around her neck!

"Oh my goodness, Eric," I said surprised. "It's beautiful."

There was a jewel box in the doll's arms. I quickly opened it to find matching diamond earrings.

"You like it?"

"I love it."

He climbed in and sat behind me. I could feel his penis on my back as the jets of the Jacuzzi flung it around. He put the necklace around my neck and I rubbed it against my chest. I put the earrings in my ears and lay back. He fed me a strawberry and massaged me while I admired my new diamond necklace and earrings.

A bigger woman would have told him to keep it and would have never accepted it. I wasn't a bigger woman. In fact, I was only five foot six, a hundred forty pounds. Besides, he could afford this plus more.

"I could be like this with you forever," he said.

"Eric, please okay. I've already had one disappointment this week. Don't fill my head with what you think I want to hear."

"I'm serious." He pulled me to lie back on his chest. "I know we haven't been really serious or anything but I think...."

"You think what? Before you start let me tell you that nothing you say is going to sway me in one way or another to have sex with you. My mind is already made up. You're gonna get lucky tonight. So you don't have to use the games or—"

"First of all, I'm about business. I'm never about games. You'll see that one day," he warned me, "and I can have sex with any woman I want to so this isn't about sex either."

"What is it about then?"

"It's about love." He fed me another strawberry like it was nothing, but did he say the 'L' word? "Mikayla, I seriously think I'm falling in love with you."

I paused for a second. "No you're not." He couldn't be. Could he? He called me constantly and we talked for hours. He met me at my job every second he had. He bought me nice things all the time. But still he only did those things because he was attracted to me and he thought I was a nice person, right?

"I don't treat everybody the way I treat you. I go to bed thinking about you. I wake up thinking about you. You're an obsession."

"No Eric, I'm something new. You don't love me."

"Look, I'm not telling you to tell me back because that's not how you feel but please don't tell me how I feel. Okay?" his tone was firm.

"I'm sorry."

He fed me another strawberry and hugged me tightly. "I'm happy to be with you tonight. I wouldn't want to bring in the new year with anyone else."

His thing got hard as he kissed my neck softly and played with my nipples.

"Can I kiss you?" he asked.

"Please," I whispered. I wanted him to.

He slid me to the side. How did he want me? Should I stand? Should I sit on the brim of the tub? How did he want me?

"Hold this," he said putting my hand on the faucet. He spread my legs apart then dove head first underneath the water. I hoped he had his oxygen mask because upon my climax I had a habit of putting a death grip on a man.

Eric palmed my butt while he tickled me with his tongue underneath the water. He was long winded but eventually came up for air only to go back under again. After a few times of deep sea fishing, he lifted me by my ass and ate the suds off my pussy. I was in ecstasy. I didn't know how long I could hold onto the faucet. My hands were getting weak. Upon reaching my climax I retained my grip both around the faucet and around his neck.

"Sit here," he told me and patted his lap. This was it. The point of no return. I hesitated for a second but he gave me a swift slap on my ass. "Didn't I say come here?" And, oh my goodness, it turned me on so bad. I straddled over him and slid it in. He moaned, "I've been waiting for this pussy."

As our bodies collided the water jumped out of the tub and drenched the floors. Neither of us worried about it. We continued a journey of lustful lovemaking.

"I'm gonna cum," he said. And I hurdled off him so fast you would have thought I was Jackie Joyner Kersey.

"Not yet. I'm not done yet," he told me. "This is so good I need to get on top."

He instructed me to sit on the side of the tub and I did. He leaned between my legs thrusting himself inside me. I looked into the mirror at his ass while he went in and out. I got wetter and wetter.

He moaned louder and louder as I gave it back to him. "I love you Mikayla. I love you," he repeated in the moment's heat.

I patted myself on the back and slapped myself high-fives in my mind, thinking there was no other female out here better than I. Then I took another look at myself as he felt his way inside of me. His wedding band reflected in the mirror as he held up my thigh. I thought to myself, 'there was no other female worse than I, either.'

CHAPTER 14

"Mikayla, don't do this again. You always do this," Eric begged three days after our affair. "Every time we do something you shut me out."

"I'm sorry Eric but I just can't. You got what you wanted. Now why—"

"I told you this was never about sex!" He smacked his lips. "I wish we wouldn't have slept together," he sulked and then hung up.

I started to call him back but changed my mind. It was better this way. I couldn't look myself in the mirror and know that I screwed another woman's husband. I needed a guy with no strings attached. No woman, no wife, no drama.

"Ready?" Gabrielle asked.

"Yup."

"Honey I'll be back soon!" she yelled to Jack. He walked her to the door. "Love you," she kissed him.

"Love you too. Have fun." He kissed her goodnight.

We walked into the dimly and basically empty café. Gabrielle and I scurried to our seats as the first performer recited his poetic speech.

"And they said, and he said, and she said. The more the conversation carried on the more I realized it was he said, she said," he preached.

Just as I suspected. Another poet speaking about losing his woman.

The waitress came over to take our order to get us started on our two drink minimum.

"Rum and Coke," Gabrielle requested.

"Sex on the beach."

She wrote our orders and walked away.

"This place is nice," Gabrielle complimented. "How'd you hear about it?"

"I saw it while waiting on Eric."

"Oh, Mr. Eric. And how is he?"

"He'll be fine."

"Got a little taste and now you're done, huh?"

"I just feel guilty. It's not something I want to make a habit of. You know?"

"Yeah I know. I also know you'll be back, too."

I didn't argue. I hoped I wouldn't but there was a possibility. I was learning to keep my mouth closed because everything I said I wouldn't do, I'd done.

The performance ended and everyone clapped as did Gabrielle and I, even though neither of us paid attention to a darn word he said. They announced a brief intermission.

We carried on our conversation, "I still can't believe I did that? What was I thinking?"

"You were thinking that Cory was full of shit and in some twisted deranged way you felt like you were getting even at him. Not to mention you have a serious problem. You can't go a week without sex and you were thinking you were at your limit," Gabrielle fed me the truth.

"Yeah, but it'll never happen again."

"Don't beat yourself up. It happened. You can't take it back."

"You're right."

"I know it. And don't take your horny ass around him again!" we laughed it off.

"Rum and Coke and," the waitress lay our drinks on the table "....sex on the beach."

"Honey, I wish!" the three of us laughed.

"Do you?"

Gabrielle and I sat in admiration at the tall dark skinned man with braids who stood smiling before us.

"That'll be twelve dollars," the waitress preceded with her business and breaking through our silence.

We reached into our purses.

"I got it Regina. Put it on my tab," he told the waitress.

"Are you sure?" we asked.

"Very," he smiled.

"Well I can't argue with free," Gabrielle said pushing her money back into her purse.

"Nothings free," I smiled at him trying to figure out how long it would be before he asked for one of our numbers.

"You're right." he said. "Everything has a price."

"What's yours?"

He laughed, "It's simple." I leaned in almost ready to call out the digits to my house, cell, and fax number when he only said, "I would like to know your names."

I took charge. Gabrielle didn't want him. Besides he was giving me the eye and I could feel the chemistry. He was cute. Tall, dark, and every bit of handsome. I never liked a man with braids but this man wore them like no other man I'd ever seen before.

"I'm Mikayla and this is my best friend Gabrielle."

"Gabrielle and Mikayla, it's nice to meet you," he shook our hands. "Are you ladies having a good time?"

"We just got here but it's a pretty nice place."

"I saw you walk in." He gave a flattering smile. Regina, the waitress, came and whispered in his ear. He whispered something back. I gave Gabrielle a look. She raised her brow giving her approval. We both looked him up and down. This nigga was the shit!

"Ladies enjoy yourselves. It was nice meeting you," he excused himself.

"Thanks we will," I said.

"Thanks again for the drinks," Gabrielle added. He gave a warm smile and waved as he walked by. "Ewww Weeee!"

"Girrrrl!"

"See that's what you need. Right there." We watched as he walked away.

She was right. That was what I needed. That's what I was going to get. I turned to Gabrielle and we chattered some more. I looked down at my ringing phone. It was Eric. I ignored it, throwing it back to the bottom of my purse. When I looked up, the guy was gone.

He must have been someone important. But what would someone important be doing in a spoken word café? No man, correction, no straight man, would go to a poetry session alone. Could he be with someone? But why would he buy us drinks? And he didn't leave a name or anything. Mr. Mystery Man. How sexy.

"I need another drink," Gabrielle said looking around for our waitress. "Oh my..." she stalled staring at the stage.

There he stood tapping the mic so the sound echoed around the room. The lights grew dim again and the silhouettes of lit candles reflected off the candy apple painted walls.

The band played a mellow tone for background sound. He smiled at his audience before taking the mic stand into his hands, caressing it gently. He closed his eyes and opened his mouth and with that deep manly voice he uttered soft sounds, almost a song or maybe it was just music to my ears.

"Love at first sight. I'm like, buy this girl a drink, invite her over for the night, body tight, mind just right, hair in place, pretty ass smile on her face...could she just be waiting for a taste...could that be the case? Then my mind's like whoa, this is Mikayla, this ain't no hoe. Not a one nighter G. Naw, naw this one here, this one might be wifey."

Did he say 'Mikayla?' Gabrielle and I looked at each other as we both covered our mouths in utter shock. No, he didn't use my name like that! Yes, he did. People applauded as he got off stage. He walked through the now crowded place and spoke to a young artsy looking woman off to the side before disappearing to the back.

Neither Gabrielle nor I could believe what we heard. And to top things off, the waitress informed us, after we drank like blood thirsty leeches, that our tab was covered. And still I had no clue of his name.

Gabrielle was ready to go. She had to make it home. She was on the wife curfew that most husbands put on their women. Jack had already called her twice.

"Why don't you ask Regina his name?" she asked in a rush.

"Because I don't see her either."

She kept watch of her clock. She needed to be home and I understood. So I gathered my things and packed up to leave.

"Forget it," I said. "If it's meant to be it will."

"Are you sure? I'll wait."

"No. I know where to find him," I said leaving. I couldn't wait until the next time I saw him. All night I fantasized about how romantic he would be to me. How romantic our love making could be as he'd recite poem after poem about us.

Before I knew it I was standing alone at the front door of the Poetry Corner Café the very next day. Again it was early and the place was empty. I looked around feeling like a complete idiot. He wasn't there and neither was Regina.

People came in and I turned to follow behind them. I found a seat in the corner, listening to performer after performer. I waited for my mystery man to come but he never did.

I had to say, I'd never been to a club so much or heard so much poetry in my life! Day after day I would drive by the café just to see if I'd see my poet. Occasionally, I'd go inside. I'm sure the people who worked there had to know my reasons for visiting. Eric was beginning to think I was crazy. I was starting to agree.

I drove home from work. Again I was compelled to stop. I walked into the empty café. I wasn't going to spend another night in a poetry café with all its romantic setting and love sounds ALONE! I started for the door and was almost run over.

"Excuse me beautiful," he said. I almost peed my pants. "Were you looking for me?" he stood confident with those bow legs. I could only think of the rumors that went along with bowlegged men.

"You know you're pretty rude," I finally said. His expression changed. "What kind of man buys a girl and her friend drinks all night, wishes her a good night, recites a beautiful personalized poem and doesn't leave his name?"

He smiled, "Hi, Mikayla. I'm Beau." He remembered my name, how cute. "You thought that poem was about you?"

"It wasn't?" I asked.

"Come on now, do you think you're the only Mikayla in the world?"

It was playful banter that I was accustomed to. Cory had done it throughout our entire relationship. I knew how to bite back.

He led me to the bar and bought me another drink.

"I think getting a girl drunk is your thing," I teased.

He laughed, "I think sex on the beach is yours."

I took a sip and licked my lips. I could feel him watching me. "Wouldn't you like to find out?" I said sarcastically.

He leaned in close to me, "Wouldn't you?"

And that's what started it all. Three or more sex on the beaches later I found myself engaged in hot and heavy sex at Beau's bachelor pad. But how it exactly happened? I couldn't say. All I know is we spent hours talking to each other, he invited me back, and it was on from there.

"You whore!" Gabrielle screamed.

"I know." With the exception of Matthew, I'd never slept with a man so soon. And his two minutes, two inches didn't count.

But WHOA, BEAU! He wasn't as large as Cory but not as short as Eric. He was just perfect. Not too long, not too short. Not too big, not too small. Just a perfect fit. And we fit mentally. He believed in freedom of the mind and soul, heart and body. Hell, I could fart in front of him if I wanted. Now that was freedom!

Eric would throw a fit if I ever performed any body function in his presence. He already made it clear that a woman should always carry herself like a lady except in the bedroom. Which meant no burping, farting, scratching, cussing, loud talking, or picking of anything should be seen. And that was fine with me. That was his image of how his woman should be. Every man has his dream.

Beau's dream was to know a person inside out. He wasn't with the false image and outer appearances. He paid attention to every detail about me as we lay in bed together.

"How did you get this?" he asked about a scar I'd got when I was nine.

"I got hit by a car when I was little."

"Really?" He wanted to hear all about it. In fact, he wanted to hear all about me. It wasn't like a one night stand. He actually made me promise I'd call him that day and insisted I stay over that night.

"Bring on the details hoe! What happened?" Gabrielle demanded.

I filled her in on all the details. I even told her about Eric blowing up my phone all night and how I completely ignored it.

I did miss Eric. I could smell his scent on my pillows and the Rainbow Brite dolls that lay on my bed. He'd spent the night after I came back looking for Beau the first time. Nothing happened ... except .... nothing happened!

But now I'd begun to devote more time with Beau. He was winning me over more and more everyday.

"Where's your girlfriend?"

"I don't have one."

"Sure," I said.

"Why don't you believe me?"

"Because everybody has someone these days."

"Then why don't you?"

"Hey, it's not by choice. I had a boyfriend but he happened to be one of the everybody's that has someone too."

He paused for a second, "Well, I don't. I'm as free as they come. Frankly I don't have time for a woman."

That was all I needed to hear. At least he was up front about his game. No lies, tricks, or waiting on phone calls. He let me know in the door he wasn't relationship material.

"So you're just out here sowing your royal oats, Akeem?" I teased.

"No, not really. I'm trying out a lot of new things and I haven't found a woman who's secure and supportive enough to give me what I need."

"What is it that you need?"

"Patience, understanding, emotional support. It's not easy for us poets out here. I'm not just putting words together to make a woman moan. This is my life, my job. Right now it's all I got and I need to know I have a woman in my corner and not someone who finds me interesting one moment and the next moment she's chasing after the first rich man that comes her way."

"So you really just don't want to be in a relationship," I came right out and said.

"I didn't say that. I said I haven't found anyone. You never know, you might be the one I'm looking for."

I smiled at the thought while Eric blew up my two way pager. "I love you," he said. I messaged him back saying that I'd call him later.

Maybe Beau could relieve me of my evil spirits and get me back right. Maybe he'd be my love potion. The next day after our conversation I found a letter in my mailbox from him. I almost tripped over myself ripping open the Crome scented envelope. I loved that cologne. I opened it and read the poem. It made my heart melt. Who thought of words like this? I was impressed by his interest in me and even more impressed when I came home the week after and found a personalized CD in my box. It listed the latest of relationship songs of how he felt about me. Week after week it was some-thing different. I anticipated every Thursday, trying to guess what I would get. It was exciting. On the last Thursday I got him on my doorstep holding a cup of my favorite ice cream.

I invited him in and shared my sundae with him.

"What made you become a poet?" I curiously asked, taking a scoop of ice cream.

"Rappers rap. I write. It's another hustle," he responded.

"Yeah, but you're so good at it you have to enjoy it. Or else why wouldn't you rap? Why would you choose poetry?"

He sat his spoon on the tablemat. I didn't mean to offend him. It wasn't that I thought poetry was gay. I just wanted to know where his inspiration stemmed from but after realizing his apprehensions, I quickly tried to dissolve the conversation.

"I'm sorry," I said still curious. It wasn't everyday that you find a poet and he not be gay. I hoped Beau wasn't a "down low brotha." He was too perfect. But his romantic characteristics and sensitive ways made him suspect.

I wondered why he wasn't a singer. He had the most beautiful voice. On a couple occasions he'd sang me to sleep right in his arms. His voice was to die for! It was a cross between Brian McKnight and Luther Vandross. It was surreal. If I wasn't fast asleep I was pulling my panties off at the sound of it.

"No don't apologize. You're just asking," he defended me. "I've written poems ever since I can remember. I gave the first one to this girl named Karen Powler. I was so nervous because she was the finest girl in school and I didn't want her to think I was a gump. She loved it. We stayed together from freshmen year 'til senior year when I..." He exhaled. "Mikayla, eight years ago...I...I was in the State Penn."

That's when the red flag went up. What had he done? Was this nigga crazy? So many thoughts brushed through my mind but I calmed my nerves and gave him the benefit of the doubt. I'd known him long enough to know I was safe. But knowing he spent time in jail wasn't soothing my suspicions about him being on the "down low."

I sat patiently and waited for the rest of the story.

"I had a situation and things got out of hand," he continued.

"What happened?"

"I accidentally killed someone," he said.

Oh hell no! How do you accidentally kill someone? In all my twenty-five years of life I never accidentally killed anyone or knew anyone who had.

"I was mixed in with the wrong crowd and just acting a fool in the streets and always drinking and getting high. My situation at home was real bad. My mom had a boyfriend that used to drink day in and day out. I'd come home and she'd have bruises all over her. For years I fought with her to leave but she wouldn't. One day I came home and saw my little sister Raquel, sitting on the porch. She told me that John, my stepfather, had hit our mother. It pissed me off but it was the same ole routine. I was just going to go in and rough him up again and kick him out of the house."

He paused for breath. "Then she told me that he tried to take advantage of her and she had to fight him off her. I saw red. How could a grown man try to make a fourteen year old girl give...give him oral sex? I just snapped. Mikayla.... I just snapped. My mother sat in the front crying with a bloody nose and a missing tooth. I ran upstairs and do you know he had the nerve to talk shit to me? I grabbed him by his throat and pulled him down the steps and beat him. My mother and sisters tried stopping me but they couldn't. I was too angry and tired. By the time I came to my senses it was too late."

I lay my spoon next to his. He was hollow. He barely looked me in my eyes. For so long, he tried to put his past behind him and now I'd brought it back.

I could only imagine the pain he felt. Though I wasn't an advocate for killing anyone, I sure could understand why he had.

"I lost everything, my girlfriend, my financial aid for school, everything. I spent four years in jail. I was dying inside. I wouldn't sleep or eat and it hurt to see my family. The only thing that saved me was a pen and paper. I haven't stopped writing since. And every time I get angry I write but nothing since then has made me that angry."

Thank God! I processed everything he revealed. It was justifiable. Scary, but justifiable. If I judged him for defending his family then I would have to be crazy myself.

"I would have told you sooner but I didn't want you to be afraid."

"I'm not afraid of you Beau. You're the most compassionate person I know. I'm sorry you went through so much."

He held his head low. I knew he was ashamed but I truly wasn't afraid of him nor did I think anything differently of him. I held his hand and stroked his skin softly.

"You're so sweet. I'm telling you, you're the only other thing that keeps my mind right. When we're together I don't think about anything else except for staying focused. I don't want to lose you to a rich man," he smiled.

"If you lose me it won't be because the guy is rich," I told him.

He gave a slight nod then looked into my eyes. "Can you do something for me?" he asked.

"What?"

"Tell me something personal about you. I've told you my deepest secret. Tell me yours."

I paused. I didn't have any secrets. "I don't have any secrets."

"There's something. What hurts you?"

I wasn't sure if I was ready but how could I deny him? I fumbled back and forth with the idea in my mind. Beau noticed my hesitance.

"You don't have to," he said. "You can tell me in your own time."

"No, I'll tell you." It was time to share my secrets. "Have you ever just not been loved?" I asked. "Even when you were growing up, with all the things you went through your mother and sister still loved you right? Even when they didn't love themselves?"

He didn't answer. His eyes were filled with such concern and sadness for me.

"My father was the only man that ever loved me. I loved him just as much. When he died I was lost. I had no one. My mom and sister hate me. They always have. No matter what I did to try to fit in, they always made me feel inferior and stupid. They don't realize or even care how much they hurt me. I constantly ask myself 'why am I the outcast?' I question what's wrong with me."

My eyes got wet but I refused to let a single tear drop in front of this man but continued to pour my heart out.

"For a long time I was totally alone with no one, I mean not a single person to love me. I wouldn't wish that on my worse enemy. It's a horrible feeling almost like dying a slow death. I jumped in and out of meaningless relationships only to be dogged one after another. But what's really messed up is I still do it and I still fool myself into believing that I love them and they love me. But none of them ever do. My last boyfriend before Cory cheated on me with a really close friend of mine which is why I only have one friend now. I've dug my claws into her and refuse to let her escape. If she wasn't married I'd probably be gay," I added a little humor to desensitize the situation.

He gave a subtle laugh. I wondered if he thought I had too much baggage. Until now, besides Gabrielle, no one in the world knew how I truly felt. Not Eric and not even Cory.

"For the record," he spoke. "You have two friends."

I lifted my spoon and took a dip of ice cream and held it up to him, "Here's to happy endings."

He grabbed his spoon and did the same. "Happy endings."

We linked our arms and ate from each other's spoon. It was a special moment. Truly special.

* * * *

Beau and I really took to each other over the next three months. Except for his trips in and out of town or at the café, we were practically inseparable. Even at the café I frequently visited him and became familiar with all his work buddies. I enjoyed my romantic weekly surprises of poems, flowers, and love notes. He knew exactly what I liked without me having to say anything.

What can I say? The man was definitely raised right. Beneath all that pain, lay a heart of gold and inside it pumped precious diamonds.

Last Thursday's surprise involved meeting his mother. She was nothing like I imagined. Soft spoken, very sweet, loving, with a beautiful smile. Her smile hid away all her suffering. A person wouldn't know she'd encountered so much in such a short lifetime behind that smile.

"Mom, meet your soon to be daughter-in-law." Beau introduced me.

She welcomed me with open arms, hugged me tight, and gave me a kiss right on my left cheek.

"Hello, honey," she said and then gave Beau the same

treatment. "Come on in! I've been waiting all day for you. What took so long?"

"She had to get pretty," he told her.

"It couldn't have taken up much time." She grabbed my face. "Look at her. She's just as cute as she can be."

I blushed while Beau laughed.

She wasted no time inviting me into their family. We stayed for dinner and afterwards we all talked and laughed. Mattie, his mother, showed me pictures of Beau in his younger days.

"Oh how cute," I said staring at his butt naked baby picture.

"Alright that's enough of that," he closed the book.

"Stop it," we both yelled at him. Mattie opened the album and continued to show pictures.

"You see how much I've grown since then," Beau whispered in my ear. I nudged him away.

Mattie turned the page to an even bigger close up than before. Again Beau tried to close the book.

"Stop it!" she demanded, "Are you afraid that she'll see your little Peter?"

I laughed profusely, "Your little Peter."

"No ma'am. Besides she's already seen my Peter."

"Beau!" I yelled in embarrassment. I pushed him out of the room.

"It's not a little Peter anymore. It's a big Peter isn't it?" he whispered in my ear.

I couldn't help but laugh while I pushed him away. What a thing to say in front of his mother!

She didn't mind. She showed more pictures of him at school dances. There was a void in the album where pictures of Beau should have been on prom and graduation. It was sad that a guy with so much potential had lost so much.

"This is where you two's wedding picture will go," she told me.

I sat flabbergasted. How cute for a mother to dream of her son's wedding.

"Beau told me that you might be the one. But don't tell him I said that though," she whispered.

He talked about me to his mother? Wow!

Beau joined us. "Okay that's enough. Mom, I'm going to show Kayla my bedroom."

"Alright fine," she said. She still had more albums to go through. We hadn't even touched the family portfolio with his sister. I was eager to see what she looked like.

"Lets go," he directed me upstairs, "so I can show you big Peter."

"You are so bad."

We made it upstairs to the small bedroom. Everything was just the same as when he was younger.

"Didn't you live here after you got out?"

"No. I moved in with my sister. I didn't want to come back here."

"Oh."

We walked around the room looking at more pictures and picking up things. I found a box full of love notes and poems. "What are these?"

He grabbed them from my hand. "They're nothing."

"Looked like something to me."

He tried stuffing the love notes written to Karen into the shoebox.

"What happened with Karen?"

"Nothing really. She decided that she didn't want to be with an ex-con and found her a new guy to be with."

"A rich guy?"

"That's the story of my life."

"Do you think you still love her?"

"No Kayla."

"Are you sure?"

"Yes I'm sure."

"How do you know when you're really out of love with someone? I mean, how do you really know that?"

He grabbed me and pulled me close. "When you have room in your heart to love someone else." Then he kissed me so soft, so slow, so passionately.

"You'd better stop before your mother comes upstairs and whoops us both."

"I'm not worried about her," he said. "I'm worried about Peter. I think little Peter is ready to do big things."

"Big things? Are you calling my thing big? Did you just call me a hoe?" We laughed and kissed again.

Our visit ended all too soon. Mattie walked us to the door and hugged and kissed us goodbye.

"You make sure you come and see me again soon."

"Okay ma," I called her by mom as instructed earlier. I left with a warm feeling. I felt secure, alive, and a part of something. Meeting Beau's mom made me feel as though I didn't have to hide or search for acceptance. For, in one day I was accepted and it was a feeling that money couldn't buy.

Eric wasn't too thrilled about my new endeavors but he still hung in there hoping that I'd see the light. I tried convincing him to make things work with his wife but he wasn't trying to hear it. There would be many nights that I'd come home and find gifts sitting on my patio from Eric. I did entertain some evenings at dinner with Eric occasionally but still refused to sleep with him except... for a few times when Beau was out of town.

I couldn't help it! He had a way of convincing me and my flesh was weak. He'd whisper in my ear and I'd catch a whiff of his cologne and all of a sudden I was putty in his hands, well... in his mouth.

Besides, there were times when I couldn't even reach Beau while he was away. I didn't know what or who he was doing. And even though he explained that he was at a club or on stage or in a meeting, I still couldn't be so sure.

Not only that, we both decided to take things slow and not rush into any decisions. While we had an unspoken agreement, we really didn't have a solid commitment to one another.

But I still found myself checking Beau's phone on the nights he slept over. I had to know. I didn't want a repeat of my relationship with Cory. I would listen carefully to his phone conversations to see if he just happen to be speaking to a girl. I'd even driven past the café along with Gabrielle and in her car, to make sure he was at the club when he said he was and that he hadn't left with anyone else. I had to keep an eye out for these things. I wouldn't be caught slipping again.

He saw right through me. He detected my paranoia so he'd purposely leave his phone out. The days I visited him at his home he would make up pretend errands leaving me in his apartment alone. You would think I wouldn't pry but I did. Of course I came up short.

He would even recite the pass code to his voicemail while he typed it so that I could check it whenever. It was very endearing to see him put himself out here like that for me. Not once did he ever put on that he knew about my snooping. I was beginning to trust him more and more everyday. I even grew attached to his company.

"Beau's going to New York to have a talk with some people from HBO," I bragged to Gabrielle as we sat at the café. "I was thinking we could go shopping this weekend. I want to surprise him with a nice suit."

She shrugged her shoulders. "Why not? You drag me everywhere else for your ex-convict boyfriend," she joked.

"Gabrielle! Don't say that. He's really sensitive about that," I yelled at her. "Okay, I won't ask you to come to the café anymore." I lied again for the hundred time.

Beau finished his poem. We watched him as he got off stage. I was so proud of my baby. He was doing his thang! Offer after offer had come in. He said I was his lady luck. He called me his lady. How sweet.

As Beau made his way off stage I reminisced about last week's trip together to LA. He had to meet with an executive at Artisan to pitch a movie idea that he'd written. I helped him put together his speech, retyped his bio, updated his portfolio, and we headed on up and flew to Beverly. He was so excited and grateful.

That night after "our" meeting we settled into our room and toasted champagne.

"Here's to finally meeting a woman who's in my corner. A woman who has been patient, understanding, loyal, supportive and all that good stuff. Rewards may not come today but they will definitely come and that's a promise." He looked at me seriously with his glass in the air. "Here's to my Lady Luck."

We kissed and kissed and kissed over the portable dinner table that room service used to tote our meal. I could feel the passion and chemistry between us. I pushed him off me. He was confused when I threw my drink on him. I was in the mood for something freaky. I licked the champagne from his bare chest and sucked his dick.

It was the first time I'd done him. I thought I was really doing something until he lay me on the bed. I was the student and he was the teacher. I closed my eyes while he poured the syrup from his sundae all over my body. He rubbed his tongue slowly across the tip of my breast then softly blew my nipples. I lay patiently while he took his time.

He turned his body and knelt at my side. Then he took his fudge filled fingers and play with my clit while I jagged him off. He climbed on top of me in the sixty nine position and sucked all the fudge he smeared on my vagina clear away.

I thought I might die in ecstasy. Cheek to cheek fudge covered his face. He took his hand and wiped it off his face then licked the back of his hand like an animal. Talk about ready to explode. I tried sitting up to take charge. He was taking too long. I was ready to have my way with him. But he immediately stopped me in my tracks. He flipped me onto my stomach and lifted me up by my thighs so that I was on all fours in the doggy style position. Then he went full throttle into my ass.

I could feel his tongue going up and down from my asshole to my vagina. Beau took a short breather only to grab for more fudge. He spread my cheeks widely and poured fudge right between the middle. It was slow and sensual. The fudge was lukewarm and took to my body like it would to ice cream. He devoured me, putting his tongue inside my asshole and sucked. I don't believe any fudge remained.

I waited for what was to come next. I had no clue. Seconds later the tip of his penis was at the mouth of my butt. Terrified, I put my hand up. He held my hand and said, "This won't hurt a bit." With his open hand he rubbed my other cheek.

Little by little, he toyed with me by penetrating me with his finger, his penis, and his tongue until finally he was inside me. At first, I felt like I was shitting on myself but as time went on the feeling got better and better. Before I knew it I was actually enjoying it.

Who would have ever thought that I would like it so

much. Cory tried on so many occasions to convince me to try and I actually did once but he damn near killed me. That was the first and last time.

But Beau had done this before. I could tell. He was too patient. He knew when to take it fast and when to take it slow.

When things were over we pulled the sheets off the bed and threw them in the tub. I know the maids were pissed at us. We left the room a mess.

Ever since then I hadn't slept with Eric and I couldn't stop talking about Beau. Gabrielle was sick to her stomach. She was happy I was happy, but she was sick to her stomach.

"When your convict boyfriend gets over here tell him to get me a Sprite." Gabrielle told me.

"Don't call him that." I laughed.

"It's the truth."

"Yeah, but he's really sensitive so don't call him that." I told her again.

"He spent how many years in the Penn and now he's sensitive?" she said sarcastically. "Who's fucking who?"

"Gabrielle!" I called to her.

"Okay, okay, I'm sorry," she laughed but then quickly turned serious. "Damn, I'm thirsty."

"You're not drinking?"

"No I've had enough to drink this week. Besides, my stomach is kind of upset. I need a sprite."

"Okay."

I waited for Beau to come over but he stopped when he was approached by the same artsy girl that I'd seen him with the first day I saw him. She hung close to him almost wrapped herself around his arm. I waited for him to release himself and return over to me but he didn't. Nor did he even look my way.

Gabrielle and I both assessed the situation. Could this

girl be just a friend? Maybe she was a poet he'd met from around the way. We glared at the girl. No, this was definitely more than a friend. They played together for a while then she kissed him on the cheek.

I wasn't about to stand for it. I didn't care if we were committed or not.

Beau led her to the back and I followed behind. By the time I got back there, the two were engaged in a warm hug. I turned the other way and returned to Gabrielle.

She gave a look as if asking what I wanted to do. "Let's go," I told her.

We packed up and left Beau still standing there with his girl. I didn't have time for things like this anymore. I'd almost got attached and lost focus of how men really are. This little reality check put me back on track real quick.

"You know you can't keep calling me when somebody pisses you off," Eric told me as he walked in my front door.

"Shut up and get your ass in here." He took his place on my loveseat and I lay on my chaise. "Why don't you come over here with me?"

"No thanks. I'm fine right where I am." He played hard to get. I knew it wouldn't take much to get him though. I walked over to him and kissed his neck. "Stop," I ignored his order. "Stop Mikayla."

"What's the problem?"

"Is that all I'm here for?"

"What?"

"You just call me over when you're mad, sleep with me and don't call again until somebody pisses you off?"

"Eric stop. Don't you want to do it?"

"Yeah I want to but—"

"Then what's the problem? It shouldn't matter how you get it as long as you get it."

He was livid. "You think this is a game?" he yelled. "You're just having fun right? This is my life! I told you I never cheated on my wife before, let alone tell another woman 'I love her.' What is wrong with you?"

"How can you get mad at me? You're the one cheating! I've tried breaking it off and not sleeping with you several times but you won't let me."

"Because it's not just sex between us Mikayla. I love you. Don't you understand that? I love you."

He looked deep into my eyes. I believed him. "Why won't you accept that?"

"Because I can't love a married man."

"Can we just forget about that? Yes, yes I am married. But you know my situation. You knew it was messed up when Victor came to you. You think Victor and I both are lying? You couldn't be thinking that," he pleaded his case. "She's never home and when she is it's like we're room mates. We barely say good morning to each other. It'll be over as soon as this school year is out for Victor. He's been through enough."

Being the boy's teacher I, too, agreed. That was the first time I truly accepted Eric's situation. I believed him when he said he loved me. I believed him when he said his wife would move sometime in the summer. But I should have waited until those two months were over before opening my heart to him. But I didn't.

I immediately gave him a key to my house and began to live fancy free. He paid my bills and I went on weekend trips to visit him while he promoted his company to various elite executives. He would send Gabrielle and me to the spa for massages and facials.

"Now this is what I'm talking about." Gabrielle would say. She enjoyed the fruits of Eric's labor much better than our times with Beau.

Every time I turned around I was being pampered in some way or another. He even slept over my house many nights. He was my boyfriend. I couldn't even tell his wife existed. I was too busy living it up.

Beau and Cory called but I was done with them both. I explained to Beau that it just wasn't meant to be and he couldn't understand why I felt that way when things were going so smoothly. I didn't feel like going into the whole 'I saw you with that other girl' spill. I could care less of his excuses.

The same with Cory. He was another man that would never get another taste of my stuff again. Every time he tried explaining about why Lisa was over his house I hung up. He could feed those lies to someone who had time to listen. My ears, heart, and legs were closed for good.

* * * *

"Come in," Eric directed me inside.

I hesitated for a moment. This was the ultimate disrespect. Though I'd pictured it a million times as we talked ourselves into delirium before going to bed, I never thought I would actually see it.

He grabbed my hand and yanked me inside. It looked nothing like I'd pictured. I imagined a bland ensemble but instead it was bright and full of colors. Ceramic tile flooded the floors. Designer artwork covered the walls. Family photos were spread throughout. I looked at one and then another.

'So this is the lady whose husband I'm stealing,' I thought. I felt so dirty. How disrespectful to come into her house.

"Go and get your things so we can go," I told Eric.

"I believe it's in my office. Follow me."

How he convinced, no, tricked me into coming over was beyond me. I followed up the stairs behind him. My feet left imprints in their plush white carpet. I would sweep those away on the way back out.

Finally we made it to hardwood floors. I tried stopping the click, clack of my high heel shoes by walking on my toes. I stood nervously as he rummaged through his desk drawers in search for his wallet and important papers.

He turned to me. "Look in those drawers please."

I did as he asked. "Nothing."

He approached me strongly and kissed me. "Eric!" I called. "You are crazy. Stop."

He refused and I fought him. We'd slept together countless times but never in his house where his wife lay her head at night. I wasn't going to allow it. I didn't care if she and Victor were out of town for another week and we had the house to ourselves. I just didn't care.

"No I can't do this!" I yelled. "That's it Eric, you're taking things too far. This whole situation is out of control. I can't do this anymore."

"Come here." He pulled me close and kissed me. My stomach tingled and my knees were ready to buckle at any moment. "You feel that? I don't get that feeling when I kiss my wife."

I tried running away but he held me. He licked my neck and kissed me more. I moaned.

"She don't make sounds like you do and," He put my hand on him and made me hold it, "Make me hard like that. You see how excited you make me?"

I tried letting go but he pushed my hand onto him even harder. "Don't." He pushed me against the wall. "Don't fight it."

He pulled apart my blouse, knelt down and licked my breast. Then he stood to his feet, shoved his tongue down my throat, and threw his finger up my shorts.

"Let me taste you. Let me taste that pussy." He didn't wait for a response before he got onto his knees, pulled my shorts to the side and began licking me inside out. He flung both legs over his shoulders. My back lay pressed against the wall.

"Mmmm she don't taste like you," he repeated with a mouth full of my orgasm. I don't know what turned me on so but it was feeding my ego to hear how good I taste or smelled or felt over his wife. He knew how to get into my head.

With my legs clinched around his neck he stood to his feet without missing a beat. I held onto the back of his head with both hands as he carried me to his desk. Finally, he removed his head from between my thighs. He fumbled with his belt for a quick second before dropping his pants and drawers to the floor.

He signaled for me to kiss him. Without hesitation I obliged. That's when I knew I was hooked as if having sex with him in his house wasn't a sign in the first place. But sucking a married man's dick was the ultimate! How did I know if he hadn't slept with his wife this morning? I didn't think about it nor did I care. I was so turned on. I slowly slipped it into my mouth and did the do.

"She don't suck it the way you do," he grunted and that took me over the edge. I got so into it that I almost climaxed myself but he stopped me. "I don't want to cum. Let me feel that pussy."

He made me stand on my feet while he lay back. I climbed on top of him and slid it inside.

"Do she feel like that?" I asked him. "Is that how she feels?"

"No baby."

"Is her pussy as tight, wet, and warm as mine?" I asked him while stroking his hard manhood with my soft womanhood.

"No." He squirmed. I could feel him getting harder and almost at the point of his climax.

"Call me your mistress," I commanded getting turned on more and more. I could feel the blood pulsating through his arteries through the walls of my vagina as I pumped slowly. "Call me your mistress. You want me to make you cum?"

"Yes."

"Tell me. Tell your mistress to fuck you harder and make you cum."

"Fuck me mistress."

"Yeah."

"Fuck me mistress. Make me cum mistress."

I dove onto him harder and harder giving it all I had until we were both at the top.

"Make me ——ughhh!" he yelled and shot all inside me.

"Are you crazy?" I snapped. "Why didn't you tell me you were——"

Ding, dong! I was interrupted by the ringing doorbell. We both jumped in fright.

"Who is that?" he asked as if I knew.

We hurried and fixed our clothes and he ran downstairs to see about the door. He returned calm and continued to search for his wallet. "Here it is," he said finding it on the shelf. I believe he knew it all along and this was all a ploy to fulfill some fantasy of his to have sex in his home with his mistress.

Minutes later we left and acted as though nothing happened. We were due to board his plane in twenty minutes for our weekend getaway to the Turks and Caicos for my birthday.

CHAPTER 15

"What do you think about this?" I asked Gabrielle.

She took a look at the watch and gave an unsure look. "It's okay. How about this one?"

I searched for a birthday present for Eric and of course I made Gabrielle tag along. She, at first, refused and complained about her stomach. She was just getting over the flu and didn't want her diarrhea to return but she could never resist me.

"Wow that's nice. I like that." I purchased the seven hundred dollar watch and we left to continue shopping for ourselves.

"Next month you should ask Jack if you can go with me to a festival in Miami. Eric can probably get us a room and you know the flight is free," I said.

She walked behind nodding and looking through the display of clothes that hung recklessly on the racks. The sales rep walked behind her fixing the clothes.

"You ladies need help with anything?" she asked.

"No thanks, we're just looking," Gabrielle told her.

"This is a nice shirt," I said walking ahead. I flipped through the shirts finding my size and modeled with it pressed up against me. I turned to Gabrielle to get her opinion.

Her complexion was pale and sweat flooded her forehead. Her eyes were dazed and rolled to the back of her head. Before I could get my first words out she hit the floor.

"Oh my—Gabrielle!" I ran over to her and grabbed her hand and felt her face. She was out cold. "Would somebody help me?" I yelled through the store. Everyone raced over in a panic. They immediately called the ambulance and we were rushed to the hospital.

I didn't know what to do or to think. I instantly called Jack and told him to haul ass up there. Then I called her mother.

I sat nervously in the emergency room. They refused to let me see her. Finally after two hours of waiting the doctor finally allowed Jack and me to come in.

Gabrielle sat in the bed like she was in the Grand Resort and Spa.

"Are you alright?" Jack immediately ran to her side.

"Yes I'm fine." She sat on the edge of the hospital bed with her feet swinging back and forth.

"What's wrong?"

"What did the doctor say? He wouldn't tell me anything," Jack insist on knowing.

"Baby, I'm fine. I'm just a little dehydrated." She pointed to me, "I told this bitch I was hot, hungry, and thirsty."

"You're always hot and hungry but your ass never passed out on me before."

Jack wasn't feeling our play. He wanted to know what was up with his wife.

"So what now? Did the doctor say you could leave or what?"

"He said it could have been stress and not letting myself recover from being sick last week. I just need to eat something and drink lots fluids. They want me to stay a few hours to check my stats and if everything is stable I can go home."

"You can't keep up those hours. Your job can survive without you. You shouldn't be running to work when you're still sick."

"I know," she didn't argue.

They'd just had an argument that morning about her working too hard. It was a repeat of every other time he'd warned her. Gabrielle never listened. She loved her job and was great at it. I never understood why Jack wouldn't leave the girl alone. It would save them both stress.

"Baby don't scare me like that." He kissed her forehead.

"I'm sorry."

"How do you feel?" Jack asked.

"I feel fine," she said smoothly, "I feel great. I'm just a little hungry." I took notice of her expression. She was lying! Something was up. Gabrielle could fool Jack but she couldn't fool me. "Would you do me a favor?" she asked sweetly.

"Anything honey."

"Would you go to the cafeteria and get me something to eat? Anything, I don't care what it is?"

"Sure, but do they want you eating regular food?"

I loved the way Jack was so cautious about his wife's condition. It was such a sweet side of him. Even though he had his ways, he loved Gabrielle to no tomorrow. I still wasn't sure why he cheated but he seemed to make up for it. At least I thought.

"They said it's fine, but if it'll make you feel better go to the nurse's station and ask them."

He did just that leaving the room for the two ladies to talk. Gabrielle kicked both feet up and flipped the channels. I jumped on the bed sitting beside her. "You're in here like this is a five star hotel. This is not vacation!"

"Do you know how much I'm paying for this room? I'm going to get every bit of my money's worth."

I lay back and watch the television with her. I could hear babies in the hall screaming. I couldn't stand hospitals. Ever since my dad spent his last six months before he died I wouldn't bring myself into another hospital no matter how sick I was. The stinky medicine smell, the nasty hospital food, and constant interruptions all made me gag.

"So what is it? Spill the beans," I finally told her during a commercial break.

"What?"

"Come on Gabrielle. I've known you way too long. Something is happening here and it's more than you're telling."

She turned away. It had to be something big. All I know is it better not be cancer.

"Kayla, I'm pregnant."

"What?" I was surprised and almost elated. But she didn't seem at all excited about the news. I had to handle the situation with care. "Is that what the doctor said?"

"I knew this last week? I didn't have the flu. I had morning sickness."

I should have seen the signs. What kind of best friend was I?

"Why haven't you told Jack?"

"Because it isn't his."

Somebody call me a doctor because I am about to die! I almost told Gabrielle to move her fat pregnant ass out of the way because I needed the bed for myself. Instead I simply asked softly, "Todd?"

"Yeah." She held her head low.

I wanted her to know that she needed to not be ashamed. I wanted her to know that I loved her no matter what. I wanted her to know that her secret was safe with me. So no, no, she need not be ashamed.

I lifted her head and with the most compassionate, most sincere voice I asked my best friend, "Bitch, what are we going to do?" It wasn't her battle alone.

"There's only one thing to do," she said.

The decision was made. We were both scared to death. We'd heard the horror stories but never experienced it. We'd been that lucky thus far.

"I'll call and make the appointment tomorrow," I told her.

"What appointment?" Jack interrupted standing in the doorway with a turkey sandwich and chips. Gabrielle and I stalled in our tracks.

"A spa appointment," I was quick on my feet. "Gabi and I are going to do a spa weekend and just relax the entire time."

I looked to see if he bought it. I don't think he was too thrilled about the whole idea of his wife leaving him again for another weekend trip with her best friend but he couldn't really deny her.

"That might be a good idea," he said finally.

It would work out great. I'd make the appointment for her abortion that morning and we'd spend the remainder of the weekend away at a spa so she could recover. It was a perfect plan. Jack would never suspect a thing.

"Pickles!" he fussed while pulling off the pickles from her sandwich, "I specifically told the lady no pickles."

"That's okay honey, leave them there. I'll eat it," Gabrielle told him.

Jack looked at her surprised. I looked at her like, 'bitch you'd better not eat those pickles.'

Gabrielle despised pickles! As much as she fussed and demanded a free meal whenever a restaurant accidentally gave her pickles? As much as she complained that pickles made a sandwich taste bitter? As much as it disgusted her to see us eat pickles in her presence, she wanted to have some now? Oh no! Not on my watch.

It was the ultimate pregnant food. What was she thinking? I'd knock that sandwich out her hands onto the floor and stomp it before I let her even attempt to put a pickle in her mouth.

"You must really be hungry," Jack said.

"I am." She gathered her senses and took a bite. "But I'm not that hungry." She handed the sandwich over.

"You have to eat something."

"I will."

The situation was a bit uncomfortable but under control. I left the hospital in a hurry and went home. Eric called me earlier and I immediately returned his call.

"Hi honey. I've been at the hospital all day with Gabrielle. It's a long story. Anyway I could use a massage, if you know what I mean. Call me back. Love you."

I took a bath and cooked up a big meal just in case Eric popped up. I settled onto my favorite plush, velour chaise and watched television.

Def Poetry Jam played on the screen and of course it reminded me of Beau. I looked closely as the people stood and presented their poetry to the world. I imagined Beau speaking his mind. I visualized his stance, his tone, his look. I bet he'd be sexy as hell up there. I wondered what ever came of the whole Def Poetry thing.

Just as I began to wonder, the host presented his last poet and out walked Beau. The pot roast almost fell out of my mouth as my jaw hit the floor. He looked debonair as he walk calmly on stage with those bow legs of his. He licked those voluptuous ass lips and closed his eyes as he started. It reminded me of the first time I saw him on stage. It sent a tingle up my spine that left me paralyzed. After he finished I broke away from my trance and immediately picked up the phone and dialed his number.

"Hello."

"Hello. Beau?" I said.

There was a silent yet uncomfortable pause until I finally broke it, "I'm sorry this is-"

"I know exactly who you are Mikayla," he interrupted.

"I'm just wondering if you have the right number."

I was flattered but his tone wasn't friendly. "Yes I have the right number."

I felt so stupid for making such an abrupt call. I hadn't spoken to the guy in months and now that I'd seen him on TV, I decided to call. He probably thought I was a groupie. I'm sure he may have wanted to hang up on me but was too much of a gentleman to do so. But I only wanted to congratulate him and tell him how proud I was.

"I saw you on TV tonight. I called to say you looked good and sounded real good and congratulations."

"Thank you." He wasn't sure of my motives.

"Sure. How ya been?"

"I've been good."

"That's nice to hear," we paused again, "well, I won't hold you. I just wanted to congratulate you. I'm happy that you're getting everything you've wanted. You worked hard for it."

I was ready to let the conversation go. Every second was beginning to feel like torture.

"What about you?" he asked. "Are you getting everything you've wanted?"

"Hey, I'm surviving."

"You always do," he said, "You always do."

"Well, um...I'll let you get to it. I know you're probably busy now being a celebrity and all."

"Celebrity?" he laughed. It was a laugh so familiar. I missed it. "I wish."

"You can't tell me that you don't have a whole A-list of friends with your new found fame," I teased.

"No, I couldn't tell you that. But what's funny is no matter how many new friends I get, I'm always a fan of yours."

I blushed. "Still a slick talker huh?"

"It's the truth."

"Thanks for the compliment."

"Don't thank me. I should be thanking you."

"What should you be thanking me for?"

"A lot of what I'm doing now, I couldn't have done it without you."

"No, you were already determined. You would have made it."

"Probably, but not so soon. You helped me put everything together. I had connections years before you came into the picture but what good are connections if you're not prepared, you know?"

"I guess," I agreed.

"So I owe you."

"You don't owe me."

"Yeah I do and I say let me take you out to a real nice restaurant. I can pay for those now."

I laughed and thought about it. He wanted to go out this weekend but I declined. Eric's birthday was Saturday and I had something planned for the entire weekend. Disappointingly, we decided to wait for the next time he came into town. Neither of us knew when that would be. He had a busy schedule for the months to come. Show after show. Taping after taping. Tour after tour. The way it was looking it could be two months from now. So we savored our moment and talked for most of the night catching up on old times.

I was really proud of Beau. Really proud.

* * * *

"Yes please." I spoke on the phone reconfirming my reservations, "That's right, Parker. Seven-thirty, that's correct. Thank you."

I rushed to get ready. He should be arriving soon. I was so nervous and put everything into place. My hair was perfect, make-up flawless, and the silk dress was sinful. I would have that man eating out of my hands before they could bring the entrée.

The doorbell rang and I slowly strolled over and open it. There Beau stood, looking down on me, smelling good and looking fresh. I wanted to skip dinner, invite him in and let him be my meal. I was a good girl though.

"Hi," I said shyly.

He opened his arms and hugged me tightly. I remembered these hugs. My face lay deeply in his chest.

"Thanks," I said inhaling the aroma. "I see you're wearing my favorite cologne."

"I'll be in town for two days only. I have to leave my mark," he kissed my cheek, "It's nice to see you again."

"Same here," I added. "You ready?"

"Yup." He walked me to the car and opened my door. Lilies lay on the passenger seat. He gave them to me.

"Thank you," I said impressed. They were my favorite flower and he remembered that.

He gave a modest nod followed by an innocent smile. The brotha was still so smooth and always a gentleman. Inside his mind was a database of tricks and romantic gestures on how to make a girl's heart skip a beat.

I watched as Beau walked from the passenger side of his car to the driver's. I felt a little bad for taking him instead of Eric but it wasn't my fault that Eric got stuck in D.C. for a meeting on his birthday. I should have flown to see him but he would be back tomorrow and I wouldn't see him tonight so that didn't make sense. We'd celebrate tomorrow night and that left tonight open for Beau.

"Right this way Miss. Parker." The maitre d' led us to our table in the back. It was a dim and private area. The table had a distinguished ambiance about itself. The floral arrangement was exact in its presentation of setting a romantic scene.

He pulled my chair out for me to sit and Beau took his seat thereafter. I felt like a queen already.

"Did I tell you how beautiful you look?"

"No." I waited for him to tell me.

"You look beautiful."

"Thank you. Next time don't wait so long," I teased.

Our conversation carried on smoothly and we ate dinner lightly. Just as I finally got over that uncomfortable first conversation he asked me the inevitable question.

"Why did you stop seeing me, honestly?"

I knew it was coming sooner or later. "Beau, you knew my history with being in relationships and I wasn't trying to be hurt again," I danced around the subject.

"Did I ever give you the impression that I would hurt you?" He kept it up, "It was like one day we were best friends and the next day you disappeared."

I listened and still held onto my secret.

"I thought I'd met that woman. I thought you were her," he told me. "What was it? I wasn't making money fast enough?"

"What?" Now he was pissing me off by making me the gold digger and him the innocent victim.

"I'm just asking. I know you're used to certain things and I worked harder than I have in life to get there, but before I could you disappeared on me."

"It wasn't about the money, Beau."

"What was it then? It's more than what you're letting on."

I hesitated, "It's nothing."

He took a deep breath, "Mikayla, I know you've been through a lot but believe me I was the one person that would have never hurt you. I was...I am crazy about you. I tried taking it slow so I wouldn't scare you off. I guess I took it too slow."

"I..."

"I'm sorry I won't ask for your excuses anymore," he politely cut me short. "You have your reasons. I'm not trying to put you on the spot. I had to get that off my chest. I don't know the next time we'll see each other and I want you to know I'm the one man if no one, who's always in your corner."

It was sweet but of course me being me, I viewed it all as game.

"Thanks I appreciate that."

He gave a giggle. "You're something else you know that?"

"What?" I asked innocently.

"Here I am pouring my heart out to you and you're just blowing me off. That's okay."

"I'm not blowing you off."

"Yes you are. That's okay. I should crack you upside your head with a club and pull your ass home by your hair instead of talking this sweet shit to you," he teased.

"Don't get me excited," we laughed and finished up our meal.

"Lets get out of here," he whispered. "Let me take you dancing. I know a nice place."

"Sounds like fun."

We paid our tab and started for the door. For those few hours I only mildly thought of Eric. It was weird. Eric kept my mind off Cory. For the most part Beau could keep my mind off Eric. Who would keep my mind off Beau? It seemed I needed another man to keep my attention off the last. It was a vicious cycle that had to be broken. I didn't know how to do it.

I led the way to the counter and waited patiently while Beau handed in our valet ticket. I turned around and suddenly grew sick to my stomach.

"Would you excuse me? I'll only be a sec," I told Beau.

"Sure."

I barely waited for his approval before I marched through the crowd of tables, chairs, and people. Eric's face turned pale as I approached him and his wife sitting intimately in the other corner of the room. The woman was deep in thought as her husband's arm lay around her. He pretended to not see me.

"Look at who's here!" I announced. "What a nice surprise."

"Miss Parker?" he put on his charade, "Wow, it is a...nice...surprise. I didn't expect to see you here."

I wanted to say, 'I bet you didn't you lying bastard' but I settled for, "Same here."

He removed his arm from around his wife. "Honey you remember Miss Parker don't you? Victor's old teacher." He didn't flinch. He stayed in character.

"I'm not sure if we ever met," I told him.

"No, we actually did," the tall, slender woman corrected me. "It was very brief at the beginning of the school year. You probably wouldn't remember. It was during an orientation and you were surrounded by a mass of parents. I was in the crowd of those parents."

"You know what?... now I remember. It's been a while."

"Yes it has. It's a pleasure seeing you again." She politely extended her hand. I accepted her lady like handshake. And after our hands met she laid hers back on his lap and cuddled underneath his armpit.

I gave a silent grunt and raised one brow to Eric. He was very uncomfortable but played it cool while his wife and mistress spoke cordially amongst each other.

She was a mirror image of the photo I'd seen in their home. Very "runwayish" with her fancy dress, wild hair, and heavy makeup. From what I could see she wasn't curvaceous but undoubtedly shaped like a pole. She wasn't ugly. In fact, she was quite pretty. Then again anyone would be pretty if they wore as much makeup as she.

I couldn't help but look at her and wonder what she had that was different from me. She was very mannerable as if she'd spent most of her years in etiquette school. And as I continued to look at her, I wondered what she really looked like underneath her mask of makeup. Normal people don't wear that much makeup on a common day.

"That's a beautiful necklace," she interrupted my thoughts as she noticed our matching necklaces. "It looks just like mine. Where'd you get it if you don't mind me asking?"

Her mind was at work I could tell. Eric told me already that the necklace was rare and that he'd special ordered it from London. He sat in his chair sipping water and sweating bullets. And being the bitch I am, I couldn't let him off that easy. I had to give an appropriate response.

"I got it from someone very close to me," I replied smartly. I didn't lie. Eric sat only five inches from me.

"Oh," was all she commented. But her eyes said it all as they cut at her husband. She tugged at her matching earrings boldly showing off. Lucky for her I'd recently lost my earrings to match or else I would have definitely thrown it in her face as well.

"Are you leaving or did you just arrive?" Eric asked while adjusting himself in his seat. A puddle formed underneath his armpit. He dabbed his forehead with his napkin.

I wanted to slap his face. For a man who repeatedly lied and said there's no romance in his marriage, he sure did have his arm wrapped around her like a cheap spandex sweater.

"Actually I'm leaving. I noticed you from across the way and had to come and speak to my favorite parent," I sarcastically said.

"Thanks," he rushed me away.

"Think nothing of it," I told him. "I'll let you get back to it. I wouldn't want to interrupt too badly. I see you guys are in the midst of celebration." I noticed the chilled champagne.

"Yeah, it's my husband's birthday," she bragged. "So yeah, we do have a bit of celebrating to do Miss...." she emphasized, "Parker right? I'm sorry, I'm horrible with names."

'Bitch you're not that horrible,' I wanted to say. I knew she was pulling rank. She could sense something in the air as any woman would. She wanted to let me know that I was a nobody and that no matter what the situation between me and her husband, she was still the head woman.

But I was smart. I wouldn't be undermined by a lesser woman regardless of who the bitch is. So I smiled and replied, "Yes Miss. Parker. Don't worry about it." I said falsely, "And happy birthday to you Eric." I used his first name purposely.

Then I added an extra touch of salt to the wound. "As a suggestion you should try the mousse de saumon et capres. And you should definitely have the tarte fine aux pommes for desert." I flaunted my years of French and mildly taunted her by throwing Eric's favorite entrée and desert in her face.

The look on her face told it all. I'd revealed just a little and not too much. His birthday would surely be less enjoyable now with all the explaining he would have to do tonight. I could care less especially since he lied and celebrated with her instead of me.

She couldn't stop giving the two of us the evil eye. 'Yeah that's right bitch I know your man!' I inwardly gloated.

I walked away towards Beau who gestured from across the room that our car was waiting. I was pissed! Of all the nerve! He'd lied to me. Out of town on business my ass!

"Are you alright?" Beau asked me.

"I'm fine. I'm just feeling a little sick to the stomach."

"Do you want to go in? We can skip dancing if you're not feeling well," he asked sweetly.

I wasn't up for dancing. Eric had really upset me. But what would I do at home except sit alone the entire night and think about it? And I didn't want to ruin the night with Beau. But still I had to. I wouldn't have been good company. I was too upset.

"If you don't mind," I reluctantly said, "I would like to go home."

"Okay." He didn't hesitate. I knew he was disappointed but what could he do?

He parked in front of my place and walked me to my door. "I'm sorry for tonight."

"Shhh," he said. "You can't help how you feel."

He was right because at that moment I felt so guilty.

"Is there anything I could do?"

"Yeah, call me when you get home," I said and turned around to go inside.

He walked away also. As soon as he got home he called as promised and checked on my well being. We talked for awhile but even Beau couldn't get my mind off the event that took place tonight.

I lay in bed wide awake thinking about everything. Who would have thought I would be sitting here staring at the seven hundred dollar birthday watch without the birthday boy sitting beside me?

The entire evening was a disappointment. I envisioned my night ending totally different. I thought Beau and I would at least kiss or keep each other company catching up all night. Instead I'd been cheated on by Eric with his wife.

I waited for his call but it never came. My night ended with me trying to think of anything but what Eric and his wife were doing. I was unsuccessful.

* * * *

Everything looked different today. Even the sun shined on my car from a different angle displaying a different color than I'd ever noticed before. My hair lay different across my face and tickled my cheek. Even my make up, I noticed as I glanced in my driver's mirror, lay rougher than usual. Everything was just DIFFERENT! But what was it?

Was my nose less wide open now that I had been smacked in the face with the truth? I didn't know.

"Have you talked to Eric?" Gabrielle asked.

"No. He didn't call me last night," I said so upset. Today I was stuck in an emotional bind. I didn't know if I should remain pissed off at Eric or depressed because he hadn't called or what. I did know that I wasn't in the mood to talk about Eric. So I immediately changed the subject. "What about you? Have you talked to Todd?"

She took a breath, "Briefly. We're meeting tonight to discuss our plans."

"Plans? What plans are you two discussing?" I was

confused. I know she wasn't considering having his baby. She couldn't have been that crazy.

"Just everything. We're fixed on the whole abortion thing but we have to decide whether we'll see each other after this. Truthfully nothing good can come from our relationship."

"Yeah, one day everything will come to light."

"I know but it's so hard to leave someone who loves you so much."

"You don't think Jack loves you?"

"Jack loves me but he doesn't love me like Todd. Todd's love for me is deep and unconditional. Jack's love is on the surface and something that he's conditioned himself to believe he needs to have for me because we've been together for so long. I don't want that kind of love."

I listened to her and couldn't help but compare my own situation. Even though I'd seen Eric with his wife I still love him. It hurt like hell and I was pissed that he lied but I still love him. It was so strange but I couldn't imagine letting him go and he wasn't even mine to begin with.

"You know what Gabrielle? You will never be able to love Jack or anyone until you let Todd go." I told her things that I needed to hear myself.

"I know. I know," she agreed.

That was the problem between the both of us. We both knew what we needed to do but neither of us would do it.

"Are you going to start cutting away from Mr. Wonderful?" she asked me.

"I don't know. I can only try," I said thinking that her and I were in the same boat. "I left my two way and other cell phone at home as a start."

"At least you started," she told me.

I pulled into the jammed packed parking lot of the gym. Inside ladies and some men pranced around in their attractive workout wear. I was there for one purpose only and that was to relieve stress. Lord knows I didn't need any new men problems.

"Gabrielle I'll call you back. I'm at the gym now."

I did my three miles on the treadmill and changed into my kickboxing gear and warmed up by beating the bag.

"Looking good," I heard a familiar voice from behind. I continued hitting the bag only this time even harder. He moved closer.

"Look stay away from me. I don't want to hear your excuses or anything. Right now I just want you to leave me alone," I snapped.

He stood dressed in his fifteen hundred dollar Armani suit in the middle of the gym. He wasn't used to anyone speaking to him in such a way. I was here to let him know he'd met his match. Without a single word, he turned away and walked out the door avoiding further embarrassment.

I couldn't believe he didn't stay and fight for me. Even when Cory was dead wrong he would fight to the bitter end and plead his case. Eric was so used to power. He felt as though he stood above all that. I was hurt but managed to finish my workout. Afterwards was a long drive home. I couldn't stand being alone. So I called Beau and confided in him.

"You feeling better?" he asked.

"Somewhat."

"Is there anything I can do?"

"Are you busy tonight?"

He didn't hesitate. "No."

"Are you lying to me Beau?" I could sense it in his voice.

He laughed, "I do have some plans but nothing major. You know I have to seize moments when you want to get together."

"I'm not that bad," I told him.

"No you're not that bad," he agreed. "But you're something else."

His favorite words for me. I smiled.

"So Mikayla, what did you have in mind?"

I thought for a second. "How about dancing?"

"Sounds good."

We made plans for later that night. I ran by Gabrielle's and talked with her for awhile. I was her excuse for getting out of the house to meet up with Todd.

"Did you make the spa appointment yet?" she covertly asked me.

I'd been so occupied with the whole Eric situation that I hadn't managed to make the call. "No, not yet. I'll do it tomorrow."

"You have to make it soon Kayla. I don't want to call from my phone and have Jack get the bill."

"I know. Tomorrow, I promise," I swore to her. "Where should I make it for?"

"I don't know. How would I know?"

"How would I?" We both racked our brains. "I guess I'll have to go through the phone book."

"Maybe I could ask Sabrina. She had one before," she whispered.

"Who is Sabrina?"

"One of my coworkers."

"You told her you might be pregnant?"

"No she told me," she explained. She leaned in close to me and whispered, "When I first began to get sick she told me my complexion had been pale lately and she thought I might be pregnant. She encouraged me to get a pregnancy test. We took it on our lunch."

"What is she, gay?" I asked. I guess I was jealous but what kind of woman notices a change in another woman's complexion? I was Gabrielle's best friend and I didn't even notice a change in anything.

"She's not gay, Kayla," Gabrielle laughed.

I didn't see anything funny. I couldn't believe I was her best friend and here she is going into the stall with a co-worker taking a pregnancy test and didn't even tell her best friend that she was pregnant.

"I'll call her tonight and ask her to make me an appointment where she had hers."

'Fine, call your new best friend,' I thought but I coached myself not to behave in such a territorial way. So I listened while she laughed at Sabrina's jokes and delegated new responsibilities. By the time I got home I only had an hour to prepare for my date with Beau. I still stunk from the gym and didn't know what I would wear.

"Hi Miss Witherspoon," I waved to her as she peeked through her blinds. She waved back.

Only the bottom lock on my door was set. Eric had come by. He probably moved his things out. My heart sank in my chest. As I started to flip the light switch I caught a glimpse of candlelight. There lay a pathway of rose pedals from my hallway to my living room. It wasn't long before I noticed that my entire home was filled with flowers of every assortment. It was like a movie.

Eric sat proudly at the dinning room table.

"Who's going to clean all this up?" I asked coldly, pretending to not be impressed. I have to say I was so excited! I thought he'd left me but he still cared.

"You don't like it?" He rose to his feet. "I saw it in a movie and the woman loved it."

I folded my arms. He would never know how much his gesture meant. "Get out of my house." I walked upstairs passing more bouquets of flowers.

He followed me into my room as I dug through my closet for an outfit to wear. "Kayla, I know you're angry just hear me out."

"What Eric? What do you have to say? Let me guess, you got in early from your trip and couldn't get in touch with me, so out of pity you let your wife take you out to dinner but you really didn't enjoy yourself. You just went because you had to. Is that right?"

"No, I lied to you."

Wow! A man who actually admitted to lying. Eric was a different breed. He certainly had my attention now.

"I lied because I didn't think you would be able to understand that I had to be with her on my birthday."

"Why? Why did you have to be with her on your birthday?"

"Kayla, how can you ask that? You know the situation. It's not like we can flaunt our relationship in front of her. I'm still married and until the divorce or separation is final then I still have a role to play."

"It didn't look like you were working on a separation to me," I told him.

"Like I said, I have a role to play."

"I never realized how good of an actor you were until now. It makes me wonder how much of an act our thing was."

"Come on Kayla don't think like that. I've never lied to you before this."

"How would I know? How do I know this isn't an act right now?"

"It isn't."

"How do I know?" I yelled, "You're buying me the same jewelry that you bought your wife!" I found my necklace and threw it at him. He shielded his face but caught it.

"Kayla," he called to me.

"I don't want it!"

"Honey—" he started but I quickly interrupted.

"Honey? Now I'm honey today?" I asked, "Last night I was Miss. Parker."

"Baby, I'll buy you something bigger and better and more expensive," he told me.

"I don't want it!"

He put his head down not knowing what to do.

"Tell me this Eric," I stopped digging, "How well of a role did you play?"

He looked confused.

"Did you play Mr. Faithful Husband? And at night did you show your appreciation for all your wife's hard work?"

He turned his head. I approached him. He at first, looked as though he wanted to run but stood his ground.

"Did you?"

"Are you asking me if I slept with my wife?" he asked me as if it were a sinful question. Then he frown his face and crossed his arms. I waited for an answer. We were two prideful people who stood neck to neck, toe to toe. "I thought we agreed to never ask questions like that."

"Just answer the question Eric."

"Why? I'm not asking you who you're sleeping with."

"That's because you know I'm not sleeping with anyone!"

"How do I know that?"

"You have a key to my house what do you mean?" I checked myself. I almost allowed him to divert all attention to me. "You're avoiding the question."

"Fine. What do you want me to do, lie Mikayla?"

I took a step back. "No Eric. I want you to get out of my house," I said calmly.

He leaned on the wall.

"I am not playing with you," I told him.

"What was I supposed to do baby? Just tell me that."
He waited but I didn't respond. I was through talking. "I'm
trying to do what's right so that everybody wins. I love you
and I want us to work."

"How do you want us to work when you're sleeping
with another woman?"

"She's my wife."

"Then why in the hell are you sleeping with me?"

"I love you. Kayla, I want to marry you."

"Shut up Eric. You sound ridiculous."

"I promise I do. Kayla, my life would be so empty
without you. Please don't end us."

"You've had it both ways for a long time. It can't go
on forever."

"Honey—" I gave him a look and he stopped in his
tracks. "Kayla baby, it won't. Give me a week and I promise
I will have proof that it's over between us."

I found the perfect dancing dress and lay it on the bed.
"What's that for?" he asked. "Where are you going?"

"Eric, lock the door behind you." I jumped into the
shower. Any other time he would have jumped in with me
but he was too worried.

"Mikayla, where are you going tonight? Why are you
getting all dressed up?" he asked.

I pulled the shower door back and showed my wet,
naked body. "Out."

"You have another clean up man to pick up my pieces?"

"I thought you were leaving?" I wrapped myself in
terrycloth robe and began to lotion up.

"Who's the rebound guy this time?" he asked.

"Did you just call me a hoe?" I asked defensively.

"What? No! I just want to know who you're going
out with."

"Don't worry about it Eric."

He waited before he asked his next question, "Are you going to sleep with him tonight?"

"I thought you just said we don't ask questions like that?"

"We don't but since you started it..."

"What do you want me to do? Lie to you Eric?" My heart jumped as my doorbell rang. Eric stood motionless waiting for me to answer. I had to pull my weight. "Lock the door behind you please." I began to walk away.

"Wait," he stopped me, "I really, really don't want you to go. I am so sorry you had to see what you saw last night but baby, I love you. Since the first day we met I've loved you."

I folded my arms and guarded my feelings while he poured his heart out to me.

"I'm not perfect and I don't always say the right words but let me say this, I will do anything it takes to keep you. Anything! I wouldn't do that for anybody. These roses and flowers and shit," he pointed around my room, "this isn't me. But you bring different things out of me. Things I've never done for anyone before. Things I never thought of doing. And baby, it's going to kill me to see you leave with another man. Literally break my heart. So please, Kayla, please don't do it. I don't know if I'll be able to handle it."

He was pulling all stops while Beau stood outside ringing my doorbell. I...I didn't know what to do. If I left with Beau my relationship with Eric would never be the same. But if I stayed with Eric then what excuse would I tell Beau?

"And what am I supposed to say to him?" I asked Eric.

"Tell him your man is back and you can't go," he tried pulling rank.

I would never be that cruel. Beau had never done anything to intentionally hurt me so he didn't deserve to be treated unfairly.

"I know this may be hard for you so do you want me to do it?" Eric asked as if it was nothing.

"No, I can handle it. Let me handle it." I didn't want to be mean and cold but my heart really was with Eric.

I took tiny steps downstairs to the front door trying to prolong the situation. I halfway opened the door to see Beau standing there looking so good and smelling so great. He gave a great grin because finally I'd answered.

"You look beautiful," he told me. "Did I wait too long to say it this time?"

He was so sweet which made this so much harder to do. I smiled. "Thank you."

"What's the matter?" his smile turned to concern.

"Beau, I can't make it tonight," I began my lie, "I was going to call you but.... Gabrielle's sick again and I need to baby-sit Jackson while Jack takes her to the hospital."

"Oh," he said. "I understand. I'm jealous as hell of that little four year old though, but I won't hate. The better man won, right? " he joked.

I smiled but the guilt was tearing me apart from inside out.

"I leave early tomorrow so maybe the next time I'm in town?"

"Definitely."

"Make sure you wear that dress." He leaned in to give me a kiss on the cheek but stalled as the candlelight from inside struck his face. Eric grabbed the door and pulled it open and stood behind me high off his own arrogance. He glared at Beau and waited to see if he would follow thru with that kiss. Needless to say Beau didn't. He had a bad taste in his mouth and took a step back.

His eyes changed shape followed by his facial expression. He was confused at first, disappointed second, and lastly pissed off. I'd never seen him like that before. He took his bad boy stance, and gave Eric the evil eye. Not once did he ever back down.

The testosterone pumped through the thin air between the men. I had to admit I was afraid and turned on at the same time.

Eric stood confidently behind me, marking his territory. I couldn't believe my position. I stood frozen and mute. My brain dropped a billion lies to tell but my mouth wouldn't register the command. I'd lied too much already and no matter what I said, nothing would be good enough.

He didn't wait for an explanation. He turned around to walk away.

"Beau wait." I ran to him but he wouldn't stop. Eric still stood in the doorway. He was interested in hearing what I'd say. "Please wait so I can explain."

"It's cool Mikayla. You don't have to explain shit to me." He cursed at me! He'd never ever cursed at me. I didn't try to pursue him any further. He got into his car and drove away. I followed his tail lights to the end of the complex. I was so disappointed in myself and even more angry at Eric.

"You're fooling around with thugs now?" Eric stereotyped Beau's braids and exterior image.

I stormed past him.

"Why would you do something like that?" I demanded to know. "Was that necessary?"

"What was I supposed to do, just listen while he made plans with you?"

"I'm a big girl! I told you I would take care of it! I didn't need you to come to my rescue."

"I had to make my presence known," he told me.

"Your presence known? What is this, some sort of competition for you?" I asked. "Really Eric, I don't think you want to play those types of games with me with the situation you're in. Don't piss me off."

"Is that a threat?"

"No it's not a threat because I'm not petty like you." I was so annoyed. At that moment I couldn't stand to be around him. I was disgusted by his behavior and only wanted him to leave. "I need time alone. Please just give me some time by myself to think."

"What?"

"The last two days have been a lot. I want to be alone. Can you do that for me?"

"It's my birthday," he said with puppy dog eyes.

I reached into my cabinet and handed him a gift bag with the Movado watch I'd bought for him. "Here," I said, "happy birthday." I walked upstairs to my room and lay down to think. I heard my storm door close. Eric had finally left.

* * * *

Rain drops tap danced across my window. I sat on my bed for hours thinking about what I would do next. How could I rectify things with Beau? What would I say to get him to talk to me again? All I could remember was the look of disgust on his face. He would never speak to me again but all I could do was try.

I stood outside his dark apartment practicing over my speech but as soon as my damp hand banged against the door, my mind went blank. I tried to regain memories of exactly what I would say but I couldn't. Before I knew it, Beau opened the door and stood before me in his boxers and eight pack abs. I wanted to lick those broad shoulders and kiss his chest from peck to peck.

He looked as though he'd been up all night. Almost as if he expected me to come. He displayed no emotion, no surprise or happiness that I'd come. He only looked me up and down in my wet hooded rain jacket and sneakers, before he rolled his eyes and walked back to his room.

I followed timidly and sat as he packed his things.

"I'm sorry," I started.

"Apology accepted but you don't owe me anything."

"Beau you're a nice guy and—"

"Guess you haven't heard about us nice guys," he interrupted, "We always finish last."

"Look I'm really sorry. I didn't know he would come over and I thought I'd avoid a conflict by lying to you. I didn't tell him to come over and I didn't tell him to come to the door." I explained. "You've never done anything to disrespect me and I didn't want you to leave thinking that I intentionally tried to hurt you."

"You came over here to clear up your character?"

"I came to apologize," I said. I opened my jacket to show off my panty and bra set that I especially picked out for him. "Can we make up?" I tried to seduce him.

He gave a sarcastic giggle. "You don't get it do you? The thing is Kayla, if I didn't care about you, I would do you like any other man that you've been with before and just fuck you and send you on your way."

My jaw hit the floor.

"You have this problem with thinking that you can solve anything by spreading your legs. I know what it is. Some man out here has told you that you have the best pussy in the world. Guess what baby, we ALL tell that lie. So please cover up and go home because I don't want to fuck you."

I was so hurt by his words I could have cried. Instead I made my way to the door but turned around for the last word.

"Um, I know you're mad but...I ..I just really wanted to apologize. I love being around you and cherish our friendship. I know that after all this you've lost some respect for me—"

"Kay, I respect you even if you don't respect yourself."

"I respect myself," I defended.

"Not by fucking a married man you don't. I saw his ring," he flat out told me. "That says it all when a man can openly walk around, screw you, and not try to hide his main woman from you. That shows how much respect he has for you and how much you have for yourself. What do you get out of it besides money and short term pleasures?"

"He's getting a divorce?" The words sounded so stupid leaving my mouth.

"You can't be that damn naïve." He stopped packing and looked at me.

At that moment I felt so stupid, so dumb, and so small.

"Okay so I've made mistakes. Who hasn't?" I began to cry. I brought out the drama queen that every woman has. No man could resist a woman's tears. No man except Beau.

"You expect me to believe that you're an innocent sweet girl who's always hurt but never hurts anyone? Come on Kayla that's not you. I used to believe that it was but it's not," he told me. "You do what you want to make yourself happy except you don't know what the hell makes you happy. You want a faithful man but when you get him you don't want him anymore. You live for drama. You're selfish and spoiled. You sleep with me and your ex and a married fucking man just because you're scared to be alone for one second.

But you're the victim? You're not the victim Kayla, you're the problem."

I was stunned. My crocodile tears turned to real tears. Never had he talked down to me and I questioned his words. Were they true? Was I really like that?

My two way pager rang. Beau gave me a look. I stalled before opening it. Of course it was Eric:

I'm sorry for tonight. I was jealous. I know in my heart that no matter how much money I have, I can't afford to lose you. I love you.

I put the sidekick into my pocket. My eyes were still filled with tears.

"Don't miss your cue," Beau told me.

Enough was enough. I couldn't hear anymore. I barely tied my jacket or threw my hood on before I ran out the door. He didn't stop me.

Chapter 16

"How'd your meeting with Todd go?"

"It went ok. It was kind of emotional but it went ok."

"What did you guys decide?"

"I decided that he and I should be friends. It's the only right thing to do," Gabrielle tried convincing herself. "If I don't end it now, then next year we'll be in the same situation. I can't go through this again. I don't know how I'll survive this time around."

"We'll survive. Don't worry," I told her.

My attitude was sober. Since my encounter with Beau a few days ago I'd become totally humble. The emotional high horse that I rode for the last few months was now a pony after I re-evaluated things.

Eric was my truest trial and biggest temptation. Since the development of our relationship, I stopped pursuing a career as a principal and revolved my future plans around him. I'd become too dependent on him, his expensive excursions, and financial securities.

But I wasn't too hard on myself. I didn't know one woman who wouldn't have gotten comfortable with a man who pays for everything from mortgage, to car note, lights and gas, phone, jewelry, clothes, hair and nail appointments and pocket change. However, catching him in a lie quickly snapped me back into reality.

"When is the appointment?" I carried on my phone conversation with Gabrielle.

"Are you okay?" she asked me.

"Yeah why?" She paused for a minute. "What?"

"Nothing. It's just that every time we talk you ask me when the appointment is. It's next Thursday."

"I'm sorry. I forgot you did tell me that."

"Are you going to be able to make it because Sabrina said she'll take me if-"

I quickly cut her off, "No, I'm taking you. Am I that selfish that you think I wouldn't make it to take you someplace important like that?"

"Kayla, you're not selfish. Hey, I told you Beau was just upset. You shouldn't take things to heart like that. Don't let it bother you so much."

"I'll try not to. I wonder if he'll ever call me again."

"He'll call you. Trust me he was just pissed that you chose another man over him. He'll call."

"I hope so."

"He will."

I hoped he would.

"On another note, do you know that Todd had the audacity to ask me to keep the baby?"

"What? What is he thinking?"

"He says he doesn't think we should make the baby pay for our mistakes."

"Uh oh Gabi, you better watch him. He may have tried to trap you intentionally."

"That's the same thing Sabrina said."

Sabrina? Okay that was enough. I'd had it with the whole Sabrina thing. Who was this broad and how did she know about this before me?

Before I could address the issue Eric snuck from behind and kissed my neck.

"Hi baby. I missed you," he told me.

"Who is that Eric?" Gabrielle asked.

"Yea it's him," he continued to kiss me all over. "Stop! Stop Eric."

He ignored my requests and continued to tease and tickle and kiss me. "Daddy's home," he said, "Come and get it."

"Eric!" I couldn't believe he was talking like that. I could have been on the phone with my mother. Not likely, but it could happen.

"Tell whoever that is bye."

"It's Gabrielle," I laughed.

"Hi Gabrielle," he spoke over the phone. "Goodbye Gabrielle."

"Ugh, you guys are disgusting. Call me back."

"Talk to you later, girl," I laughed.

He pulled me on top of him and pulled off my clothes. "How bad did you miss me? I asked.

He didn't say a word. His actions said it all.

* * * *

The morning sun blinded my eyes. I reached for my pillow and felt the empty cold bed next to me. I jumped up. He was gone. He'd vanished during the night without a single warning. I instantly picked up my phone and dialed his number. His phone rang over and over again until I got his voicemail. I didn't leave a message.

I rose out of bed, got dressed, and drove by his house. As crazy as it seemed I had to know if he rushed out of bed with me to run to her. I didn't see his car parked in their driveway so he was safe for now. I waited for signs of him inside thinking that maybe he'd put his Range Rover in the garage. It wasn't until I noticed the neighbors that began to pour out by what seemed like the dozens walking their dogs that I asked myself a serious question. Had I gone totally mad? Why was I stalking this man?

The older white lady walked her shiatsu and stared into my car. I put the car into drive and pulled out of the private area.

"Hi Linda," I spoke to his secretary, "Mr. Lareau made it in yet?"

"Mr. Lareau is not expected in until later this afternoon," she said in an annoyed voice. The lady couldn't stand me. She knew something was up between Eric and my relationship.

"Thank you," I ignored her tone and then hung up on her.

I made my way over to Gabrielle's and knocked on the door. It was only seven in the morning. Jack was going to kill me for coming over so early.

He answered the door.

"Good morning," I said and walked right passed him.

"Good morning," he closed the door behind. "Where's Gabi?"

'Huh?' I thought. What did he mean? I was looking for her myself.

She must have spent the night out and used me as an excuse. I was going to kill her! Didn't she know she should always cover her tracks and at least tell the person who's the alibi that they're the alibi? Now here I was in her house in front of her man without an alibi to tell.

I did the first thing that came to mind and ignored him. I pretended I didn't hear him.

"Oh my goodness, I gotta go to the bathroom so bad!" I said.

I rushed to the bathroom and used my cell phone to call her. Her phone must have been dead because it sent me directly to her voicemail.

"Where's Gabi?" Jack asked again through the bathroom door.

I was sweating bullets. "She had to stop at the ugh!!...oh my stomach," I squealed trying to stall for time, "I must have eaten something bad."

"She stopped where?" he was relentless.

"Excuse me Jack, but do you mind getting your ass away from the door so I can boo boo in peace?" I snapped, "Thank you."

He moved away from the door. I sat on the toilet and repeatedly dialed Gabrielle's number only to get her voicemail every time. I didn't know how much longer I could remain in the bathroom.

I tried her number once more but was interrupted by the sound of the front door closing. I heard Jack's footsteps coming from the back to the front.

"Hey where you been?" Jack quickly asked his wife as soon as she got in the door.

I quickly hurried off the pot and slammed the bathroom door causing a distraction. "Whew! I feel sooo much better. Don't anybody go in there!"

Gabrielle was mortified. She didn't know if I'd blown her cover or not. I had to let her know exactly how much was told.

"What took you so long? You better stop letting your tank go all the way to empty. I know you don't do that with my godson in the car?"

Her face was still uptight but she managed to go along, "No, mother."

"And you," I teased and pointed my finger in Jack's face, "you need to stop talking to people while they're trying to handle private business."

He grabbed my finger and bent it back. "Owe, owe, owe," I yelled. He let go and walked away.

Gabrielle and I both gave a sigh of relief. I was so happy it was over. I scolded her for not letting me know what was going on while Jack showered.

"I know I'm sorry," she said. "I thought you would be with Eric. You never come over this early. Why in the hell are you here this early?"

"I just left from stalking Eric's house for about an hour," I said nonchalantly. "What about you? Where in the hell have you been?"

"I had one last fling with Todd," she whispered. "It's over now."

"You are one crazy bitch."

"I'm one crazy bitch but you're stalking someone at seven in the morning," she sarcastically added.

We laughed.

"You want breakfast?" she asked.

"Yes, but please wash your hands." She playfully rubbed her hands across my face. "Ugh! Stop it!"

She laughed hysterically and cooked breakfast.

"Um, it smells so good." I said sitting in front of the plate of food. I couldn't wait to dig in. I grabbed a slice of bacon and munched on it.

Jack entered the room wrapped in a bath towel. "Whew sexy poppa!" I teased with a mouth full of bacon.

He didn't smile. In fact his face was expressionless. He stared at his wife but spoke to me.

"Kayla, I need to speak to Gabrielle. Can you come back later?" he said.

He'd never asked me to leave before. Not even when I test drove his brand new Benz and scratched it. He wanted to tell me to go home then but he never did. So this had to be something heavy.

I wondered if he found out about Todd and how. I bet Todd spilled the beans. I knew it. He was too attached to Gabrielle and he wanted her to keep the baby.

But why did Jack have to find out now? Just as I was about to eat breakfast. I should have known better. I hadn't had a meal at their house since I could remember. Soon I'd learn my lesson and stop trying.

I grabbed the rest of my bacon and got up to leave. Gabrielle wanted to come with but there was nothing I could do.

"Call me later Gabi," I told her before walking out the door.

I munched on my bacon on my way to my car but it didn't satisfy my hunger. McDonalds wasn't too far so I drove through to grab breakfast.

I noticed a familiar car in the gas station across the street. The owner, also a familiar face, pumped gas oblivious to my observing eyes. My next move I contemplated seriously. Should I go over and speak? Of course I should.

Chapter 17

"Thank you." I accepted my food from the girl at the counter and made my way across the street. I would just speak and leave.

I pulled over to his car pretending that I would hit him. He was surprised and almost jumped out of his skin. I laughed, "Hello handsome."

He looked at me strangely and continued to pump gas. "Hey what's up girl? How you been?"

His conversation was unusually cold. Normally he would have come over, given me a hug and kissed me. This time he half recognized me.

"I've been alright. How about you?"

The gas station door flung open and out walked Lisa with juice and snacks in hand. Her radar was on target that hour. She didn't give us more than a minute to get comfortable.

"Baby," she called to him. I wanted to choke the hell out of both of them and especially her with this new found level of confidence. Where did she get it from?

"Would you open the door for me? My hands are full." She flaunted her diamond ring. They were engaged! I almost gagged but kept my composure.

He obliged her request and opened the door for her. She sat inside but followed him with her eyes. He continued to fill his tank. I felt stupid for even stopping to say hi.

"I've been okay," he said.

"Looks like you've been more than okay," I told him, "Congratulations."

"Thank you," he spoke softly and looked away.

Lisa sat impatiently in the car and waited. I looked Cory up and down but cried inside. Before today I thought I was over him. Now that I knew that he had truly gone on with his life, I wasn't so sure if I'd truly gone on with mine.

There were so many questions and the first one was why? Why her? Why not me? What had she done to deserve him? I'd put in years of work with this man and now she wears his engagement ring. She barely did anything and he was falling over her feet. Nevertheless I refused to ask.

Instead I put my car in drive and told him to have a nice life. The long car ride home was a mere distraction from all the thoughts that raced through my mind. And my throat was dry from having my mouth wide open in surprise.

"I'm going. I'm going," I said as I moved along. Cars honked behind me. My mind was so gone. I was totally unaware of the green light.

I thought Eric took away any stitch of love I had for Cory but I guess he hadn't. He was just another layer that lay on top of every other man problem I had in the world. Then again maybe it was my pride that had me down.

After driving around aimlessly, I finally made it home and slowly strolled inside. I'd forgotten all about my pancakes that were now as rubbery as the sole on my shoes. I threw the entire meal in the garbage. A Sanford and Son marathon played on TV-land and for the life of me I couldn't get into it. The same questions haunted me for hours. I sat and waited for Gabrielle to call and tell her news. At least then I'd be put out of my misery of thinking about my own drama.

I sat on my chaise and began to doze. My ringing

phone broke my sleep.

"Hello," I answered.

"Hi baby, did I wake you?"

"Where have you been?" I got right to it.

"I had to go to an early meeting today. I didn't want to wake you."

"Really? I called your office. Linda said you weren't due in until noon."

"I know. My meetings weren't at the office. I met a few clients on the golf course," he explained. "How's your day been?"

"Just peachy," I said sarcastically.

"Are you mad at me?"

"Why would I be mad? It's eleven o'clock at night and I haven't heard from you all day. Why would I be mad at you Eric?"

"Baby," he called. "Don't be like that."

"Whatever."

"I got a surprise for you."

"You're full of surprises lately, among other things."

"Yeah but you'll like this surprise and yeah, I am full of other things too but you'll help me get that out. I'll be over in ten minutes...if that's alright? Can I come over? Is that alright?"

"You've already invited yourself. Why are you asking me now?"

"Because baby I want you to invite me over. I want you to want to see me. If you don't want to be bothered then I won't bother you tonight."

I not only wanted to see him desperately but I needed to be with him tonight. But of all nights he wanted to play this game. The night when I needed to be with him the most. The night of which I'd seen my ex and his new fiancé. I hated giving Eric this much control. He knew I wanted to see him and that I couldn't turn him down.

"Am I invited?" he asked.

I exhaled a deep breath. Sometimes I could be so prideful. I didn't like the fact that he knew he had me right where he wanted me.

"Don't play with my emotions," I told him.

"What?" he asked innocently.

"You know I want to see you. That's why I'm fussing. But if you're going to be a dick about it then you can stay where you are and I can stay home by myself."

"I'm not trying to be a dick."

"Yes you are," I cut in and continued to talk and complain. He cut me off.

"Listen, listen. Kayla, honey, listen," he tried getting a word in. Finally, I gave him the floor. "Baby, I don't want to fight. I'm coming over in five minutes to see you and make love like we've never made before. Got it?"

He tried being firm. That was my man, Mr. Business, always calling the shots and taking control. I loved that about Eric.

But I wouldn't bend too much. "You better do something. I need some type of recollection of why I'm still dealing with you."

"Five minutes," he said.

I quickly showered and sprayed his favorite perfume. I could hear him in my bedroom as I fumble around in the bathroom.

"I'll be right out," I yelled. I didn't dress myself in anything seductive. Even though we'd done the wild thang on uncountable occasions, I didn't want him to think I was easy. There was no way this bad boy was going to get a goodie bag from me for free this time. He had to earn this tonight.

I walked out of the bathroom. The lights were dim and Eric lit candles.

He stood on the far side of the bed. His sexy silhouetted body reflected boldly off the shadows of freshly scented candle light.

"Come here," he commanded and I slowly obliged by his order. "What's all that fuss about?" he held my chin, "You missed your daddy?"

I smacked my lips and turned my head trying to pretend I wasn't in the mood. He grabbed my hand and kissed each finger one by one. Next, from his pocket he took a diamond ring and placed it on my finger.

"What's this?" I asked him.

"A promise ring," he said. "I promise to be everything you want in a man."

He grabbed my chin again and lifted it. Then without warning he threw his tongue down my throat. It was the roughest, most passionate kiss he ever laid on me. I instantly got wet.

"Now take all that shit off and lay on the bed." he demanded. I didn't resist. I undressed myself and lay submissively on the bed.

He fumbled with a bag and brought it to the bedside. "What's in there?" I asked but he shushed me.

"Shhh," he said. He lifted the bag over my body and I lay anxiously waiting. Seconds later money poured out by the dozens. He flooded my bed with hundred dollar bills.

"Why are you carrying so much money?" I asked.

He ignored me and climbed onto the bed. "Who brings home the dough?" He laid on top of my body and kissed my breasts softly. "I didn't hear you. Who brings home the money?"

"You do baby."

"That's right." He stood on his knees and held a handful of hundreds. "You smell that?" He put it under my nose.

"Yes," I sniffed the bitter sweet smell of freshly made hundred dollar bills.

He smiled then one by one he threw them on me. "That's one incentive why you stay with me," he said throwing one hundred, "And that's another, and another, and another," he kept on.

He lifted me up. "How much for a private dance?"

"Five hundred, plus tips."

"Not a problem." He counted off five hundred dollar bills, planted himself in my chair that sat in the corner of the room, and waited for the show to begin.

I adjusted the sound on the radio and selected random love songs to play. I performed like a pro. A minute into the song I began lifting my leg in the air, doing splits, and bending over touching my toes and spreading my cheeks. Eric couldn't keep his eyes off me. He tipped me at least two thousand dollars. It wasn't long before he requested something else.

"How much for a blow job?"

I looked around the bed. "A thousand."

"You got it." He threw a thousand dollars on the night stand and assumed his position. I climbed on my knees and did the do until it was done.

He rolled over, and with money stuck to his back, went down on me, returning the favor. I moaned and grabbed at the sheets only to come up with a fistful of money. 'I guess some fantasies do come true,' I began to think to myself. How much better could it get? Making love on a bed full of money had to be heaven for most women.

Eric flipped me over and penetrated me deeply. "Who paid for this pussy tonight?"

"You did."

"I own this now. This is my pussy. I own this pussy now right?" he asked.

"Yes."

"Yes what? Let me hear you say it." He gave me a smack on my ass, "Say it."

"You own this pussy baby," I finally said it.

He was pleased. His ego was on top of the world even after we both climaxed. He and I lay comatose on the bed. An hour later I felt him ease his arm from underneath my head. He began to get dressed.

"You're leaving?"

"Yeah, I have meetings in the morning."

"More meetings, huh?" I asked sarcastically. I snatched the covers on top of me. "If this is how things are going to be then at least be up front with me.

"What are you talking about?" he asked agitated.

"I'm talking about you sleeping with me and then running home to her."

"I'm not running home to her."

"What do you call it?"

"I call it keeping the peace. You might not know it but I've been catching a lot of heat since that day at the restaurant. What am I supposed to do? If it's up to you I would never leave."

"And that's a bad thing?" I asked. "You're right you wouldn't leave. If it were up to me your home would be here with me. If it were up to me I wouldn't share you with someone else! But it's not up to me.

"Baby I promise it won't be like this forever."

"Eric please, okay. I don't want to hear it. I lie well enough to myself. I don't need your help so please just go home to your wife."

I walked into the bathroom leaving him to get dressed to return home. The bedroom door closed and my heart dropped. The mirror reflected my sorrow filled face. What was I doing? Why was I doing this to myself? How could I have fallen for a married man?

I questioned everything about my relationship with Eric. Did he really love me like he said? Maybe he did have to do things to keep the peace in his home. But I really needed him tonight. I wanted him tonight.

Reluctantly, I walked from the bathroom and there he lay on the bed waiting for me. It almost frightened me to see a man in my bedroom. I thought maybe he was a prowler at first. It couldn't be Eric. He would never stay when asked to leave. That wasn't him.

"Come here honey," Eric said.

I slowly walked over and lay my head on his arm.

"I'm sorry I upset you." He kissed my forehead. "I love you. If you want me to stay I'll stay."

It was like a breath of fresh air. No longer did I have to question his love for me. He was willing to take a chance of getting screamed at by spending a night with me.

"Thanks. Sometimes I just need you. I can't wait 'til this is over. I know it won't last forever but sometimes it feels like it."

He wrapped his arms tightly around my side.

"A couple weeks. I promise. Just trust me," were his last words before we both fell into a deep sleep.

Chapter 18

Today is the rebirth of Beau. August seventeenth, the day he was released from jail. We still hadn't spoken since the last time in his home but my heart told me to send a card. It was a day of celebration. I knew he would do it for me.

What began as a short passage ended as a three page letter. Determined to resolve our differences, I apologized and explained how special of a friend he is and asked if we could start over. I wasn't sure of the possibilities but I'd keep hope alive and I'd wait just like I'd wait for Eric's relationship with his wife to end. A new school year had begun and still he hadn't separated or filed for divorce. My ears were tired of hearing broken promises and the "it won't last forever" speech.

He continually pleaded for my patience and often did things to make me feel special, important, and like the only woman instead of the other woman.

I began to make appearances at corporate dinner parties, social gatherings, and company trips. Pretty soon I was well known and accepted. No one asked questions or looked at me strangely. They treated me as if I was the first lady. And it was probably because all the men had their special lady other than their wife who accompanied them everywhere. Nevertheless, the feeling of involvement quieted my complaints.

"Don't you feel weird going around his business and everyone knows he's married?" Gabrielle asked as we sat a local restaurant for dinner.

"I did the first couple times but everyone knows he's getting a divorce soon so they act pretty cool."

She gobbled her cheeseburger and sucked down her fries. "You want your fries?" she asked me.

"You are going to be huge Gabi."

She dug into my plate. "I can't help it. I'm hungry all day long."

I watched as she devoured my last few fries. "So you're actually going to have the baby?"

"What else can I do? Now that Jack told my mom I can't have an abortion. She'll never forgive me and well...if I can't keep my husband then I at least need my ma."

"I still can't figure out what would possess you to keep your medical papers in your work bag."

"I can't figure that out either. Just stupid, I suppose. I never thought Jack would search my things. That's not like him. It's like he knew where to look."

"How many times have you told me that men are like women?"

"I know. I know. I should have followed my same advice but it's too late now. He knows I'm pregnant, thinks it's his, and refuses to let me have an abortion."

"What about Todd?"

"He's not sure of it all. He didn't want the abortion but he isn't sure of how he'll feel once the baby gets here and starts calling Jack daddy instead of him."

"I bet."

"At least he'll get to be the Godfather."

"What?" Was she serious?

"Yeah, I convinced Jack that it's important that our

baby have a righteous man as the Godfather. Todd is the baby's Godfather."

She looked at me for feedback. I couldn't give her anything. I didn't know what was going through the girl's head, then again I wasn't in her situation.

"I'm just trying to make everyone happy. I don't want any trouble and if this is the only way I can be somewhat fair and have Todd involved in his baby's life then so be it."

"I hear you girl."

We finished up. Gabrielle ordered a milkshake to go. Just watching her eat made me feel like I'd gained ten pounds.

She walked her tired, four month pregnant ass to the car and demanded that I drive.

"I have to make a stop at the teacher store."

"That's fine. I'm just too tired to drive." She fastened her seat belt. "You all ready for your first day?"

"I'm as ready as I'll ever be. I don't think any teacher is ever ready for her first day. I can only imagine what tomorrow will be like."

* * * *

I rounded my crew of kids. They bounced all over the place as if they'd just finished a punch bowl of sugar.

"Come in and have a seat at the desk with your name on it."

The children scrambled around and found their seats. My day had begun. It was a long day and full of surprises. Only half way through the day and I anticipated lunch time already. But what I thought would be the highlight of my day turned out to be its downfall.

There they stood gaping at me as I directed my children. I could only wonder what the problem was.

Just as I sat to eat, "Miss Parker," the principal called to me. "You have a parent in your classroom waiting to see you."

I packed up my sandwich and started for my room. There was an immediate distinctive smell of Chanel perfume as soon as I approached my classroom door. Upon entering I noticed the expensive Louis Vuitton bag on my desk and then the fair skinned woman sitting comfortably in my chair at my desk. Who did she think she was?

"Hello Mrs. Lareau," I greeted her.

She approached me extending her arm. I held out my hand and prepared for a handshake. But this wasn't an ordinary handshake. This one left me a little treat. After she let go I opened my hand and discovered an earring. Not just any earring, my earring. And not just any one of my earrings. The earring I lost a while back that matched my necklace Eric bought me.

"What's this?" I pretended not to know.

"I thought you might want it back," she said. "I noticed at dinner you weren't wearing the earrings that match your necklace. And since I know that the jewelers only sell the piece as a set, I thought you might want your earring back to make it complete."

"Excuse me?"

"Our maid found it in my husband's office the other day. She thought it was mine. Hell I thought it was mine too until I realized I had both earrings in my jewelry box. Then I asked myself, 'Michia did you grow another earlobe?' and I answered, 'No, that dirty bastard of a husband of yours had some whore in your house."

"I'm sorry Michia but I —"

"Michia? No dear, that's MRS. Lareau to you."

"Okay, Mrs. Lareau. I don't know what you are trying to say-"

"I think you and I both know what I'm trying to say Miss. Parker but let me spell it out for you."

She grabbed her bag from my desk and started for the door. Michia detoured over to the chalk board and wrote me a message.

She lay the chalk down and cut her eyes at me. "Se comprendre l'un l'autre?" she now flaunted her French asking if we understood one another. Then she sashayed confidently out of my classroom as if nothing was said.

I couldn't believe the balls of this model chick to come to my job, threaten and curse at me. I wondered how long she actually practiced that phrase. All lies aside, I was scared as shit. She'd definitely intimidated me. She could stir up a lot of commotion and have me fired if there was any evidence of me having a relationship with Eric.

Private schools were so political. They had a strict policy against parents and teachers intermingling. There was an even stricter policy if that parent's child was in the teacher's class. I could only imagine what they'd do if the parent was actually married.

I hurried to erase the board as soon as she left. It would have been pretty difficult to explain to my principal why, *"Leave my fucking husband alone!!"* was written on my chalkboard.

Needless to say, her words were bien compris...well understood.

* * * *

The rest of my day I remained unfocused. I couldn't contact Eric because I'd left my pager and cell phone on the counter at home. I was stuck. What a bitch!

Finally two forty-five came. I barely released the children to their parents before I rushed out the door myself. What a day to leave my phone at home!

I burned rubber into my parking space and bolted inside. My cell phone lay just where I left it. I immediately called Eric. Of course I didn't get an answer. He'd warned me earlier that he'd be in meetings all day.

I two-way messaged him and called Gabrielle.

"What are you doing?" I asked her.

"Oh nothing just sitting here with Sabrina."

"Humph, really?"

"Yes, really," she noticed my tone. "You should come over and join us."

"No thanks. Maybe some other time."

"You sure?"

"Positive."

"What's up? You sound like something is wrong. Is everything ok?"

"No, but I wouldn't want to interrupt you and your new best friend. Besides, I don't discuss my business in front of others."

"Stop it Kayla," she warned me about my whiny attitude.

"Hey, you know, maybe I'll join you guys next week if Eric's wife doesn't kill me first considering she knows about me screwing around with her husband."

"Shut up! How?"

"When you have time, call me."

"Wait."

"Bye Gabrielle."

"Kayla," she called but I hung up.

I paced the floor not knowing what to do with myself. Today was one of those times when I needed Gabrielle. I was sick of that broad Sabrina. Who was she and where did she come from?

Two hours later Eric called me back.

"What's going on baby?"

"Your wife came to my job today. She knows about us Eric. She found my earring in your office. She told me to leave you alone."

"Wait a minute. Calm down," he told me.

"Calm down? I could get fired for some shit like this. I knew this was a mistake. I knew it."

"Mikayla, baby, calm down. You won't get fired. I'll call and talk to her tonight. Everything will be fine, okay?" he assured me.

"Okay." I believed him and calmed myself. "Tell her to stay away from my job."

"I will. She will," he told me. "I'll see you tonight."

"I don't think you should come over. Things are too crazy. You don't know what she might do."

"I'm coming over."

"I don't think you should. She may follow you."

"I know my wife. We'll be fine."

"No, Eric. This is a mistake. It's all been a mistake. I think it's time we end it now."

He was never good at accepting no. "I have to get back to this meeting. We'll discuss it later. I love you."

I didn't respond.

"We'll talk about it. I have to go."

I hung up the phone and paced the floor. Paranoia really settled in. I closed my drapes and constantly checked my window for suspicious cars all night.

Eric showed up anyway. I knew he would.

"Don't start saying we're a mistake, Kayla. Don't start thinking like that again," he pleaded.

"You should go home. She's probably looking for you now."

"I'm not worried about her. Why do you think I'm here with you trying to clear the air and make sure you're not thinking anything crazy about us?"

"Eric-"

"Do you love me?"

"That's not the issue."

"Do you love me?"

"Yes I do love you. You know I do but that doesn't change anything. What we did was wrong and it's over now." I was serious. I'd had enough. He hadn't given me anything to stand on except broken promises. What happened to give him two weeks? "Please leave. I don't want this anymore."

"Are you serious?"

"Very."

He took a breath and looked me into my eyes.

"Come here."

"Eric no."

"Come here," he pulled at me, "I have a surprise for you. Come go with me."

"Where are we going?"

He pulled me to the car and took me for a drive. We drove downtown through all the buildings and pretty lights until we got to a specific building. He walked me upstairs.

"Where are we? Who lives here?"

"We do."

He walked me around the empty loft.

"What?"

"This is ours. I've been saving this as a surprise but I see it can't wait."

"This is ours?" I asked still in disbelief.

He smiled. "I have people coming to finish repairs but we can move in as early as October."

"You're lying. Eric don't lie to me."

"Honey I wouldn't play with you like that. Look here." He pulled papers from a kitchen drawer. "Read it."

I read over the contract that included both our names.

"The only thing that's missing is your signature." he handed me a pen.

A million thoughts raced through my head. "What about my home and it's so far from my job."

"Would you rather be closer to me or your job?"

He asked a simple question and I had a simple answer. I took the pen and signed the contract to our new loft.

We spent hours inside the loft talking about our plans while we overlook the lights of the city. I couldn't believe it. I felt on top of the world. Finally my dreams with Eric were coming true.

* * * *

"When is he going to tell his wife?" Gabrielle asked me.

"He's waiting for the best time."

"When is that?"

"When they're finished with all the repairs. I don't know within the next week or so. We're moving in next month so it has to be soon."

"And you're sure you're ready to move in with him?"

"Sure? Gabi, I am positive!"

"I hope it works out for you." She didn't sound so sure.

"Me too. I am a little scared. I know he loves me but I hope ....you know?"

"Yeah I know. Don't I know." She thought for a second. "If it doesn't, my firm is in charge of marketing for Beau's tour. I have his entire schedule."

"His entire schedule?"

"His entire schedule," she repeated. She reached into her briefcase and pulled out a sheet with performance dates, times, and hotel information of where all the acts would stay.

I gave it some thought. Eric and I were having good times but I couldn't lie to myself. I'd thought about Beau a time or two. I wondered what he was up to. Was he thinking about me or did he truly hate my guts?

"I'm over Beau," I lied and threw the paper and back-stage pass into my purse.

"Really?"

"Yup. It's all about Eric and me."

Her doorbell rang. "Well that pass will get you back-stage to any of his shows if you change your mind." She opened the door. "Hey, what are you doing here?"

'Who is that?' I asked myself.

"Sabrina, meet my best friend Mikayla. Mikayla meet my girl, Sabrina."

The tall, cocoa complexioned female waved her hand politely. At first sight I didn't like her. Not because she was stealing my best friend but because she had sneaky eyes. What was she really up to?

"Hi." I gave a bogus smile.

"It's nice to finally meet you. Gabi has told me so much about you." She was so giddy.

Gabi? Who told her she could call Gabrielle, Gabi?

"Nice to meet you too," I lied

"Hey Gabi, where's Jack and my baby Jackson?"

Her baby? Since when was Jackson her baby? And why was she so concerned about Jack's whereabouts?

"They just left to buy sneakers."

"Jack is such a good dad," she complimented.

What a suck up.

I sat in the background as they talked and joked about work related issues. Then Gabrielle's situation became a topic.

"I haven't talked to Todd in what feels like... forever."

"You're doing good. Keep up the good work," I told her.

"I'm trying but I miss him so much. Certain things he used to do like how he used to kiss me and hug me. Sometimes I can't help but think about him."

"I don't blame you," Sabrina said, "From what I've heard it sounds like he's an animal in bed."

If looks could kill, Sabrina would be buried eight feet under. The situation was crazy. No matter how I tried to deter Gabrielle's attention away from Todd, Sabrina would come back saying how much she understood and if she was Gabrielle, she'd do the same thing.

Gabrielle's head switched from side to side. It was like she had an angel on one shoulder and the devil on the other.

"I'm just saying it's too late now," Sabrina continued, "She may as well have fun. What's the worse that can happen?"

I grew agitated. "Did you forget she has a husband? The worst that can happen is that she can lose her marriage and family, that's the worst that can happen," I snapped. "If that's the case why doesn't she just fuck everyone in the entire congregation. Oh sure, she may get herpes but at least she won't get pregnant!"

Sabrina was offended. Gabrielle quickly sided with her.

"Kayla, she's just giving her opinion."

"And that's fine but I think it's in bad taste for her to try to convince you to sleep with Todd, especially if you're trying to be right."

"I'm not telling her to sleep with him. It's apparent that she already did that. I'm just saying what I would do."

'Shut up hoe! No one was talking to you,' I wanted to say so badly but I didn't want to disrespect Gabrielle.

Sabrina was getting on my last nerve. She didn't see Jack and Gabrielle grow up together and how in love the two were. I was there when he nervously asked her out on their first date. I was there helping him pick out only the best ring his money could afford. I was there when he cried while preparing his wedding vows because the words couldn't express how much he loved her.

Yes, he slept with another woman but he loved Gabrielle and wouldn't trade her for the world. I was surprised it hadn't happened sooner. In all honesty, I thought Gabrielle would be the one to have an affair first. I definitely knew someone would experiment. Two virgins being together and staying together was totally unheard of. We all knew one of them would cheat one day.

"So you think I'm wrong, Kayla?" Gabrielle asked me. "Jack cheated on me first but I'm wrong?"

"What are we in fifth grade Gabi? You cheated on him second."

"I can't believe you out of all people are judging me."

What was that supposed to mean? First of all, I was deeply offended that she wanted to have this conversation in front of Sabrina. But since she wanted to take it there I needed to make things clear.

"I'm not judging you. I'm only saying that Jack didn't get a woman pregnant. Gabi, you're pregnant by another man and are about to have his baby and pass it off as Jack's. You think you're right? You know you're not right, that's why you're trying to leave Todd alone. And I wouldn't be a friend," I whipped my neck around to Sabrina and back at Gabrielle, "if I told you, you're right when we both know you're wrong."

"You're going to tell me about right and wrong?" Gabrielle asked angrily, "YOU! A girl who's fucking her student's dad? You know the little boy is fucked up in the head already but you still fuck his father? Some great teacher you are but of course Gabrielle is wrong and as always Kayla is so right," she gave a sarcastic giggle. "You can't tell me shit Kayla because you don't know shit yourself."

This was the first fight that Gabrielle and I ever had. In all the years we'd known each other we never had a blow out this big. We never argued. Now all of a sudden another broad comes into the picture and Gabrielle and I were having the fight of the century. But I dummied up. I wasn't about to go back and forth giving Sabrina total satisfaction. I decided to leave and when things cooled down tomorrow, I'd call Gabrielle and talk sensibly.

"Whatever, Gabrielle." I grabbed my jacket and stormed out of her house. "Whatever."

Chapter 19

It had been almost two weeks since my big argument with Gabrielle and we still hadn't spoken. I called her at least six times and she was either too busy and put me off or refused to answer. I wanted to talk things over but she'd say, "I don't want to talk about it Kayla," and in a nonchalant tone she'd say, "I'm fine. It's over with."

But I knew better. I knew she was still angry but how could she get so angry at me for telling her the truth? We always told each other the truth no matter how brutal it was. Why'd she get so angry now? Maybe it was her hormones. I tried being sensitive to her pregnancy but hell, a girl can only do so much. I was never an ass kisser and Gabrielle or nobody else was going to make me into one. Screw them all!

I told Eric what she said. He didn't speak badly about her, but only told me to wait it out before I wrote her off. I would of course take his advice because not only was I crazy over the man but I also missed my best friend desperately.

She wouldn't stay on the phone long enough to hear me tell her that Eric and I finally did it. He'd finally told his wife he was leaving and we both began moving our things into our loft downtown a whole week ago. He even stopped going home to her. When he left work, he finally came straight home to me. He and I had slept together an entire week in the same bed. We waited eagerly for our new bed to arrive at our new place. Like kids in a candy store, he and I would plan all the nasty positions we'd break in the bed.

But of course, we still kept our dealings undercover. We both agreed it was too early to reveal our relationship. Victor could be permanently mentally damaged and Eric informed me of Michia's recent rampage and crying spells. Who could blame her? I'd cry if Eric left me for another woman too, but her instability could ruin my career at school.

I set a relaxing mood. Candles lay around a fresh hot steamy bubble bath while soft music played in the background. Tonight I'd planned time for myself. The children at school managed to get on my last nerve and my home was in shambles ever since we started moving. I gave the place a thorough cleaning, cooked dinner for when Eric arrived, and settled in the tub with a good book. Before I could turn the first page my phone rang.

"Hello."

"Where's Eric?" Michia asked in an unfriendly tone.

"I have no idea," I responded agitated, "He's not here."

"I just bet," she said sarcastically.

"Believe what you want."

"I will and I believe that you know exactly where he is."

"Okay, Michia. Whatever. I'm not about to argue with you."

"Sweetie, I'm not arguing with you. Why would I argue over someone I already have?"

"If you have him then why are you calling my house looking for him?" I asked her. "Sounds like to me you only have him part time, if at all."

"I'd rather be a part time wife and have the house and checkbook than be the part time whore getting fucked—"

"Don't forget sucked," I added.

I could hear in her voice I'd gotten to her, "Maybe,

but the house still sounds better to me. You're selling your-self cheap."

"Whatever, I already told you he's not here. I'm not looking for a cat fight. Doesn't he have a phone? Why don't you call him?"

"Because I'm calling you!"

"That's the problem. Stop approaching me and confront Eric."

"No, the problem is secondhand whores like you pursu-ing married men making it easy for them to cheat on their wives."

Did she just call me a whore? And not only a whore, but a secondhand whore? Didn't she know that anything I did was done to the best of my ability? I wasn't secondhand anything.

"First of all, I didn't pursue anyone. Get that straight," I snapped. She yelled as I spoke but I kept going, "And sec-ond, I'm not going to be too many more whores."

"I doubt that you slut, you bitch, you whore," she carried on.

The woman was crazy. I slammed the phone and called Eric.

"Your wife just called my house and cursed me out again," I squealed. "Call me back."

I decided to go on with my evening. Michia wasn't go-ing to ruin my peaceful night. The water was still hot and steamy. Slowly, I slipped my feet into the tub and took a deep breath.

My hair barely had a chance to sweat before I heard three knocks at the door followed by the rambunctious ring-ing of my doorbell. I wrapped myself in my satin robe and opened the door.

It was Michia, standing angrily on my doorstep. She must have called me from her car because not even five min-utes had gone by since we spoke.

"I told you Eric wasn't here. What in the hell do you

want?" I asked frustrated.

She glared at me through my screen door. "I wanted to see the whore's whose life I'm going to ruin up close one last time."

This broad was truly crazy.

"You are a psycho bitch. No wonder he left your dumb ass," I scolded her.

She spit at the screen and tiny droplets hit my skin. I was disgusted and wanted to whoop her ass but instead I slammed the door in her face and called Eric.

"Open the door you whore!" she yelled and screamed. "Be a woman. You can fuck my husband but you can't face me like a woman."

My phone rang. "Hello."

"What's going on?" Eric's voice echoed on the other end of the line.

"Your wife, that's what's going on. She's yelling and screaming and trying to kick my door in!" I made her seem like the big bad wolf when indeed she had every reason to be angry.

"Where is she now?"

"Are you listening? She's at my front door," I was impatient with the situation.

How could he be so stupid? How could he allow his wife to come to my home and invade me like this? Didn't he know how to keep better tabs on the situation? Men never knew how to do anything right.

"I'll be right over," he said.

Michia continued to scream and pound at my door. Half an hour later she stopped. There was a brief silence.

From my window I saw Eric grabbing at Michia. She threw her hands in the air.

"Why Eric?" she asked, "Why her? Why do you keep doing this to me?"

"What are you talking about? What are you doing here?" he asked her, "You're acting crazy."

"I'm acting crazy because my husband is sleeping with another woman."

He gave a sigh, "I'm not sleeping with anyone."

Oh really? He'd denied me. What was up with that? I slid on my clothes. It was time to clear the air. Eric would either be with his wife or with me. There were no ifs, ands, or buts about it.

I opened the door and caught the tail lights as they turned the corner exit of my complex. He'd left with her. His car sat parked in my visitor space where he'd left it. I sat alone.

I figured Eric left with his wife to diffuse the situation. I figured he wanted to get her away to calm her down and stop the embarrassment. But after three days passed of not hearing from him and no return phone calls, I didn't know what to figure anymore.

Day four I came home and noticed he'd come by and taken his car. No note, no warning, no anything. For the first time in a long time I cried over a man. I cried tears like I'd never cried before. Once again another woman had been chosen over me. And that wasn't a good feeling.

The entire weekend I moped around the house. I should have been well rested by the time Monday came but I wasn't. Mentally I was exhausted. Every hour I checked my phone but to no avail. I'd given up on calling him.

School so far was the only thing that kept me a little occupied. I walked into my classroom bright and early Wednesday morning since I wasn't getting any sleep lately for the most part anyway. There was a substitute at my chalkboard.

"I'm sorry I believe you're in the wrong classroom," I told the girl.

She looked confused, "I'm supposed to be subbing

for Miss Parker today."

"I'm Miss Parker, but I'm here today."

"Miss Parker," Mrs. Lewis, the principal's secretary called from behind, "Mrs. Rinaldi wants to see you."

I hoped it was about the substitute situation. There must have been an accident. The secretary must have called the sub in for the wrong teacher. I was so naïve.

I sat at the desk. Mrs. Rinaldi got up to close the door. It silenced the entire room. She returned to her seat, looked over the papers on her desk then at me.

"Something has been brought to my attention," she started, "A parent called me at home last night,"

My heart pounded in my chest. I instantly went into shock. Mrs. Rinaldi continued to talk. I noticed her mouth moving and sound coming out but everything else was unrecognizable. It was almost as effective as listening to Charlie Brown's teacher. I couldn't understand a damn thing except for 'Mrs. Lareau' and 'you're suspended indefinitely until our investigation is complete.' And that was that.

She wasn't mean about it and she gave reasons why in their policies it had to be this way and blah, blah, blah. I didn't ask questions. I didn't defend myself. I let the lady talk and dismissed myself. Now I'd lost everything.

Michia kept her promise, that's for sure. She was definitely making my life a living hell. I grabbed my things from my classroom, got into my car and called Eric. I cried hysterically on his voicemail, "Eric, I lost my job. They just fired me. Where are you?" I cried.

I still held on to some hope that he wouldn't desert me in my desperate time of need. I hoped he would call me and tell me that everything would be okay.

By Friday my two-way pager and cell phone were disconnected and that's when I let go of all hope. I went over to the loft and it was up for sale. How he did it without my signature, I didn't know. What I did know was that Eric was cutting me out of his life.

I felt my world shatter at my feet. Emotionally I was a wreck. Still not speaking to Gabrielle, I had no outlet to release my problems. And I needed so badly to get away from it all. I needed a break. I needed something...someone.

* * * *

I must have been crazy. I asked myself the entire ride there. But it didn't matter I was here now and there was no turning back. I bought my ticket and took my seat in the eighth row behind a couple who seemed to be so in love. I envied them being at a concert together while I sat by myself.

The lights went dim and I danced around in my seat. These were great seats but the show was even better. Beau ended his last selection with a dramatization of my poem that I wrote and mailed to his house. I hadn't even known if he'd read it. But the way he acted it out on stage I could tell he read it a million times. Once again the man impressed me.

At the end I rose to my feet in celebration of each poet, especially Beau. They took their bows and retired to the back where I hastily put my backstage pass into effect. I should have used it at the beginning instead of paying for tickets but I didn't want him to see me before the show and become distracted.

I stood at the back entrance waiting nervously for him to come out. Then, there he stood, ten feet away from me, built as ever, sexy as all outdoors, and confident. He joked with another poet before the two went their separate ways.

He turned and started in my direction but stopped. He wasn't sure if his eyes were playing tricks on him or if I really existed.

"Hi." I smiled nervously.

He approached me and stared in disbelief.

"Yeah, it's Kayla. I flew all the way to Philly just to see you," I told him. "You must be somebody special."

"Did you enjoy the show?" he asked coldly.

"I really did. I especially enjoyed the part where you said 'lovers on a different path will eventually have a crash course of love, and you can't escape the impact it will have on your life, leaving you paralyzed forever,' or something like that."

He looked into my eyes, "I didn't say that. Craig Boyd said that."

"Oh," I said feeling stupid, "well, you should have."

"Maybe but I'm not paralyzed with love. I went on with my life Kay, maybe you should go on with yours," he said.

Somehow, I didn't believe him. Maybe because he avoided eye contact. Maybe because I just didn't want to accept another rejection.

"I'm happy you came out here and you enjoyed the show but I have to go say hi to my audience and sign autographs. Have a safe trip back." He began to walk away.

"If you've gone on with your life so much then why are you using my poem that I wrote you? And you say it with such passion."

"I'm a poet. It's my job to sell good poems. It doesn't matter if it's yours or Maya Angelou's."

"That's bull Beau. Tell me that you don't feel anything for me. Tell me."

I thought he couldn't do it but he walked right to my face, looked me in my eyes and said, "I don't feel anything for you." This wasn't television. It was the real thing. People didn't fall for that drama in real life. Beau tried to turn away. I grabbed his wrist.

"You told me that if I ever needed anything that I could come to you. I need you. You said that you would be my only friend if I had no one. I have no one Beau. I'm all alone and I'm not asking for anything except for understanding. I need someone to understand me, to talk to me and you're the only person in this world that I could think of," I poured my heart out to him.

"Please, I know I've made mistakes and I deserted you that first time but only because I saw you with that girl with the curly fro and I thought that she might be someone you were interested in..."

He looked confused but I didn't stop for air, "I didn't want to be hurt again but I promise I won't desert you again and I'll be honest to you. I really just need a friend tonight. My world is empty and I know that even if you and I could never be lovers again we can at least be friends."

I reached into my purse and pulled out my hotel key card and directions. "I'll only be in town 'til nine o'clock tomorrow. Come tonight, please. You don't have to call, just show up. And if you don't then I'll take the hint and never bother you again."

I slid it into his pocket and left before I burst into tears.

In my hotel I continually watched the clock and the door. I showered but didn't slip on anything sexy. I played a CD on my laptop but nothing too over the top. I didn't want him to think I was trying to seduce him. I sincerely wanted to talk. Tonight wasn't about sex and it wasn't just about me clearing my head. I wanted to repair a friendship that I totally destroyed.

Hours passed and it became evident that he wasn't going to show. I took one last look at the clock at six o'clock in the morning and one last look at the undisturbed door. He wasn't coming. My last stride to the finish line to repair the last relationship in my life was now dead. My world felt like it was coming to an end.

This time I accepted it. I didn't cry no matter how bad I wanted to. 'What doesn't kill us makes us stronger' was now my favorite quote. Even with that in mind, I still didn't know if I had the strength to go home and face everything that waited for me.

Regardless, I packed my things and checked out of my hotel.

"How was your stay ma'am?" The woman at the counter asked.

Disappointed, I responded with a half smile, "Very quiet, thanks." She didn't know what I meant and I didn't want to explain either. Why ruin her day?

She checked me out and I stood outside along with others, waiting for a taxi.

"It was my sister," a voice said from out the blue.

Still in a daze, I looked beside me. It was Beau wearing the same clothes from last night.

"Hi," he said softly.

"Hi," I responded the same. "What?"

"The girl from the café was my sister. My sister Raquel."

"Oh." Didn't I feel like a first class ass.

We stood waiting for each other to say something but I didn't know what to say.

"I'm kind of hungry. You want to grab something to eat?" he offered.

I looked at my watch. I had only half an hour of

playtime before I had to be at the airport. He noticed my apprehension.

"Don't worry about it. We'll make time."

He grabbed my luggage and we walked to a little breakfast spot around the corner from the hotel. It was a peaceful walk. Two old friends taking a walk in the park catching up on old times. He'd playfully push me and make me fall off the edge of the curb. I'd give him a slap on his arm. We carried on the entire time as if we hadn't lost out on the last few months of each other's life.

Once at the restaurant I didn't find it as important to talk about all my issues. I'd harped on them enough for a lifetime. Instead we talked about him and his new lifestyle and about us and our new start.

He apologized for not coming to the hotel that night and explained that he'd been out there for most of the night contemplating whether he should or shouldn't.

"Stay with me tonight," he asked. "Forget about your plane ticket. I'll get you a new flight tomorrow." And well since I didn't have a job anymore, I didn't refuse.

His hotel room was junky. Clothes lay everywhere and he immediately began picking things up. I sat on the bed and waited while he straightened up. He joined me on the bed and rubbed my hair and talked to me.

"I lost it all Beau. Gabrielle, you, my job, respect and dignity for myself. It's all gone," I whimpered.

While I was feeling down and out about life and myself, I'll never forget the next words from his mouth, "Now you're free. Sometimes you have to be stripped of everything to appreciate anything."

He was right. For a long time I didn't appreciate anything except myself. I took everything for granted. Now I had a fresh start.

I lay my head on his shoulder and fell fast asleep. Hours later, I could still feel his hands stroking my hair. It was dark outside and he hadn't moved an inch while I slept peacefully in his arms. Finally I appreciated that.

"What can I do for you?" I asked him. "You've always been here when I needed you and you make me feel so special and important. What can I do for you?"

He didn't blink. "Mikayla, I don't want you to need me," he said, "I need you to want me."

As deep as it was, I understood.

Chapter 20

I returned home with a new attitude. Changes were underway. First things first, I began looking for a new job. I grabbed a directory of schools and started sending out my resume. Normally positions weren't available until January so I'd have to sit tight and just wait.

Also on my agenda was to repair my relationship with my mom and Paris. They weren't good family but they were my family. But before I could do that I needed to restore my friendship with Gabrielle just in case I needed some reinforcement.

I started my way out of the door when, I was stopped, to my surprise, by Gabrielle.

"Hi," I said stunned.

"Hi," she looked sad and apologetic, "You're on your way out?"

"Actually, yeah I was." I folded my arms.

"Oh," she said.

I put her out of her misery. "I was on my way over to your house to kick your ass for avoiding me!"

She was relieved. I didn't want to go through the whole scene of apologizing and explaining and grudge holdings. We were friends for too long and were beyond that.

"Come in," I invited. We went inside and I fixed her

favorite, peanut butter and jelly sandwich. "Wow what a difference a month makes," I said noticing her huge stomach.

"Yeah, the doctor says I'm getting too huge. All I do is eat." She peeled a banana.

"How's Jack and Jackson?"

"Besides getting on my last nerve everybody is doing swell."

"And Todd?"

"Todd is Todd. He's adjusting. He's begging to be more involved in the baby's life."

"That's a good thing in a way. It could be worse. At least he's not threatening to tell Jack."

"God no! I'm so thankful for that."

"And what about Miss. Sabrina? She still hanging in there strong?" I almost bit my tongue asking about her. I still couldn't stand the girl.

"Sabrina is still around. We're actually getting ready to plan my baby shower and I thought I could do it without you, but I can't."

What a knife to my back that would have been. I'm happy she came to her senses.

"Sabrina is cool but when we started going over things we couldn't agree on anything. She thought I should have this or that. And I started thinking, if that were you it wouldn't have taken us a day to put it together. You know?"

I nodded my head.

"I don't know, she and I connect on one level whereas you and I connect on all levels. There's a difference. I'm sorry for acting like a—."

"A bitch." I helped her out.

"Yeah a bitch. I just didn't want to hear the truth that day but I always knew, if you couldn't give me anything the least you would give me was the truth."

There it was all on the table. All was forgiven.

"Let me give you a last little bit of truth," I started, "I don't know what it is but I still don't like that bitch."

"And you don't have to. I'm not asking you to anymore. But... my shower is next month and I would like you to just manage her presence. Please, I don't want her in charge of planning it."

"I can do that." In the back of my mind I asked myself, 'Can I do that?' I'd try.

The next couple weeks we planned and organized and Gabrielle and I overruled Sabrina's every idea. She wasn't too happy but I didn't care. It felt good to be a team again.

Beau and I kept in touch. He called me every night after his shows and we'd stay on for hours. Next weekend he'd have a break and we planned to go over his mom's for dinner. His sister would also be in town. It would be the first time I'd get to meet her. I still felt like an ass for thinking he had an interest in his own sister.

But that was the past now. Things in my life were starting to look up. I actually had an interview with two schools next month for positions in January. It would be so great to get one of them. I didn't mind that it was three months away. I enjoyed my vacation. Because I'd saved so much money while Eric and I were together, I wasn't experiencing any financial hardships. Thank God I hadn't gone on endless shopping sprees and exhausted all my funds. I was smart enough to not do that.

I did at times wonder what Eric was doing but the whole ordeal left a bitter taste in my mouth. I sat on my bed reading a book when out of nowhere my two way pager beeped.

Hi stranger. I miss you.

What a bunch of bologna! Now he wanted to call me? After he abandoned me for almost a month? I started to text back and lash out at him but I stopped in mid sentence. He wasn't worth my energy. In my most vulnerable time he wasn't there even after I told him I got fired. He could have called at least once. Almost four weeks later was inexcusable.

The page went unanswered and any other that followed would be handled just the same. Beau had given me a reason to look forward instead of back. I didn't even miss Eric. I missed a man's company but I didn't miss Eric. I couldn't wait for Beau to come in town. I knew that after dinner with his mom and sister it would be straight back to my place for dessert.

*   *   *   *

The conversation was great and his mom was as sweet and warm as the first time I met her. His sister showed up late.

"Sorry," she said, "I had a couple late buyers at the art gallery." She walked over and laid her hand on my shoulder. "So this must be her," she smiled at her mom and brother.

Beau began to blush. "Kayla this is my crazy sister Raquel."

"Nice to meet you," I politely extended my hand.

"Girl you better get up," she insisted. "We're practically family." I stood uncomfortably to my feet and she hugged me tightly. "I've heard so much about you."

"Same here."

We took our seats and carried on with our conversation. His sister's energy and smile lit up the room. She had the deepest dimples and curliest hair. She and her brother shared a commonality of artistic ability. She painted and he was a poet.

The man was so sexy and I was so horny. I couldn't resist Beau's invitation of playing footsies underneath the dinner table while his sister carried on about the new painting she was working on.

"Have you two ever thought about putting together a book?" I blurted out. Without realizing, I began to throw out ideas, "It could be a children's book almost similar to Dr. Seuss with rhymes and stuff. I hear there's a huge market for children's books and you see how big Dr. Seuss' books are to this day."

The entire table looked at me as though I spoke a foreign language. Then Beau said, "I told you she was smart."

So thanks to my big mouth, after dinner we all sat around and brainstormed on what topics they could target. While I was having a great time, I was ready to go and get my groove on. But they were serious. Even their mother was in on the idea.

"I think you should talk about esteem issues," she suggested.

"That's good mom," Raquel reinforced that idea.

Here was a family that had been through so much and never looked back. Why wasn't my family like this?' I kept thinking and Beau would give me the warmest hug every single time the thought crossed my mind. It was like he knew I was thinking it.

By the time the night ended we'd developed a series of twelve books. It was crazy. I promised to call Gabrielle and have her research the market and find us a deal on how to promote the book. Everyone was excited.

Beau and I finally made it back to my place.

"I had a nice time," he said.

"Me too."

"Well," he started, "it's late so I'll let you get some sleep."

I grabbed him by his collar and tongued him real good. Then I snatched him into the house. I know he didn't think he was getting off that easy. I'd been a good girl and not even mentioned sex but tonight he was giving it up or I was taking it. Luckily, he gladly gave it up without a fight.

And it was sooo good! Every time I had sex with Beau it felt like the first time. He knew exactly how to touch me and never under my direction. That, I think was the best. He knew what speed to switch it to and just how deep to go. And after it was all over, he knew how to hold me. It was like being in heaven because everything seemed perfect.

"Hey," he whispered in my ear.

I turned to face him and gave him a soft kiss on the lips. He squeezed me tight.

"I love you," he whispered.

........I drew a blank. I wanted to say it back but I had to be safe. I'd told two men in the last two years that I loved them. One was married and the other was about to marry someone else. But neither of those men ever made me feel like Beau did. Neither one of those men respected me as much as Beau did. Most importantly, I didn't feel the way I did about either of those men the way I feel about Beau.

I was in love with Eric's money and power. As for Cory I was in love with his colossal dick. But I was in love with Beau's heart and his spirit and in love with the way he loved me back. He was the total package but I was still reluctant to say it back. I thought about someone other than myself. I thought about Beau and if I said it now and didn't mean it then it would kill him later.

"I—"

"Shhh," he interrupted. "I didn't tell you that so you

could tell me back. I told you so you would know. My family loves you. They think you're great and I just wanted you to know that they're not alone."

He kissed my forehead and made love to me again. Leave it up to Beau to make a great night perfect.

I slept hard in his arms until interrupted by the shine of my bedroom light. I opened my eyes as much as I could. Beau lifted his arm from around me and that's when I realized something was very wrong.

Eric stood over my bed gaping at us. We sat up on the bed and covered ourselves.

"Get out! Get out!" I shouted.

Eric ran out of the room and I quickly slipped on my robe while Beau slid on his shorts. I raced to the bottom of the steps.

"What the hell are you doing here?" I asked. "Are you crazy?"

"I only came over to talk," he explained.

"Talk? Talk? Get the fuck out of my house!" I was livid.

"That's your new boyfriend?" he asked.

"Eric give me the key to my house and get the hell out!"

"That's how it is with us? What about moving in together and everything else?"

"Your wife happened to it. That's what happened to it," I yelled, "And you! You haven't been seen or heard from in over three weeks."

"I had to lay low until things died down. Kayla she found everything. The phone bills, the loft, everything. She was about to give it to her attorney. I had to get rid of it all or she would have taken everything I worked for."

"Eric, that's neither her nor there." I told him. "The bottom line is it's over between us."

"You don't mean that," he said handing me my pager.

He'd taken it from a box of things I'd packed. Who knows how long Eric was actually in my house before he even came upstairs. "Keep it, I had the number changed."

"I don't want it. I already told you, it's over."

I threw it back at him. He allowed it to hit the floor. I stood strong. Beau had to be jumping for joy in his boxers right now as he listened quietly upstairs.

"I can't believe you can't see my side of things." He laid the guilt trip on really thick.

"Your side of things? How about you seeing my side Eric?" I yelled at him for being so one dimensional. "You left me alone! No phone call, no reason, no anything. You turned off my phone, pager, sold our loft and I lost my job. So believe it. Believe that I can't see your side of things, I'm too busy fighting through mine."

He gave the saddest look that I was almost taken in by. We paused for a long silence.

I held out my hand for the key.

"I still pay the bills here," he said softly.

Beau stepped out from the bedroom and stood at the top of the steps.

"Not anymore," I told Eric.

He looked into my eyes with great regret before handing over the key. His money held no power over me anymore. It only controlled him.

After he left I went back to bed and continued to let Beau hold me tightly.

* * * *

"Awe how cute," they all shouted as Gabrielle opened another gift.

We all sat around and oohed and aahed over all the cute little things that Gabrielle got for her arriving daughter. So many guests showed up and brought so many nice things. It was a beautiful turn out for Gabrielle until she got one last surprise.

I stood at her side as she opened the last gift. Just as she tore the gift wrap off Sabrina announced, "Everyone this is the Godfather."

The crowded room of ladies turned to Todd who stood nervously in the middle of Gabrielle's front room. Jack went to greet him. Gabrielle's face turned pale as she looked at me. I had nothing to do with it. I was just as clueless and speech-less as she. We both were thinking fatal attraction.

Nevertheless, we carried on as if the surprise was noth-ing. The end of the party couldn't have come fast enough. The three of us whispered lightly in the kitchen as Jack and Todd spoke cordially.

"What is he doing here?" Gabrielle asked.

"I have no idea," I said.

"Do you think he's going to tell Jack?" she asked.

"I don't think so," Sabrina cut in.

"Why would he come here?" Gabrielle looked around suspiciously.

"Didn't you invite him?" I asked her.

"No, I didn't even tell him about it."

"I invited him," Sabrina informed us.

Our whispers stopped and stares began. Words can't describe how hard we stared at the girl. I think we both were trying to see inside her brain to figure out what in the hell she was thinking to make a move like that.

"You what?" Gabrielle finally asked her.

"All at work you've been saying how you wished Todd could come to the shower."

"Yeah, but if I wanted to invite him I would have done

it myself. Where do you get off inviting another man to my house and without asking me first?" Gabrielle snapped.

She was pissed! I'd only seen her this angry a few times and tonight was one of those times. I didn't butt in. I allowed Gabrielle to let her have it.

"I'm sorry. I thought I was doing something special by saving it as a surprise."

"Didn't you think that I would somehow be very un-comfortable with my husband," she took her whisper even lower "and my lover in the same room? Didn't you think that?"

"Not really." Sabrina had this dumb look on her face. "I really didn't think it would cause such a commotion since you named him the Godfather anyway. I figured you could play along with it."

"What an idiot." Whoops did I say that out loud?

Sabrina cut her eyes at me. Gabrielle cut her eyes at her. I knew she wanted to curse me so badly and I wanted her to because we would have been scraping right in Gabrielle's kitchen. But now was not the time to fight. Gabrielle would have kicked both our asses if we even passed a single word.

"You better hope he doesn't say anything to Jack," she warned Sabrina.

We all peeked from the kitchen to the front room at the guys who seemed to be enjoying each other's company.

"I'm so happy there was another man in the house to-night," Jack told Todd. "It would have been hard being surrounded by all that estrogen. Gabi has enough to fill the entire room."

They laughed. We took a breath and returned to our conversation. "When you leave you take him with you," she told Sabrina.

The girl stood so uncomfortably in the kitchen and she had every good reason to. Of all the dumb things a person could do, Sabrina had done them all. Better her than me.

Chapter 21

"I love you," Beau told me over the phone before hanging up.

"Thanks sweetie. That makes me feel good," I said back.

I still hadn't told him I loved him. I wished he would stop telling me. It always made me feel bad to not say it back but he told me not to say it until I was truly positive. I did love Beau but I wasn't sure if I was ready to love him with my all. Somehow inside me, I thought he was better than me. And while I was sure he wouldn't break my heart, I wasn't sure I wouldn't break his.

Though I stopped all dealings with Eric, he had pulled out all stops to get me back. He sent me texts constantly throughout the day telling me to take him back and that he loved me and would do anything to keep me in his life. He gave me a second promise ring with bigger diamonds that I kept in my jewelry box. Then a plane ticket to Costa Rico for the weekend for next month suddenly arrived in the mail. He even had a tailor come to my house with all the latest designer clothes for me to select from.

But I wasn't falling for any of his expensive tricks. I still held out for Beau who wouldn't return for another month. I would soon visit him in Houston if he didn't get back in town first. There was a slim chance that he would.

When I returned home from an afternoon workout to

find a letter on my doorstep I knew that, the slim chance wasn't slim anymore. It was a poem of directions of where to go to find my next clue. I showered, threw on my clothes, and drove to my destination for my next clue. Beau was home and I was going to find him!

I stayed on the phone with Gabrielle the entire time through my scavenger hunt. She was excellent at solving riddles and useless trivia. At every stop there was a certain gift. The first stop was an apple, symbolic of my career. The second stop was a rose. The third stop was candy. And the last stop was a bottle of champagne to bring with me to my last destination where I would see my baby.

I arrived at the park and immediately noticed the blanket, candles in the form of a heart shape, and a picnic basket. The sun was just beginning to set so the candles reflected beautifully off the sky. I walked over, sat the champagne down and looked around frantically. On the blanket lay a blindfold with directions for me to put it on and wait to be kissed by my prince. I followed the directions. Soon enough I felt his soft wet lips against mine.

"See, I can be romantic too."

I snatched off the blindfold. Disgust settled in. Eric had tricked and manipulated me again. I stood to leave.

"Wait," he said.

"What is this? What is all this? Another trick for you to get me back to accept you so you can hurt me all over again?"

"No, Kayla please, just listen. My life has been so incomplete without you. I feel like I'm suffocating. I miss you so much. Can't you tell? Didn't it feel good to kiss me again? Didn't it? We belong together."

He went on and on. Before I knew it he was back at my place making love to me. The feeling was indescribable. More like unbelievable or better put...regrettable! I didn't know if it was worth it. All I could think about was Beau. Beau would have given me a lily instead of a rose. He would have brought music to set the mood just right. And he wouldn't do it to me this way. He would have kissed my neck first and would have would have undressed me slowly instead of asking me to take my clothes off. And Beau wouldn't have orgasmed so fast either. And he would have rubbed my hair and wrapped his arms around me afterwards.

Everything was Beau, Beau, Beau. If Beau and Eric were running a marathon, Eric would have been left at the finish line. There was no competition. I felt lower than dirt for having another man in my bed instead of my man. For the first time I felt guilty for cheating.

Eric lay comatose. I looked at him and tried to figure what I saw in him in the first place. Then my phone rang. I knew it would be Beau. I slipped out of the bedroom and into the next room.

"Hello."

"What are you doing?" he asked.

I instantly became on edge. What did he mean by that? "Nothing. Where are you?"

"Huh?" He asked. "I'm in Phoenix."

"Oh, I don't know what I was thinking. I'm still half sleep. How was the show?"

"It was fine. It would have been better if you would have been there but it's cool."

"We'll see each other in Houston."

"I can't wait."

He continued to talk. I could hear through my end of the phone, someone picking up the receiver in the other room. I almost pissed my pants. I rushed into my bedroom so fast and threatened Eric. I waved with my hands for him to put the phone down. Instead he playfully pressed buttons and made faces. How mature. It was such a turn off.

He had a devilish look in his eyes. He wanted to mess things up between me and Beau. And if he did there would be no chance in hell of us ever getting back together or even speaking.

Finally, he hung up the phone.

"Hello?" Beau asked.

"Yeah I'm still here. I had to switch phones. That one was going dead," I quickly lied.

"Okay."

I let him get in a few words before I ended our conversation.

"Baby, I'm sorry. I'm so tired I can't even think straight. Let me call you back in the morning as soon as I get up."

"Alright," he said unsuspectingly, "Good night."

I hung up the phone. "What is wrong with you? Why are you acting so petty?"

"I'm jealous," he confessed.

It was kind of cute, I had to admit. We lay back in the bed except I couldn't sleep. Eric had no problems. He slept hard on my Sealy mattress. But too many things raced through my head. Why was he here? Why was he so bent on making things better after three almost four weeks of not talking to me? Why?

Maybe I was looking for a reason to kick him out of my bed and ultimately my life. I always left someone when they'd done something bad to me. I always waited for that point in my relationship because I didn't know how to leave a person unless I had an excuse when all along my excuse should have been 'I don't want to be involved anymore.'

I paced the floor and I noticed it. His pager lay openly on the nightstand. He took for granted that I'd never go through his things. That was his first mistake.

I locked myself in the bathroom, opened that pager,

and read all his messages. 'Please take me back,' he begged. 'I miss you,' he said. 'I could never love anyone else,' he wrote. 'I'll do anything to get you back in my life.' They were all the same exact pages he'd sent to me this week but instead of my number being the recipient, it was his wife's number.

At first I didn't quite comprehend. Then it hit me. The slick bastard! He'd been sending her and I both the same pages. Every time he sent me a message, he'd forward it to her. How dirty! She must have kicked him out of the house and now he was trying to get in good with either of us by sending us the same pages. It was all I needed to see. It was my last straw.

I grinned to myself on my way back in the room. I couldn't wait for this disastrous moment to occur. Eric had manipulated me for the last time. I wasn't accepting it this time which is why I two way messaged Michia and told her to get her no good husband out of my bed. Just in case she was having second thoughts of why she should keep him I would let her catch the motherfucker naked in my bed. Let her take him for everything he has, I didn't care. And even if she did still want him, that was even better. Just get his ass out of my house and keep him out.

Half an hour later I met her outside. She wasn't happy to see me and vice versa but we didn't argue because tonight we were on the same team. I led her upstairs where Eric still slept soundly.

She took her purse and slapped him across his face. He jumped in fright.

"You're so sorry right?" she asked. "You want me to let you back home so you can be a better father and husband right?" she slapped him again. This time he guarded his face but still felt the whip of her Louis Vuitton purse on his cheeks.

"Ow! Stop! Michia! Stop!" he yelled.

I stood back with my arms folded and rooted for her. I wanted him to get everything he deserved. He grabbed his clothes and ran into the bathroom. She banged and kicked at my door. Then she rushed downstairs to his car and flattened the tires and left.

"You can come out now, she's gone," I told Eric who now had come out of the bathroom but locked himself in my room.

He fumbled around for a minute. I could hear him mumble underneath his breath before he opened the door slowly. He held the telephone in one hand and his shoes in the other. I asked myself who was he going to call. But couldn't ask him because I was too busy laughing at the whole situation.

Until he said deviously, "Telephone."

I grabbed the phone and curiously said, "Hello?"

"You're not sleepy anymore?" Beau asked.

Eric walked from my bedroom smiling. He'd gotten the last laugh.

"Beau listen. I—"

"No you listen. Fuck you, Kayla. What I do today, you won't appreciate that shit tomorrow. And what I do tomorrow you won't appreciate that a month from now. I'm tired of trying to impress you only to find that you're not worth impressing. It's cool though. Sometimes you just have to let go. Can't save every hoe."

Click. The phone disconnected. I didn't know whether to be offended or what. I didn't know what all Eric told him but I did know that he hated my guts and my relationship with Beau was over. There was no chance he would ever speak to me this time. No way possible.

I saw fire and at once attacked Eric. He fought me off him.

"You played that game first," he told me.

"Get out! Get out! I don't want to ever see you again."
He didn't argue. He carried his shoes to the car and drove away on all four slit tires. If I never saw Eric after today that would be too soon.

As soon as he left I called Beau repeatedly. Not once did he answer. I left message after message. Still he didn't return my call. It was over this time for good.

* * * *

I kicked Jack out of his room early the next morning and cuddled up with Gabrielle in her bed. He didn't mind. In fact I think he was relieved. He needed a break from his wife and her crazy hormones. He left right after I arrived.

"Gabrielle what am I going to do?" I asked her.

"There's really nothing you can do except wait until he cools off and call him."

"Your theory sucks. I'm just going to wait until he cools off and call him," I repeated.

"Yeah your way sounds so much better," she teased.

"Ooh Gabi, what am I going to do?" I pouted.

"That's it!" Gabrielle screamed. She rolled out of her bed. "I am so sick of you moping around. Get some life in you girl. It's just a man."

"But you don't understand Gabrielle. I really f'd up this time."

"Yeah you did," she agreed.

I got angry. "Stupid Eric. I hate him."

"Good, lets get into some trouble. Lets slash his tires and run."

"Run? You? Gabrielle you can't run to the toilet and back," I told her. "Besides I don't want anymore trouble with that man. I only want him to leave me alone."

"You're right," she looked in the mirror, "I am kind of fat."

"Kind of?" I said.

She gave me an evil look. "Do something. Go get high or something. Do something reckless."

"I don't want to get high. Beau is my only drug," I whined and put the pillow over my head.

"Are you serious?" she took the pillow off and hit me with it. "Is this my best friend talking?"

"I think so," I said. "I don't know, where's Sabrina?"

"Very funny. "

"Did you two make up?"

"Yeah we're fine. At first I was mad but I kind of understand why she did what she did. I do walk around talking about Todd. She didn't know any better."

I wanted to speak up but I didn't. Had that been me, Gabrielle would have stopped speaking to me for another month but because sweet precious Sabrina did that, then it was 'she didn't know any better.' What a crock.

"Whatever," I said sarcastically.

"Don't start."

"Hey, I haven't said anything."

"You know what we're going to do? We're going to plan a nice ladies night out. Dinner, dancing, and most of all drinking."

"You can't drink."

"No, but you can and I can at least watch. When's the last time you went out?"

"When Beau and I went dancing while he was in town," I sulked.

"Oh brother, you got to be kidding me," she teased, "I'm just going to be honest, this is not about you. I need this. I need some excitement in my life. So bitch, you're going."

We both laughed.

We shopped for her an appropriate dinner outfit then the two of us went out. It was the craziest night. To see Gabrielle dance around with a huge belly was hilarious. But we had a great time. I only thought about Beau when Gabrielle went to the bathroom which was about six times during our evening.

After mostly talking about how we turned out so damn crazy there was very little time for discussing men. But we managed.

"I love Jack but we were so young and naïve about marriage," Gabrielle told me. "We thought it was going to be a fairytale and for a while it was, then it wasn't."

"Do you regret Todd?" I wanted to know. Now she was seven months pregnant and due to have his child. What did she think about that?

"As crazy as it may sound, my five second affair with Todd will make me love and appreciate Jack for a lifetime."

We finished our meals and I drank my third apple martini and we headed home. I was so drunk by the time we got into her car. My stomach turned and my head began to spin.

"Ohhh," I moaned in despair. "I feel horrible."

"We must be getting old. You can't even drink three apple martinis without getting sick? I have to stop hanging out with you."

"Who will you hang with? I'm your only friend," I teased while holding my stomach and keeping my eyes closed. "Oh no that's right, you have Sabrina."

"You are so childish."

243

"Sabrina, your new best friend," I teased more, "I forgot about her."

"I don't know what's wrong with you sometimes. That girl is not my best friend."

"That's why she has four front teeth and Dumb and Dumber bangs," I mocked Sabrina's big teeth and her short bangs. Gabrielle burst into tears of laughter. "Let me stop talking about your friend before you get mad and stop talking to me for another month."

"Girl please," she got serious, "I would never let anyone, not even Sabrina, ruin our friendship. Please believe that."

I paused for a second.

"Did we just have a moment?" I teased. "Bitch are you trying to get sentimental on me or am I just really, really drunk?"

"I love you man," she teased and shook my aching head profusely.

"Stop it!" I squealed. "You better stop it unless you want apple martini all on your beautiful interior."

My two-way beeped. I looked down. Eric wrote: I'm sorry. I miss you. Can I please see you?

I sat the pager back in my purse. I didn't want to see him ever. At least I didn't think I did. He'd messed everything up with Beau and now he decided to call me. But something inside me must love to be mistreated. Otherwise why would I still carry around the pager?

"Listen!" she yelled and turned up the volume on the radio. Shirley Murdock's song *Husband* play. I opened my eyes and sat up. We loved the song and it was so fitting for both our lives. We lifted our voices and sang our hearts out.

"I know, I know you are her husband. That's why I got to let you go. So I'm let-et-ting you go. Letting you go," we sang and waved our hands around getting into it.

Gabrielle slapped me five. "Let him go girl," she told

me. I looked into my friend's eyes. She gave a serious yet warm smile. "Let him go. He's not worth losing someone special."

And before I could say anything, before the song was fully over, there were bright lights, a loud horn, and a loud crash. Within seconds everything went black.

Chapter 22

Beep. Beep. Beep. I could hear in the distance and it seemed to get louder. I slowly opened my eyes. The room seemed tinted. There was almost this haze of cloudiness that lay among it. I lay in confusion wondering where I was and how I'd gotten here.

My body lay stagnate. Only my eyes moved, scanning the entire surface of the room.

A big brown door with a pull back handle for a knob. White walls and a high television. Machinery to my left that beeped and beeped and beeped.

A hospital? What was I doing in a hospital? I scanned my body overlooking the white sheets that I lay upon. At my stomach I noticed a hand and a familiar grip around my waist. I must be dreaming. I looked further this time moving my head to see the feet.

"Kayla?" he said to me. "Wait Kayla, lay down."

I did as he said. He fidgeted around the call button and paged a nurse.

"Do you know where you are?" he asked me.

I tried speaking but my voice was rough and my head hurt at the smallest attempt to open my mouth. My chest felt like five fat people sat on it but I tried speaking again and was unsuccessful.

"It's okay honey," Beau said, "Don't try to talk."

He held my hand and kissed my cheek. I knew something was terribly wrong but I couldn't ask what. Tears rolled down his face and I wondered how bad things really were.

The nurse rushed in and asked me a million questions. "Do you know what year it is? Do you know where you are? Do you know your name? Do you know who he is? Do you remember what happened?"

I could answer yes to all but one. I didn't know what happened but I would find out very soon.

The doctor came in shortly after, looked at my chart, asked more questions, did a few tests to see if I could follow his finger with my eyes and if I could feel him tickling my feet.

Then he said, "Good. It all looks good."

Beau stood behind watching. He looked so worried.

I tried to speak again. "You won't feel that soreness in your throat after a few hours. We removed a breathing tube this morning. Miss Parker, you were in a serious car accident. Do you remember any of it?"

I thought about my last night out. I remembered being in the car listening to the radio. I remembered seeing bright lights fast approaching and screaming before everything went dark. That was all I remembered.

I blinked twice as instructed if my answer was 'no.'

Beau, the doctor and nurse all looked at each other then back at me.

"You've been unconscious for two days. You had your poor fiancé worried about you." The doctor referred to Beau.

Damn, when did I get engaged?

"Luckily, everything looks good," he said again. "You have a sprained left wrist and a couple of fractured ribs and a bump on your head which caused your lapse of consciousness. We're going to keep you here for a few days. We don't want any surprises do we?"

I cleared my sore throat.

"Can she have some water?" Beau requested.

The doctor barely gave the nurse a good look before she rushed to get me a cup of water. Beau was so sweet and effective. He knew exactly what I needed and he was there when I woke up.

The doctor excused himself and Beau followed behind. I could hear them whispering on the other side of the door but couldn't make out anything either of them said. Beau returned to the room with my cup of water. He helped me drink it.

"How do you feel?" he asked standing at my bedside rubbing my hair.

I smiled although I felt like crap.

"I'm happy you're alright. I was afraid I wouldn't get to talk to you again. Afraid you wouldn't get a chance to give me more excuses," he smiled.

He smiled but I didn't. I was so grateful he was here. After all the things I put him through he was still here for me like no one else.

"I'm sorry," he apologized. "You need anything?"

I blinked twice.

"I had to tell the doctor and nurses I'm your fiancé. They wouldn't let me come in," he explained and pulled a chair close to my bed. He continued to stroke my hair and rub my face. I closed my eyes and enjoyed it all.

"I was so scared for you. The hospital found your cell phone and called me. I left my show and got here as fast as I could. I've been here ever since." He lifted my hand and kissed each of my fingers. "I love you," he said uncomfortably.

He rubbed my hair until I fell fast asleep. In my dreams I got flashes of the accident. The longer I slept the more and more I remembered. There I was, in the car, smiling having a good time, listening to the radio with Gabrielle. Gabrielle....Gabrielle?

I awakened in fright. The bump on my head must have given me a lapse of common sense also. Beau's head lay on my bed while he still slept in the chair. I rubbed his frizzy, braided hair.

He lifted his head and looked at me groggy eyed. "I need a hair cut."

I smiled. "Where's Gabrielle?" I said roughly.

His smile slowly vanished. "She's okay."

I gave a breath of relief. It was all I needed to hear. If anything would have gone wrong with Gabi and the baby I would have died on the hospital bed.

"Good," I cleared my throat. "Where is—"

"You should save your voice," he interrupted. "Let it get a little better before you start talking."

"It's okay. It feels better already."

"I called your mother and sister and practically every-one else in your phone," he successfully changed the subject. "I even called Cory. He came to visit while you were out."

"Really?" I was shocked.

"He left you a card," he pulled it from the drawer. "You want me to read it?"

I shook my head 'no.' I was grateful enough that Cory had even cared that much.

"Okay," he said softly and put the card away. "Eric called you." I gave a curious look but Beau wouldn't look me in my eyes. "I figured he didn't know what happened so I answered your phone and told him."

Still he barely looked me in my face. His heart was so kind. I knew that even the thought of Eric made Beau's blood boil but he did the honest and noble thing of informing him of my condition anyway.

"He didn't come to visit yet but I'm sure he will," he assured me.

I held his face in my hand. "I'm happy you're here." He smiled and kissed me. Yuck! I hadn't brushed my teeth in two days, hadn't moved from the bed to wash my ass in two days, and this man still could kiss me? He must have really been sprung.

The nurse interrupted us. "I see you're feeling better already," she said. We smiled while she checked my monitors and did whatever. Then she pulled out the biggest needle I've ever seen. "Scoot over sweetie unless you want one too."

"No thanks. I have to go to the bathroom anyway." Beau gave me another kiss and went to the restroom.

The nurse didn't hesitate to give me my shot. "Ouch."

"There, there," she wiped my arm. "It's all over."

"What room is Gabrielle in?" I asked the nurse.

She focused her attention away from my IV and onto me. She looked confused.

"My best friend," I said. "The girl that was in the accident with me?"

"No one came in here with you," she said still confused. "I could check it out but I'm almost sure."

Beau entered in.

"The nurse said Gabrielle isn't in here. Was she already discharged?"

I was curious. Why wasn't my best friend visiting me? Beau had a stupid look on his face. He was hiding something.

"Beau, where is Gabrielle?"

He stood in the doorway. The nurse excused herself for us to talk. He walked over to me and held my hand.

"The accident was really bad," he started and all of a sudden I felt sick. I knew the accident was bad already. Why was he telling me this again? And where in the hell was my

best friend? "The guy was drunk and hit you almost head on."
"No, no!" I yelled. "Don't tell me any more. No!
Please don't tell me! Just tell me where she is."

Tears filled his eyes.

"Kayla, I'm sorry but Gabrielle and the baby didn't make it."

"NOOOO! NOOOO!" I screamed. Nurses rushed into the room. Beau held me tight and fanned them away as I cried in his arms. "She did make it. Yes they did. Stop lying. Please, Beau stop lying," I cried hysterically.

He shook his head 'no' assuring me that she hadn't. It was true. My best friend was gone. She was gone forever. I burst into even more tears. It hurt so much. It was a pain I'd never felt. I felt as though I'd lost my life.

No more late night conversations or complaining about my love life. No more cuddling up in the bed with her or going on binges to retaliate when someone breaks my heart. No more swapping stories about our sexual endeavors. No more anything. No more anything at all.

My best friend was gone forever and this was the biggest heart break I'd ever had. No pain could compare and no man or medicine could dissolve it.

"Make it stop. Please make it stop," I pleaded with Beau. But the pain just kept on. He couldn't do anything about it.

Beau held me tight. "I'm sorry. I'm sorry," he repeated.

* * * *

Precious Lord take my hand
Lead me on
Help me stand

I am tired, I am weak, I am worn
Through the storm, through the night
Lead me on, to the light
Take my hand
Precious Lord
And lead me home
Precious Lord
You're the one
That I built my life on
You're my rock
You're my hope
You are my song
You picked me up, made me strong
When my way was all wrong
Here's my hand
Precious Lord
Now lead me home

When my way grows drear
Precious Lord, linger near
When my life is almost gone
Hear my cry, hear my call
Take my hand lest I fall
Take my hand
Precious Lord
And lead me home

Take my hand Precious Lord
And lead me home

    I sat numbly as the soloist sang those beautiful words to Thomas A. Dorsey's, Precious Lord. And even though she sounded like an angel, her words escaped me.

Jack and little Jackson sat to my left. Jack bit his lip and fought back tears while holding his son in his arms. I could hardly look at either of them and as horrible as it may sound, I knew that when he looked at me, he wished that it was I who sat in place of his wife in that casket. I didn't blame him because in many ways, I too, wished the same.

But just when I thought I would lose it all, just when I wanted to throw my hands up and fall to the floor begging to be taken instead, I felt the warmth of Beau who sat to my right, holding my hand, keeping me strong.

"Gabrielle wasn't just a friend to any of us. She was our light, our rock, our doctor, our psychiatrist, our teacher. She had a smile...." as he began to get into his speech, Todd broke down. He grabbed at his stomach as if it the air was being pushed out of him. He bent over and tried to gain composure but the tears continued to bucket from his eyes.

Another deacon patted his back and the crowd yelled, "Go on. Amen!" and more sobs were heard.

Then finally he stood. His voice all broken up, he said, "I'm sorry, but to me Gabrielle was more than just an ordinary person."

I glanced at Jack, whose eyes now bleed an abundance of tears because of Todd's touching words. His ignorance ran deep and he clapped loudly and encouraged his wife's lover to continue.

Todd went on to deliver the most beautiful eulogy that I'd ever heard. It came from his heart. For the first time I saw past all my judgments of church people not practicing what they preached and I saw him as the godly man that he was and didn't look at him as God.

His love for Gabrielle was true. It may have been many things to many people but one thing it wasn't, was a fake.

Jack listened and applauded Todd, as everyone else

did. I took his hand and also my best friend's secret to my own grave.

* * * *

Certain thoughts haunt me. I meditate in my mind of how to confront past ghosts and bury them. Here I sat in Beau's house another day, after weeks of rehabilitation, physical and mental. Eric still two-way messaged me everyday but I was sick and tired of him. I was fed up with his excuses, his expensive gestures to get back with me, and anything else affiliated with Mr. Eric.

I couldn't believe he had the nerve to ask to see me after he disregarded my being in the hospital for almost a week and didn't show up to my best friend's funeral. Now he wanted to see me after all my bruises healed and I was pretty again. What he didn't realize was that the scars and bruises ran deep. While I'd healed outwardly, inwardly my insides were damaged more than ever.

"I couldn't see you like that. It was too hard for me."

"For you? Why is everything about you? When are things about Kayla? Kayla could have died in that crash not you. Kayla lost her best friend in that accident not you. Kayla lost her job, not you."

"Why are you bringing that up? That's the past," he told me.

I stood against Beau's bathroom wall in disbelief. Did he just say that? I couldn't believe he opened his mouth to say that. How selfish!

"Your bills are paid, you don't have to ask for anything. What's the problem? You don't need to work anyway," he went on.

My hand grew weak. I could no longer hold the phone. Before I knew it, I watched as it sank to the bottom of the toilet. He was where he needed to be, in the toilet with the rest of the crap.

I returned to my favorite section of Beau's couch and watched television. Minutes later he walked through the door with a bag of groceries.

"They had green grapes but not the blue ones," he told me.

"Blue grapes? When have you ever seen blue grapes?" I laughed.

"In the store," he said confused, "What color are they?"

"Sweetie they're purple not blue," I teased, "If you ever find blue grapes please don't buy them for me. Or orange, red, hot pink either."

He laughed it off and put away the groceries. I loved this man. I didn't know where it came from all of a sudden. I only knew that I couldn't see myself without him.

He pulled his shirt over his head to avoid sweating while he fixed up our entrée. Then he brought my plate and took his place next to me. I watched him bless his food and eat.

"What?" he asked with a mouth full of food.

"Nothing. I just, I...nothing."

He placed his fork down and gave me his undivided attention. I knew that look. He tried to figure out my soul but this time he couldn't. This overwhelming feeling I had for him right now was, oh so different. It was indescribable. He'd never received it from me because I'd shielded it for so long.

"It's something. What is it? You know you can talk to me about anything."

He was right. I could. "I was thinking." I nervously started. "Things have been so great and you've been so nice and perfect. With the whole job thing and funeral and just everything, you've been my rock. I don't want it to end."

He moved around in his seat anticipating my next words.

"I was thinking that maybe we could live together."

He was quiet. It was not the response I expected. He sat his plate on the table and moved away.

"Kay, you don't want to move in together."

"Yes I do," I assured him.

"No you don't," he said firmly. "How could you want to move in with someone you can't even tell you love?"

He was right again. I hadn't said those three words but I felt it inside. I really did.

"You're just enjoying the pampering and support and attention because right now you're vulnerable. But I already told you once, I don't want you to need me. I need you to want me. I never wanted to be your roommate. I always wanted to be your husband one day."

"I know that and I'm not asking for a roommate."

"What are you asking for? Kayla, we've been through so much. I don't think I can handle trusting you and seeing you go back to another man again. I can't deal with that. I'm still dealing with you lying about being in bed when you were in bed with Eric. I might not say anything about it but I think about it everyday when we're playing checkers, watching TV, eating dinner, or while you're sleeping. I still think about it everyday. The truth is, I don't know if I'll ever be able to trust you again. And I can't be with anyone I can't trust."

"Oh." I was speechless, "Alright, I understand."

I'd turned a beautiful evening into an uncomfortable one. He finished his meal in the kitchen.

"I understand." I said again to myself. I understood that things would never be the same once I left Beau's home.

Chapter 23

The next day I returned home. I decided not to torture myself by staying with someone who didn't want to be with me any longer. It was evident that my feelings for Beau were stronger than his for me. That was never a good thing.

"How was the shoot?" I asked Beau. He'd returned back to work touring and making his first debut in a film. "Good. I'm happy to hear it went well. No I understand you're tired. Call me when you get up. Okay. Bye."

I tried getting my mind off him but I missed him so much that I didn't know what to do with myself. So I did what I usually do. I called Eric and he came right over.

"I missed you," he hugged me tight. "You smell so good."

"Thanks."

He handed over a bouquet of colorful roses. Eric still didn't know my favorite flower. He walked inside and made himself at home finding my favorite place on my chaise.

"Come sit next to me." He patted beside him.

I gave into his request. He pulled my feet onto his legs and began to massage them. Five minutes later he was all over me. He tried taking off my blouse but I stopped him. The whole scene felt all wrong. The way he smelled, and touched me, talked, and brought the wrong flowers. None of it felt right. And I was still upset about his absence at the hospital and my best friend's funeral. How selfish could one person be?

"Stop," I said, "Eric, stop it."

"What's the problem?"

"I don't want to do this."

"Why not?"

I looked deep into his face. He wasn't the handsome, debonair, irresistible man I fell for in the past. I did not love this man nor did I lust for him. Every bone in my body ached for every second I kept him near me.

"I want you to leave and," I paused for my next words, "never come back."

He gave a huge sigh.

"Eric just listen. I don't feel anything for you anymore. What happened between us happened and now it's gone."

"Are you saying this because of your little boyfriend?"

"No it's not about him. It's about me."

For a change, it was about me. All about me.

"Stop lying Mikayla. You can tell me because I honestly don't care if you have a boyfriend. I mean I have a wife, right?"

His words totally blew me. They hit me like a brick. I had to have been the dumbest, most stupid bitch in the world! What was I thinking all this time? In so many words he was willing to share me as long as I was willing to share him. Eric never planned to leave his wife. Never. But none of it mattered. I was done entirely. Unlike the times before when I'd say I was through and allow him to return. Tonight was different. Tonight was the last time I would see Eric.

"You're right, you do have a wife. And now go home to her."

"Come on don't act like that Felicia-" he caught himself.

I knew he didn't call me by another woman's name. He looked around aimlessly trying to cover his shame. Then

I realized he did just call me another woman. To top it off, he hadn't confused me with his wife but rather with some unknown woman.

"Felicia?" I said. "No, I'm Mikayla. Get your hoes straight."

"I know who you are Mikayla. Felicia is an intern-" he tried explaining but I cut his excuses short.

"Eric, I really don't care who Felicia is. The point remains the same. I don't want to see you again. I don't want your money, gifts, sex, or anything from you. So please stay away from my home."

"And if I don't?" he tested me.

I'd reached a point in my life where I was tired of the same situations with the same outcomes. I wanted Eric erased from my world. Desperate times like these call for desperate measures.

"Then me and Michia will have a long serious heart to heart," I threatened.

"You wouldn't do that." He smiled confidently. "You're not going to leave me alone Kayla so stop talking crazy. I'm your go to guy and you're my go to girl."

"Eric the only thing you can go to is hell. And try me. If you don't believe me then go ahead and call my bluff." But he didn't. "You're the only liar here Eric. I've always told the truth. Anything I said I would do, I did it. You haven't done a damn thing and now, your time is up."

He wasn't amused by my threat and turned his back on me. And that was it. It was just that simple. He didn't ask or say anything about it. He left out of my house and out of my life for good or rather until the next day when I showed up at his job because of regretful feelings for being so evil.

It was noon and Linda, his secretary faithfully took her lunch at that time. I baked cookies as a peace offering and took the elevator to his floor.

Eric was a man of great pride and an even bigger ego. Of course he'd called me by another woman's name. He wanted to get back at me for trying to leave him again. I should have noticed last night but I was caught off guard. Today, I was prepared to reconcile our differences and be friends and only friends.

Just as I expected, Linda was gone and a good thing too because we couldn't stand the sight of each other.

I opened the door to Eric's office. He sat at his desk at first extremely relaxed but his posture quickly changed to nervously tense.

"Mikayla!" He shouted.

"Hi."

He didn't stand to greet me. I completely understood why.

"I came to apologize for last night," I said, "I know some things were said that neither of us meant. I don't want to end our friendship on a bad note."

"Don't worry about it," he said still sitting, "apology accepted."

His tone was friendly and I could only accept it as being sincere.

"I baked you cookies." I walked towards him.

He raised his hand to me, "Thanks, put them on Linda's desk. I'll get them on the way out."

"Aw, come on. You have to try at least one. I slaved all morning making the perfect-"

I stopped frozen in my tracks reaching his desk. The once hidden girl who knelt under Eric's desk with smeared lipstick rose to her feet. He immediately pulled his pants from his ankles to his waist as the girl fastened her unbuttoned blouse.

"Felicia, right?" I asked the girl who tried walking away. "No sweetie, you stay. I'll leave."

I grabbed my cookies and didn't look back.

Ding! The elevator sang. The doors barely opened when I marched off the empty elevator.

"Pardon me." I spoke to the woman who I almost trampled over.

"Of course," Michia started until she realized she was speaking to her rival. We both took a step back but I didn't give her a chance to belittle or lash out at me. I didn't want her to waste time on me but rather go upstairs and deal with Eric and Felicia. I ran outside and put the key to my car inside the lock.

"You drink coffee?" I heard a voice nearby. Michia stood on the sidewalk yelling for my attention.

Her eyes sensed my vulnerability.

* * * *

Michia walked into the coffee shop as if we were life long friends catching up on old times. She walked with confidence with her model cheek bones that sat up as high as her breasts in her two hundred dollar Victoria Secret push up bra. Her purse sat tightly underneath the pit of her arm as if she expected someone to steal it.

The waitress sat us at a table by the window. I fidgeted nervously trying to not throw up the three cookies I'd ate on the way over.

Michia was just the opposite. Her voice was soft and

warm as she ordered her coffee. She then gave me the go ahead to order whatever I wanted.

"Can I have a ginger ale please?" I asked the waitress. Michia sat softly across from me. Her eyes were hidden behind her four hundred dollar Chanel glasses. She raised one brow scoping and evaluating every fiber of my flesh.

Then she finally said with a hint of sarcasm, "So Mikayla," my eyes watched her like a hawk as she reached into her purse and pulled a single cigarette and lit it before finishing her sentence. "What brings us here?"

I looked at her as though she was crazy. Had she forgotten she called this meeting?

She took a pull from her cigarette and blew smoke from the corner of her lips. Either this bitch was beyond confident or she'd done this a million times before.

I could see what Eric spoke about. He'd always told me she appeared unaffected by anything. Nothing moved or excited her. I believed him now because here she sat in front of her husband's ex lover and she handled it like a business deal.

"Relationships," I finally began.

"Relationships?" she asked, "Is that what they call it these days?"

I took a breath. "I don't know what to call it."

We were briefly interrupted by our waitress. Michia accepted our drinks and sent the lady away for a cup of fruit. Few seconds passed and we both remained quiet until I couldn't take it anymore.

"Look, I'm sorry. What I did was wrong and I should have faced you sooner but I didn't. I thought I loved Eric so I carried on in a way I thought I never would. I want to apologize for all the hurt and confusion I've caused in your life."

She lay back in her seat. I wondered about her thoughts and it wouldn't be long before she revealed them to me.

"Tell me something," she started, "when you met my husband you knew he was married correct? He didn't lie about me or anything like that right? You knew all along right?"

Shamefully I responded, "yes."

She blew a cloud of smoke in my face and smacked her lips before putting out her cigarette.

The next question was followed by a set of even more brutal intensifying, embarrassing questions. I gave honest answers. I didn't know why I told her everything or why I even agreed to meet with her in the first place. Somewhere inside me I believed I owed her this much and just wanted things to be over. I wanted things to be over for good. I knew that by betraying Eric that there would be no us anymore and I was ready and more than willing to live with that.

* * * *

I gathered some things and caught the next flight out to St. Louis. Beau's show was over by the time I got in but I knew what hotel he stayed. After arguing with the airline about my lost luggage and leaving my purse at the airport, I arrived at Beau's hotel two hours later.

"I'm a guest for Beau Sims. Would you ring his room please?"

The lady at the counter did as I asked. I turned and watched people as I wait. Beau sauntered in the hotel lobby with a beautiful woman attached to his arm. Neither of them noticed me.

"I'm sorry ma'am but the guest is not answering his phone," The receptionist told me.

"That's fine. Thank you," I said distracted.

Beau and the woman started for the elevators. I didn't stop them but I wanted to grab them both by their hair. I knew what he would do to her upstairs in his room and I was instantly jealous. But I was also embarrassed to show up again unannounced only to find he had gotten over me.

I decided to leave. Why fight it? Why fight over a man who didn't want me? I walked away from the desk and wait for a cab outside. As I waited I realized, I'd fought over every other no good man in my life before, why wouldn't I fight over a good one?

I marched inside with a mission at hand. Beau stood by the elevators where I confronted him and her.

"Kayla?" he asked in confusion.

"Hi," I said softly. Then I waved to the woman so not to be disrespectful. She returned with an unsure wave.

"What are you doing here?"

"Can I talk to you for a minute?" I pulled him over to the side. "I love you. Okay?" Beau stood in shock. His new girlfriend was less than pleased, "I love you. And if you think I'm here because I need you then you're right. I do need you. But I want you too. I want you so much."

"Kayla, I have company," he said uncomfortably.

"I know and I'm sorry. In a minute you can go up and you can sleep with this girl and I won't say anything about it. It'll hurt like hell but it's only physical. I know what we have is something deeper than that."

"This is all nice to hear," he whispered in that deep hoarse voice of his. He fidgeted around, "Lord knows I've waited for so long to hear you say all this stuff but it's too late. I'm moving on."

"I noticed," I said sadly.

"This isn't about Shana. It's about us Kayla. I can't throw myself out here like that again. Not with you."

"This time is different," I pleaded.

"Kay," he called for me to stop.

"Say it again," I closed my eyes and whispered softly to him. "Call me Kay again." I melted at the sound of the nickname he'd unintentionally given me. No one else in the world called me Kay except my dad. I'd never told Beau about it. The way the sound rolled off his tongue made everything in my life seem right at a time when everything was so wrong.

"Say it again, please." I begged.

His guards were getting weak. For a brief second he wanted to take me in his arms but he resisted.

"Beau," the agitated girl called to him.

He looked at me in shame. "I gotta go."

He walked off and boarded the elevator. He didn't even look back.

I returned back home empty. But for the first time I didn't call on another man to fill my void. Instead, I decided to work on a separate project of my own. I changed my mind about returning to work. I'd suffered a rough year. Enjoying this long vacation could be the start of something good.

Day and night I sat on my computer working on the children books for Beau and his sister. I made frequent trips to Gabrielle's old job to speak with Sabrina. Her attitude stunk. She made it apparent that she didn't have to deal with me now that Gabrielle was gone. So I chose not to bother her anymore but rather reached out to another one of Gabrielle's coworkers, Renee. She was more than willing to extend a helping hand. Come to find out the two of us shared a common disinterest in Sabrina.

Renee was a huge help and finally I finished the

project. I mailed it off to Raquel and took a long breather. I went on a binge of fine dining alone and pampering myself. Then me and my positive attitude eloped to Vegas where I partied and gambled all negative energy and attitudes away. Dedicated to Eric's contributions of course.

For the first time in my life I learned to love myself and didn't depend on any man or anyone to love me. I learned to be alone and not be lonely and to love Mikayla unconditionally because if I didn't, how could I expect anyone else to?

Upon returning from Vegas, I immediately went to visit Jack to share the love.

"Hi," I said standing at the door, "How ya been?"

"I've been alright." His behavior seemed evasive and he blocked the doorway.

"Are you going to let me in to see my son?" I asked sarcastically.

Undecidedly, he cleared the way and let me in.

"Stay here. I'll go get Jackson," Jack instructed.

He was cold towards me. I didn't know why but assumed it was because we were both used to Gabrielle being around. Whatever the reason, I wasn't going to let Jack push me out of his life. I wouldn't allow him to go into hiding.

I took my seat at the kitchen counter. The baby monitor sat to my right just as Gabrielle had left it. Voices echoed about. I stood in a daze as I listen to Jack deliver multiple directions.

"That's Mikayla," he whispered, "she wants to see Jackson. I'll bring him out. You stay in here."

"Alright," a familiar woman's voice responded.

Jack returned to the front with Jackson.

"Hey Jack, Jack," I exclaimed and pretended not to know anything. I watched closely as Jack made frequent trips to the back to check on his guest.

"He was just about to take his nap," Jack interrupted our playtime.

"Okay," I said disappointed. I gave Jackson a kiss. "I love you," I said before sending him to the back with his dad.

Once again Jack returned to the front, this time ready to see me out.

"Thanks for coming by," he told me.

"Who is she?" I asked, "Who's in the back?"

"What?"

"I can hear you two on the monitor, Jack."

He hung his head low, "That's not important."

"Not important my ass," I said as I angrily approached the back.

Maybe it wasn't my business but I had to know. I had to see the woman who was taking my best friend's place.

Sabrina sat comfortably with her shoes off and hair wild, in the family room of my best friend's house.

"What is going on here?"

"Nothing," Jack lied. "Sabrina just stopped by to see how we were doing."

"Really? And where's her car?" He was at a loss for words. "How could you do something like this? How could you stoop so low to sleep with someone who claimed to be her friend? In your wife's house with your son?"

I walked over to Sabrina. Her body language turned defensive. "You are so fucking lucky my godson is in the other room or I would have your ass on the floor pulling all your hair out."

"I would like to see you try it."

I rolled up my sleeves preparing for war. "Would you?"

Jack stood between us. I was ready to kick her over the couch she sat so calmly on.

"How could you do this to her?" I screamed at Jack. "Why? She loved you. You were her life. Why, Jack?"

"I was her life? How? She couldn't stand to see me half the time. At first I couldn't understand how she even got pregnant. I thought it was by some sort of miracle until I realized the baby was Todd's and not mine."

I stood in shock. "What?" I acted stupid.

"Come on Kayla. Sabrina told me everything."

I gave that bitch, excuse me, that WHORE the dirtiest look. I had so much fire in my eyes that her ass should have been in flames.

It became apparent why she encouraged Gabrielle's cheating and invited Todd to the baby shower. She had her own plan.

"And you believe this scheming, conniving whore?"

"That's your mother." Sabrina defended.

"That's your ass if you say another word to me." I warned her.

She waved her hand at me. I didn't speak another word. I grabbed her by the hair and punched her in the nose and again in the lip and again in the eye and again in the jaw. I hit that girl as many times as I could before Jack pulled me off her. Finally, blood shed after all the bad blood between me and Sabrina.

Jackson peeked from the hall in fright.

"Kayla, leave." Jack demanded "Leave now."

I was so hurt. You would have thought Jack cheated on me. I took one look at the boy's face. I should have held back and not behaved so animalistic but I just COULDN'T HELP IT! I had to defend Gabrielle's territory. I couldn't stand by and watch Sabrina ruin my best friend's image and wreck everything Gabrielle stood for and loved. I couldn't allow her to do that without a fight.

"It's real messed up that your wife's body isn't even cold yet and you've brought another woman into her home already. I guess I was wrong about you. I guess you didn't love Gabrielle as much as I told her you did," were my last words to Jack before he closed the door in my face.

I threw a fit in my mind. None of it was fair. I was fighting a battle for someone who wasn't here anymore. It was like I took on all Gabrielle's pain, anger, and rage. I wanted to slap Jack back into reality and release him from Sabrina's web of manipulation. I wanted to steal Jackson and not let him grow up around Sabrina at all. I wanted to do so many things but couldn't do any. I was fighting a losing battle and because of my loyalty to my best friend, Jack had closed the door on me for good. It would be the last time I'd see Jack, Jackson, or Sabrina.

* * * *

Saturday morning the sun shinned brightly on my face but it wasn't the sun that awakened me. I heard the soft sounds of the doorbell. I slid on my robe and answered its call.

"Hi." I said surprised. "How are you? Come in."

"Hi!" Raquel walked inside with her peppery attitude.

I directed her to the dining area. "You want something to drink or eat? I'm gonna make myself breakfast."

"No I just ate."

"Okay." I reached in the fridge and grabbed all my essentials for my meal. "Did you like the books?"

"I loved them. I read all four at least twenty times."

"Great."

"But I'm actually here because Beau is back in town. He's doing an appearance tonight at the café and I wanted you to come and support."

"I don't know if I should. He might not want to see me."

"Trust me he wants to see you. I know my brother and don't tell him I said it but you're all he talks about still. I know it'll mean a lot to him if you came to his last show."

I thought about it. I really didn't want to go. I already threw away his schedule and all the tour information I had on him. I vowed to never make the mistake of surprising him again and humiliating myself by throwing myself at his feet. There was no way.

"Here's the ticket." Raquel said laying it on my counter. "Just in case you decide to come."

I walked her to the door and saw her out.

"You should really come, Kayla. I know you love happy endings just as much as I do," she said getting into her car.

"Yeah but I stopped dreaming about them a long time ago." I said to myself.

The ticket sat on my counter watching me as I ate breakfast. I left it there but somehow it ended in my hand and I ended at the parking lot of the cafe.

I took a deep breath. Was I ready to do this again? Nevertheless, I was already here and may as well go in. I opened my car door slightly when, out of nowhere, a shadow figure appeared and flung it the rest of the way. I turned in fright and the man yanked me out of the car before my body could even manage a scream.

He grabbed me by my throat and pinned me against the car.

"You know what your problem is?" Eric asked me. "You never knew your role. You never knew how to be happy and accept the finer things in life and not complain. With Felicia I don't have to pretend or play games. I don't have to sleep over or claim love. She knows her role as the other woman. She knows she will never be first and doesn't try to be. So I can just be myself."

"I'm happy for you. Now can you go be yourself somewhere else?" I said sarcastically.

I was a bit intimidated. Eric or no man had ever put his hands on me.

"That's funny because when I tried being myself I came home to an empty house. No wife, no son, nothing except a tape recorder in my mailbox. You know who was on the recorder?"

"It's not my business so I could really care less."

I tried to move but he slammed me against the car.

"It's you and Michia talking about everything you and me ever did." He tightened his grip around the collar of my shirt. He squint his eyes and gritted his teeth. I took a deep breath and prepared for a swift punch. At that moment I really regretted talking to his wife and didn't even know why I had in the first place.

"I had you confused for a whore that could keep her mouth closed but I see I was wrong," Eric told me and tightened his grip even more.

I prayed for help but there was no one in the lot of the café and I was afraid to yell figuring that any sound or slightest movement could set him off.

But out of nowhere an entourage of people came to my aid. Eric fell harshly on the ground after being struck by Beau. Other guys asked about my condition while Beau stood defensively over Eric.

271

"I'm okay," I told them as I watched Eric get off the ground.

"Twinkle toes the poet." Eric said sarcastically while brushing himself off.

Even covered in dirt his arrogance still shined through. Beau stood still. He had a look on his face that I'd never seen before in my life. Not in him or in anyone. He was like a soldier ready for combat.

Eric gave a cocky smile. "What you gonna do tough man? You want to battle me in a rhyme?" he laughed.

But Beau wasn't amused, "Don't you ever put your fucking hands on her ever again."

"Or what?" Eric approached him. "What are you going to do? You gonna fight me over her? Save yourself the embarrassment. She ain't worth it. She's not yours, she's everybody's. All it takes is a nice bracelet or a free night out and she's yours. In the car, hotel, your place, you name it. She ain't nothing but a hoe and not even an expensive hoe."

I burst into tears of embarrassment. Almost simultaneously to my first sob I saw Beau punch Eric with all his might. For a second time Eric lay on the ground. Beau jumped on top of him and continued to beat him.

"Don't you ever talk about her like that!" Beau shouted over and over again.

Raquel came running over yelling and screaming to the top of her lungs. "Beau no! Leave him alone Beau! No, no not again!" she cried but was unable to stop her brother.

I was too afraid to move and only cried the entire time of Eric's beating.

All I could think about was 'God please don't let Beau kill Eric and go back to jail. Especially not over me.'

It took all seven of the men standing out there to pull Beau off of Eric who now bled from everywhere. They dragged Beau to a corner of the lot, a great distance from Eric, to keep him calm.

Others helped Eric up but he snatched away and refused to accept any gesture of kindness. He took his handkerchief from his pocket, wiped himself off, gave me the dirtiest look, and drove himself away from there.

Once again the men checked on my state of mind. "I'm fine, thank you," I said gratefully and they focused their attention back on Beau. He calmly walked inside along with others.

Slowly the lot became less crowded until finally, I stood alone. I wanted to go in to check on Beau and tell him thanks for saving me but another part of me said to just leave. I'd caused enough trouble.

"Kayla," Maria, the waitress from the café called to me, "They have your table waiting inside."

How could I refuse? She led me inside to my seat next to Raquel who held my hand and comforted me. I accepted her 'it's not your fault' gesture and smiled politely. Beau sat uncomfortably on the other side of me. I wanted to clear the air. I couldn't stand the tension.

"I'm, I'm sorry for involving you in something like that," I began to whisper to Beau. He barely paid any attention to me but kept his eyes on the performers. "But thanks anyway for helping me out. You really didn't have to."

He gave an indescribable stare. I didn't know what to think of it. It was almost as if he looked right through me, discounting everything I was saying.

Then he turned his head and continued to ignore my presence. I was sure he was angry for retorting back to past behaviors that got him thrown in jail in the first place and was trying my best to rectify the situation but he never once looked my way.

"Beau, I-"

"We have a special performer tonight. You've seen him on TV ya'll," The MC began to announce abruptly interrupting my attempt to pour my heart out to Beau. "from Def Poetry to cameos, and a new movie coming out soon! This man is making all stops!"

The butterflies in my stomach were uncontrollable and I felt like I was sweating as he praised Beau's accomplishments. I didn't know how Beau would concentrate on his performance tonight after everything that just happened. I could barely concentrate myself.

"Give it up for Beau!" the MC finally said. Beau took the stage and closed his eyes. Then he licked his lips as he always did just before he spoke. "Does a man scorn run as deep?" he began. I instantly knew what or who this poem would be about. "love is what she preached but made me teach. I was no prophet but I saw our future."

Every sentence brought me back to us. The crowd screamed at their own experiences.

"Give me you. Let me be your all. Be my air in my lungs, let me breathe you. Can I come inside you and be you? Be my food to survive, let me eat you." The ladies screamed again.

I couldn't take it. I refused to sit through another second of Beau's poem and not let him know how I truly felt. I swallowed my pride and every inhibition inside of me and ran on stage and snatched the microphone away like a mad woman.

The crowd muttered different things and security was about to take me away but Beau politely waved them away.

Then he gave me a nod, the coolest and sexiest nod ever to say the floor was mine. I looked around the room in embarrassment. It was my time to shine and prove my love for Beau. I closed my eyes and took a chance in front of what felt like the world and said,

"I know everybody came here for a show. I'm sorry that I'm not a poet but I do have something to say and I believe that words spoken from the heart can be just as poetic as any song, script, or whatever. Let me ask everyone in here, specifically for my ladies, a question."

I had the room's attention.

"Have you ever been dogged before?"

The crowd of ladies erupted of reminiscent experiences.

"I know." I agreed with most. "I've had my bad times too. But for some reason in your mind when you're with that dog you convince yourself things will change, things will get better even when you know in your heart they'll only get worse. I know there have been many nights where I've cried to God and prayed for a good man to take me away from the pain, love me unconditionally, or even just give me back half of what I put into the relationship. But when he sent me a man so sweet, endearing, and sincere, I was so damaged and broken that I couldn't trust that anyone like that existed. I'd convinced myself that I alone was the only person in this world who could love unconditionally."

"Well I'm the first one to tell you ladies, I messed up. And when I started thinking like that, that's when I found myself alone. See, instead of chasing after the good guy... I chased him away. And I just want to say, I'm sorry," I turned to Beau, "I'm sorry Beau. And I know I couldn't say it before but damn it, I love you. I promise you, I will not give up on us. I will chase you to the end of the earth if I have to. What can I do?" My emotions ran deep.

"Take your shirt off!" a man yelled from the back of the café and the crowd burst into laughter.

Beau only stared but didn't respond. I looked around the room in complete embarrassment as I began to have second thoughts. What in the hell was I thinking getting on stage like that? Who did I think I was?

I got ready to make a break for it, when he grabbed my hand and stopped me.

"Stop running." He said in front of everyone, "I love you Mikayla. Just like you I'm scared too but everything we've been through from a year to twenty minutes ago, is in the past. I swear to be right to you. I promise in front of all these people that I will never hurt you but I want you to promise me the same."

"I promise," I didn't give a moment's hesitation.

We kissed and the crowd cheered at our display of affection for one another. We'd turned the evening into our moment and Beau didn't stop there. He reached around his neck for the platinum chain with a key attached and handed it over to me.

"What is this?" I whispered.

"It's the key to my place. Our place."

I hugged him and never wanted to let him go. Hopefully it would be forever.

"Awwww," everyone said.

"Get ya'll ass off the stage." The MC joked. We did get off stage. In fact we left altogether. He and I celebrated that night in OUR home.

It was a special moment. I felt like Cinderella finally getting her prince. And even though I hadn't resolved issues with my family or got another job, I got my knight. And he wasn't my ending, he was just my beginning. I guess even my fairytales deserved to come true.

EPILOGUE

Gabrielle

(Continued from Chapter 16)

I watched nervously as Kayla left me behind to fend for myself and face the wrath of my husband. As Jack slowly took his first breath to begin, my heart beat boldly against my breasts and my limbs went numb. I could only anticipate what he would say but I waited anxiously so I could deny it all. If he didn't start speaking soon there would be no need to have an abortion because I would have the baby right here and now.

He walked over slowly towards me. I stood frozen, "What?"

It always frightened me whenever Jack was angry. He was so quiet and I never knew what to expect. He'd get this crazed look on his face while he analyzed in his mind how to handle the situation. It was a look that I assumed to be similar to a murderer or a crazy person. If he found out I'd been having an affair with the deacon at church and was now pregnant by him I wouldn't have to assume anymore because I would be a dead bitch tonight.

"I found these in your work bag," He said laying papers on the counter before me.

There was no need in picking them up. I knew exactly what they were.

"When were you going to tell me? Or were you even going to tell me?" I put my head down in shame. How in the hell was I going to get out of this? My hospital papers indicating that I was pregnant lay freely on the counter but Jack assumed it was his. So far I'd only been guilty of concealing a small secret. Instead of burying myself further, I let him do all the talking.

"You weren't going to tell me were you?"

"Jack... I don't know."

"Yes you do know," he told me. "You were going to have an abortion weren't you? That's the trip you were going to take with Kayla isn't it? You weren't going to the damn spa!" he shouted and flung the flowers from the kitchen table. Glass shattered everywhere. I jumped and instantly began to cry.

"I'm sorry. I didn't know what else to do," I told him "I didn't think now was a good time to have another baby."

"You're right, you didn't think!" he point his finger in my face.

"Our marriage hasn't been right in over a year."

"And killing our child would make it better? Keeping a secret like this from your husband would help us regain trust?" he asked me.

I stood in the corner of the kitchen weeping. I wouldn't move just in case he went on a rampage of destroying things. But then to my surprise he began to cry.

"Why would you hide something like this from me? I thought we were working on things. Haven't I been good to you? I've made mistakes but I... we were working through those," he took a deep breath, "Gabrielle you know I love you more than anything in the world. How could you consider this?"

I looked into my husband's tear filled eyes. He was so naïve, so clueless, and so hurt. He loved me so much but he had no idea of how dishonest and deceiving his wife had really been. Every guard and every shield I'd built were lowered and I stood behind it so small. How could I hurt a man I loved so much for so long?

I walked over and wrapped my arms around him and kissed his forehead. "I'm sorry."

"Do you want a divorce?" he asked fearfully. I looked into his troubled eyes. He was fretting over what my response would be. "Is that what it is?"

"No," I sniffed, "No I don't want a divorce. I want my family."

"Then why?" he asked. He hesitated before unveiling his next question, "Is the baby mine?"

My arms fell loosely from around his neck. My first mind was to get defensive and scream at him for calling me a whore. But he and I had been through so much that he waited for the day I would stray. He believed it was the inevitable while I pretended it would never happen. But it had.

A smart woman and honest wife would confess right now and get everything out on the table. But I couldn't. I couldn't look into the anguished eyes of my husband and tell him that I'd been unfaithful and gotten pregnant by another man. I just couldn't. So I looked him directly in his eyes and lied.

"Of course this is your child sweetheart. Who else's would it be?"

He kissed my lying lips and squeezed me tight. Then he kissed my stomach and rested his head there.

"I love you," he said, "I love you so much. This baby will change everything. You'll see."

This baby would change everything that was for certain. I rubbed my husband's head as my cell phone silently called for my attention. It was Todd and it was our time to meet.

Your Wife Is The OTHER Woman

Made in the USA
Lexington, KY
23 November 2015